RENKIN FAMILY
1515 Shasta Dr. #1204
Davis, CA 95616 - 6676

# For Whom
# The Minivan Rolls

*An Aaron Tucker Mystery*

Jeffrey Cohen

bancroft
press

Baltimore, MD

Published by Bancroft Press ("Books that enlighten")
P.O. Box 65360, Baltimore, MD 21209
800-637-7377
410-764-1967 (fax)
bruceb@bancroftpress.com
www.bancroftpress.com

Jacket Design: Stephen Parke/What? Design parke@imagecarnival.com

Book design by Theresa Williams, theresa@visuallee.com


1-890862-18-5 (cloth)
1-890862-19-3 (paper)
Library of Congress Card Number: 2002109251

Printed in the United States of America

First Edition

*To Jessica, who knows the only thing
I haven't exaggerated is how much I love her.*

# *Prologue*

Eeeeuuuuurrrppp!

The noise—wherever it was coming from—woke Madlyn Beckwirth, and she nudged Gary, who was snoring beside her. Every few seconds, eeeuuurrrp!

If she just lay there and listened, it was enough to drive Madlyn crazy. That's the way things are at two in the morning. So she got out of bed and went downstairs to investigate.

Madlyn carefully checked the living room and the kitchen, but no one was there. She realized now the noise was coming from somewhere outside the house.

Nothing else to do. Madlyn took the chain off the front door, checking to make sure she had unlocked both the dead bolt and the lock in the doorknob. The last thing she needed was to be locked out of her own house. Especially with a man upstairs who wouldn't wake up if you bounced him out of bed and screamed at him through a bullhorn.

Nothing on the doorstep, nothing on the lawn. Where the hell was that sound coming from? A-ha! There at the curb. Madlyn let the air out of her lungs, just now realizing she had been holding her breath.

Somebody's car had lost a hubcap while riding past her house. When the stupid thing had stopped rolling, it had come to rest on a sewer grate, and wedged itself there. Every time the wind blew, it made a metallic scraping sound—eeeeuuuuurrrppp!—trying to break free.

She'd never get back to sleep with that racket going on. So, resigned to venturing even farther outside the house dressed in her bedclothes, Madlyn headed toward the curb and reached down. Even with both hands, she couldn't pull the hubcap out—it was stuck too tight.

Madlyn looked up the street. All the usual cars were parked in front of their owners' homes, though a blue minivan she didn't recognize was parked a couple of houses down, in front of Diane and Bill's.

Well, she couldn't bear that noise anymore, so she decided on a new strategy. She picked up a stick lying near the curb, wedged it in under the hubcap, and pried. Sure enough, after a few tries, the hubcap came loose, but the Herculean effort caused her to stagger backward a few steps into the street.

It was at that moment that the blue minivan, its headlights now on, started down the street with a squealing of brakes and the smell of burning rubber. Madlyn didn't realize at first that it was headed directly at her, and by the time she did, it was too late to even put up her hands or scream.

# Part One: Searching

## Chapter 1

"Do you like mysteries?"

Milt Ladowski sat behind what must have been, for him, his cheap desk. For me, the real-wood monster with five drawers would have been an unaffordable luxury, but Milt is a high-priced attorney, accustomed to private practice extravagance. In his part-time position as borough counsel for Midland Heights, New Jersey, however, he had to accept an office in nondescript Borough Hall, and the government-issued desk that came with it. To serve his community, in effect, he had to go slumming. Many are called. Few are chosen. Or was it the other way around?

"Yeah," I told him. "I love mysteries. I just got done reading the latest Janet Evanovich. Why, do you want me to write one?"

"No. I want you to solve one."

Well, that was a mystery in itself. You want somebody to solve a mystery, you generally don't go to a freelance writer. Nine times out of ten, you might want to consult, say, a private detective. Or a cop. Freelancers are more likely to be consulted when your goal is to publish a thousand-word feature about the dangers of cholesterol in the newspaper's Sunday health section.

"That's not really my line of work, Milt."

He nodded. "I know. But Gary Beckwirth insisted. He said to call you, and only you."

"Beckwirth? Which one is Gary Beckwirth?"

"Beckwirth. You know. His wife is managing Rachel Barlow's campaign for mayor."

I stared blankly at him. I follow municipal politics with the same enthusiasm I muster for the cricket scores from Bath.

"Their son Joel is a patrol kid at the middle school," he said, seeing if he could jog my memory.

"Oh, is he the one who busted Ethan for going to the bathroom without a hall pass?"

I remember everything that anybody has ever done to and for my children. The little Beckwirth son of a bitch hadn't even bothered to check with Ethan's teacher, and he'd practically forced my 11-year-old son to have an accident in the school corridor. After that fiasco, Ethan had come home and locked himself in his room with Pokémon Stadium for three hours, which is a half-hour longer than usual.

"You're going to take that to your grave, aren't you, Aaron?" asked Ladowski. "The kid did what he thought was the right thing."

"So did Lee Harvey Oswald. Okay, so that's Beckwirth. The father looks like some rich guy off a daytime soap, right? And the mother . . ."

"Madlyn is the mystery. She's been missing for three days, and Gary's worried. She never goes anywhere without telling him, and then in the middle of the night, Monday, she vanishes right out of their bed."

My eye was distracted by a flier on Ladowski's desk that mentioned the start of the Recreation Department's little league baseball season. Both Ethan and Leah would probably want to play. And they'd both want me to coach. That's three nights a week, and Sundays, from early April until late June. I'd look like a member of the walking dead by the time the season was over. I don't remember my parents coaching me in anything. They took me to the games and watched me strike out a lot, but coaching . . .

"Aaron?"

I was jolted out of my "Dad-of-the-Year" reverie. "I still don't get why you're telling me about this, Milt. Did Beckwirth go to Barry Dutton?"

Ladowski's mouth straightened out, making a horizontal line that perfectly displayed his displeasure. His face doesn't look so good when he's smiling, so you can imagine. "Our esteemed chief of police has made some inquiries. Gary and Barry don't get along very well."

"That's the title of a children's book, isn't it? *Gary and Barry Don't Get Along Very Well*, by Dr. Seuss?"

"You're very amusing."

"I'm a goddam riot, to tell you the truth, but I'm still not a private detective. So Beckwirth thinks the cops aren't doing enough to find his wife. So fine. So go out and hire yourself an investigator to, uh, investigate. And why are *you* dealing with this, anyway? Did the borough hire you to ask freelance writers why a woman gets out of bed in the middle of the night and doesn't come back? Our first two questions almost always are going to be: 'When's the deadline? And how much per word?'"

Ladowski didn't like the way this conversation was going, but he had expected it. He'd known me a long time. Hell, everybody in this town knew everybody else a long time. Half of them went to high school together. I'd been living here nine years, and they still considered me the "new guy." Nobody ever left Midland Heights. Except, it seemed, Madlyn Beckwirth.

Milt stood up, to better emphasize the difference in our height. In other words, he has some. I'm 5'4", and pretend I'm 5'5" when I want to intimidate someone. Ladowski, on the other hand, is about 5'10". But it's not like I notice height.

"Gary asked me to look into it because I'm his attorney, and his friend. I'm not handling this for the borough, I'm doing it for Gary. He's too upset right now to deal with people much. And he doesn't want a private detective. He wants someone who knows the people in this town and how it works. We don't have any private investigators living and working in Midland Heights."

"No, but we have more social workers, therapists, and shrinks per capita than any other square mile of property in the known universe. Come to think of it, a shrink would probably be a better fit for Beckwirth right now than a freelancer."

Ladowski sighed. He knew this was stupid, but his client had insisted. "He wants someone who can be . . . discreet. And when he heard that you've been an investigative reporter . . . "

Now it was my turn to sigh. Loudly. "Oh, come on, Milt, that was 20 years ago, and I only did it for six months. I wasn't even a *good* investigative reporter. I was rooting out bad cops for the *Herald-News* in Passaic, and I found exactly one. The rest of the cops were so impressed with my work that they refused ever to speak to me again, and I ended up losing my job because I got scooped by two other papers on a regular basis. I'd hardly call that a stellar investigative record."

"Gary heard the word 'investigative,' and that's all he needed," Ladowski said. His voice was calm, but he was eyeing the window with the definite thought of throwing himself or me out of it. Luckily for both of us, it was a first-floor office. The borough, thank goodness, couldn't afford a view for Ladowski, either.

"This is stupid, Milt. I'm not a detective. I don't solve mysteries. I read them. I write newspaper and magazine features about electronics. You want to know about new DVD players, I'm your guy. You want to find a missing woman, you go to the cops or to private detectives, wherever they live. I can't help Gary Beckwirth."

Ladowski did the last thing I'd have expected him to do. He smiled.

"Fine. *You* go tell him that."

# Chapter 2

I walked out of Ladowski's office feeling a little light-headed. I had stepped into an alternate universe, where the word "investigative" was enough to get you invited to dig into people's private lives and unearth God knows what. Maybe Madlyn Beckwirth had left her husband. Maybe she was sleeping with someone else. Maybe she left because *he* was sleeping with someone else. Maybe she had gotten up to go to the bathroom in the middle of the night and her Fascist kid had sent her to the street for peeing without a hall pass. In any event, it was none of my business, and I was happy to leave it that way.

All that left my mind when I caught a glimpse of a woman leaving Borough Hall. Short dark hair. Well-fitting tan linen suit. Navy silk blouse. And legs. I'm not even going to tell you about her legs. Think about the best legs you've seen this month, add a couple of exclamation points, and you'd be getting close.

Clearly, this woman needed investigating, and since I was now considered an investigator, at least by some, it was my duty to plunge right in. Maybe there was an upside to this investigator stuff after all. I doubled my step, and caught up with her just outside the door to the street, at the top of the stairs.

"And why aren't you in Livingston today, where you belong, Ms. Stein?"

Abigail Stein turned around to face me, her large brown eyes hiding their delight behind a transparent mask of annoyance. At least, that's how I like to think about it.

"Some clients have taken exception to the Midland Heights police, who, the last week of every month, ticket every car they don't recognize. I'm here filing a brief," she said. "Like that's your business."

"You'd be amazed what some people think my business is," I told her. Best to lend an air of mystery.

"Would I?"

"I'll tell you about it over dinner. I've been thinking of asking you to marry me, and this might be the night."

"You're married," she reminded me.

"If you're going to get hung up on details ..."

"It's been nice seeing you, Mr. Tucker. But I have actual work to do, and you have to go write your little stories." This time, there was definite amusement in her eyes. I spent a few seconds getting lost in them.

"They're screenplays. And I bet you'll have dinner with me when Spielberg comes by just to have a bite."

"I'll check my calendar," she said. "Ask your wife if you're free that night."

"I'll do that," I told her. "See you later."

"Not if I see you first." She walked away, and I couldn't stop watching. Did I mention she has really great legs?

# Chapter 3

Gary Beckwirth opened the door to his house after checking through the peephole to see if it was me. It was me, so he let me in.

About six months ago, Beckwirth and his wife had moved into what the kids in town call "The Castle." The site, way back when, had been a farm, where corn and tomatoes grew, and there was a beautiful farmhouse. Midland Heights' first structure, it was affectionately known as the "White House," and served as both fixture and landmark.

Because the original four acre tract, owned by Midland Heights' founding family, was one of the largest undeveloped pieces of land in Central New Jersey, it could not be subdivided. But when the last member of the farm owner's family, known not so popularly around town as the "Mean Old Man," died, his will stipulated that the farm-house be torn down. An outcry from the town's citizenry (and an effort to get the site listed as a National Historic Landmark) failed to prevent the bulldozing of the elegant structure.

When Gary and Madlyn Beckwirth moved into town with passels of money, the site had lain dormant for a number of years. They quick-ly bought the land (rumor had it for as much as $1 million), and, though it took a few years, built on it an enormous fake mansion to out-fake practically every fake mansion ever known to man.

It was huge and brick, and it had two rounded protrusions, one on each side, that suggested towers. If there had been a moat and turrets for pouring boiling oil on invading Visigoths, I wouldn't have been surprised.

The Beckwirths' regal estate also boasted a swimming pool, a tennis court, and for all I knew, Beckwirth's own version of the Pirates of the Carribean in the backyard. The front door was only about 15 feet from Hayes Street, but the other three sides of the house were so far removed from the neighbors, the Beckwirths could pretend they had no neighbors—this in a town so overdeveloped the guy next door usually yells "gesundheit" whenever you sneeze.

Beckwirth and his wife, despite their atrocioius taste, were clearly doing quite well. But I had no idea how they made their money. And my mind still couldn't summon an adequate picture of Madlyn Beckwirth.

Her husband, standing before me, was a shade under six feet tall. And, as I'd remembered, he was unusually handsome. But, if that supermodel on TV could keep imploring me not to hate her because she was beautiful, I couldn't really hold it against Gary Beckwirth that he looked like he belonged on one of the classier Aaron Spelling shows—one without any of Aaron's kids in the cast.

He had those blue-green eyes that women tend to melt into a puddle over, and dark brown, almost black, hair, fashionably coiffed. Normally, you could see the dimple in his chin, but he hadn't shaved in a couple of days, and the dimple now looked like a belly button with hair growing out of it. And he still looked better than me.

He embraced me and hugged me tightly to his chest (which was roughly as high as I reached), and began to sob. I was gasping for breath, because he had my nose buried in his shirt.

"Thank God you've come," he wailed, as my eyes widened from lack of air. "I was afraid, so afraid ..."

I gave the front door a backward kick with my left heel so the neighbors wouldn't think Gary and I were having an illicit liaison. Then

I raised my hands to his shoulders, and gently pushed away, normalizing the flow of oxygen to my lungs. "Gary," I gasped. "Nice to meet you."

He ushered me into a living room that could have come out of the 19th century. In fact, I'm not sure it didn't. Every piece of furniture was an antique, every rug an Oriental. The room was devoid of televisions, stereos, computers, or any device other than lamps requiring electrical power. If they'd been able to get gas jets up and running there, they likely would have gotten rid of the lamps, too. The Beckwirths probably had a home theatre set up elsewhere, but this was the main room, and they kept it this way so they could tell their friends they never watched TV, and then sneak off to catch *Nash Bridges* when nobody was looking. Was I being judgmental?

Beckwirth managed to control his weeping until we were inside. He actually had coffee in a silver urn on the coffee table, and poured me some without asking. I don't drink coffee, but I mimed taking a sip and put the cup down as he composed himself.

"I don't know how much Milton told you . . ." he began.

"He told me that Madlyn hasn't come home in a few days," I offered. "And you're worried. That's certainly understandable, but . . ."

Beckwirth nodded, and ignored the "but." "That's why you've got to help me, Aaron. You're the only one I could think of."

*I* was the only one he could think of? I could think of dozens. In fact, I'd sooner go to the dry cleaner for help than a freelance writer. At least *he'd* know whether she took her clothes with her. What the hell was I supposed to do about the guy's wife leaving him? Pitch a story to *Redbook* on ways to lose those last 10 pounds before running away from your husband?

"Can you think of any reason Madlyn might want to . . . take a few days off without telling you?"

It took him a couple of seconds to absorb what I was saying. "You think she went away *on purpose?*"

"I don't think anything. I haven't the slightest idea what happened.

I'm just asking."

For a moment, his face darkened, his eyebrows lowered, and his voice gained authority. This must be the Beckwith his employees saw. "My wife did *not* leave me, Aaron. She was taken away against her will."

This time it took me a moment. "She was kidnapped?"

"Exactly. She was kidnapped. And I want you to find out who did it, and why, and get her back."

I pretended to take another sip of coffee. Lord, that stuff smells great, but it tastes foul. "Gary, this really isn't my line of work. What you need is . . ."

"Don't tell me about the police, Aaron," Beckwirth said with a voice that must cause young stockbrokers, or whatever the hell he is, to tremble in their boots. "I've spoken to our esteemed chief of police, and he's barely raised a finger. The lazy bastard sends out a fax to other police departments and thinks that's going to get my wife back. An affirmative action appointment if ever I saw one." Barry Dutton is African-American.

"If you think the police aren't doing enough, Gary, get yourself a private investigator."

Beckwirth smiled his best "aren't-we-all-friends-here" smile and leaned toward me. "I've got something better. I've got *you*."

"I'm not better. I'm worse. I write articles about cellular phones for a living, Gary. If my wife didn't have a full-time job, I would be considered indigent." I figured the allusion to money would impress him.

Once again, I had underestimated the depth of Beckwirth's fantasy life. "You know investigation, Aaron. You're an investigative reporter."

"*Was.* I *was* an investigative reporter. I used to be a teenager, too, but that doesn't mean I can come up with a cure for acne."

He got up and sat next to me on the couch. In another minute, I might have to scream and otherwise fight for my virtue. Beckwirth's tone was hushed and intimate. I searched the coffee table for a butter knife, or something I could use to fend off his advances, should it come to that. I found nothing. Just to give myself something to do, I picked up the cup, with two sips taken out of it, and made a big deal out of "freshening" it with hot coffee. If I had to drink the whole thing, I'd be a raving caffeine addict by lunch.

"You know the tricks, Aaron. You know who to call. You know where to look. You can find my Madlyn and save her from these people."

"Gary, I have trouble finding my car keys in the morning. I don't know how to save anybody. Try and listen to me. I'm a freelance writer. I send query letters to editors, they give me assignments, we agree on a rate, which means they tell me how much they're going to pay me and I say 'okay,' and then I call people up and ask them questions. When my deadline's approaching, I write up the information the best way I can and I send it to the editor, who then does whatever he wants to it, and prints it in a magazine or a newspaper. That's what I do. I don't save people, I don't find missing wives. It's not that I don't want to help you. I just don't have any idea at all what to do. You understand?"

He stared into my face, wheels turning in his head. Then Beckwirth decided on a strategy. He drew a deep breath and sighed painfully.

"Fine. *Don't* help me. Let me live through this experience alone, with no one to end my suffering and no chance of bringing my Madlyn home."

"Gary, doing an impression of my mother isn't going to help. I told you. I'm a freelancer. I do freelancer stuff. Look in the Yellow Pages, find a detect ..." I stopped just from the expression on his face.

Beckwirth's face was made of stone. But it started to crack, and tears began to fall silently from his eyes. I felt like I was telling Charlie Brown that Snoopy had been run over by a bus. Beckwirth stood, turned, and walked out of the room.

I guessed the job interview was over. So I left. Outside Beckwirth's house, a sixty-ish woman walking her dog scowled at me as I headed back to my minivan. Probably thought Gary and I were having an illicit liaison.

# Chapter 4

It was after noon when I walked through the front door of my own house. The place was in its usual state of disarray. Ethan had left his socks the night before on the floor in front of the living room couch, and Leah had simply taken off her pajamas while watching *The Wild Thornberrys* that morning, and left them on the couch. Toys and school papers obscured the coffee table, which was not an antique but was old, and there was a distinct smell of cooking oil in the air, because I'd made some french fries to go with the hamburgers I'd cooked for dinner. Two nights ago.

Home, sweet home.

I took off my jacket and hung it on the banister at the bottom of the stairs, then took a left and walked past the $25 thrift store armchair into my office, otherwise known as the playroom, where action figures and fax machines co-existed peacefully as an example to objects world-wide. It made one proud to work at home.

The answering machine light was flashing, and there were three messages. One from the pediatrician's office, confirming Ethan's check-up for the next day at 4:30. One from my mother, who in fact doesn't nag like Gary Beckwirth, but sometimes you have to exaggerate to make your point. The last was from Dave Harrington, an editor I'd worked with before at the *Press-Tribune*. My mother was fine, and wondered why I wasn't in my office at 11 a.m. on a Thursday.

I called Harrington back first, since it was unlikely that talking to either the pediatrician or my mother would result in a paycheck. And I got him on the second ring.

"City desk. Harrington." My eyes wandered to the lithograph of the Marx Brothers over my desk. Once, I'd had this idea for a screenplay where Groucho had to solve a murder mystery. Then some guy actually started writing Groucho Marx detective mysteries. All my best ideas have been used by other people. It can wear you down after a while.

"Explain to me how you can have a city desk when all you cover is suburbia."

"You're not starting this again, are you, Aaron?"

"Just doesn't make sense, that's all. There's no city. What's the desk for?"

"Holds paper clips, stuff like that. Without it, I'd just be sitting in a swivel chair with nothing to do." City editors are damn witty people.

"How you doing, Dave?" Next to the Marx Brothers lithograph, which my parents had bought me when I was 14 and probably didn't think I'd keep for 29 years, was a Bullwinkle clock. How would Rocky the Flying Squirrel solve this puzzler? Hell, there were only two criminals in his known universe. If Boris and Natasha hadn't kidnapped Madlyn Beckwirth, I was out of luck.

"Not bad. You up for a feature?"

This was a bit of a surprise. So far, the best I'd gotten out of Harrington had been a business profile on a company that makes lottery tickets. They had made me sign a non-disclosure agreement when I entered the building. Imagine asking a reporter to sign a non-disclosure agreement. It's my *job* to disclose things. But, I digress.

The point is, the lottery company story was just a sidebar, nothing major, since I hadn't worked with the *Press-Tribune* very much yet and they didn't know if they could trust me with something bigger. A feature, a longer piece with better placement, meant more money, and was definitely a step up on the paper's pecking order.

"Sure. What's it about?"

"It's an investigative piece." Harrington's voice sounded funny, and I don't mean ha-ha funny. "Woman from your town went and got herself missing and her husband thinks the cops aren't looking into it enough."

Wow. And it's only a five-minute car-ride from Beckwirth's house to mine. If I hadn't stopped at the supermarket for a gallon of one-percent milk, I'd probably have gotten Dave's call live. That Beckwirth sure moved fast for a guy consumed with worry.

"Madlyn Beckwirth?"

"Yeah. How'd you know?"

I groaned. "I'm incredibly intuitive. Who gave you this piece, Dave? Who mentioned my name? It wasn't your idea, was it?"

"As a matter of fact, no. I got it from the exec editor maybe ten minutes ago. Funny, because I've been talking you up for weeks, trying to get you something better, and today they ask for you by name."

Beckwirth must have walked straight out of the room with me, picked up a phone, and called Harrington's publisher. Money knows money. The rest of us are from Central Casting.

"It figures. What does your exec want me to do?"

"The way I hear it, he wants you to forget the cops and find the wife. Apparently the guy thinks she's been kidnapped, even though he has no note, no phone call, nothing from any supposed kidnappers. And for some reason, he thinks you are Sam Spade, Phillip Marlowe, and Woodward and Bernstein all rolled up into one. So, you want to write it for us, or what?"

"What's the deadline?"

"I can give you a week."

"A week!"

"Yeah, with a breaking story it would have been less, but I don't think anybody else has this yet. A week's as far as I can go." He actually thought he was giving me a break. In a week, I might find my way back out to my minivan.

"How much?"

"Money?"

"No, how much sour cream fits into Tom Cruise's swimming pool? Yeah, how much money?"

"I've been told, uh, to go to a thousand dollars."

I stared at my headset for a moment. A thousand dollars? That was about five times the average paycheck from a local newspaper.

"What did you just say?"

"You heard me, Aaron. You can draw from that whatever conclusions you choose. Now, do you want the story or not?"

I don't think well on my feet. And the fact that I was currently sitting down didn't help.

"Sure," I said, idiot that I am.

# Chapter 5

I called my mother back about an hour later. It took me that long to recover from the shock of my latest journalistic assignment. She was physically well, but emotionally shook up. Apparently the Shop-Rite near her house was selling orange juice after the stamped expiration date, and she had given them hell about it. It was almost on par with the lawn service fertilizer scandal of '97.

I still had a couple of assignments with deadlines approaching, and I made phone calls on them until the kids got home. Ethan barreled in first, flinging the front door open, stomping into the house and hanging his backpack on one of the banister rungs currently unoccupied. We run a tidy household around here.

Normally, I don't like to brag, mostly because I have so little bragging material when I'm talking about myself. But my son is a different story. He is a remarkably handsome boy, having inherited his mother's big brown eyes, thank goodness, and her even, pleasant features. He even stood a chance, according to his pediatrician, of achieving something nobody in my family had ever dreamed of—average height.

Right now, Ethan's face was expressionless. He was thinking about something other than being home. He didn't notice me until I hung up the phone. Nobody can ignore you better than an 11-year-old boy. Except maybe a 13-year-old girl, but I'll get back to you on that in six years.

"Hey, Skipper. How you doin'?" Best to show them you're their friend. They can smell fear.

"Hi, Dad." Kids with Asperger's Syndrome, like Ethan, tend to have unusual vocal expressions. Some speak with little inflection. Others mumble. Ethan's voice is unusually high. Nobody knows why.

Asperger's is a form of high-functioning autism. The kids speak quite well, compared to more severely autistic children, but their social skills are underdeveloped. They don't read body language. They don't understand idioms. They tend to have physical "tics," or what the experts called "stimming," which is a way of saying that they flap their arms or continually run their fingers through their hair as a way of getting the physical stimulation they lack in everyday life. They need more sensory input than the average person, and so they create as much of it as they can, wherever they can. But the worst thing is that they don't really read another person's tone of voice in a conversation, so they can't understand sarcasm. It is a huge handicap for a child growing up in my household.

Ethan was diagnosed with Asperger's when he started kindergarten, and since then, we've attended conferences, enrolled him in a yearlong transitional class between kindergarten and first grade, learned the meaning of an "IEP" (Individualized Education Plan), something that school systems do for children with "special needs," asked for and gotten an adult aide (called a "para-professional") to help get him through the school day, and gotten him Occupational Therapy for his slowly developing fine motor skills, and social skills training and speech therapy, so he can learn how to use speech in a conversation. He also takes Ritalin twice a day to help him concentrate, and anybody who thinks we're unnecessarily medicating our kid can share a week with him with no medication and see what they think when they're done.

He is the sweetest 11-year-old on the planet 85 percent of the time. But when the Asperger's kicks into overdrive and he gets into a dark mood, you'd better give him a wide berth and lock away the sharp objects. An Asperger's tantrum is like a regular tantrum, but on Jolt! Cola.

"How'd the day go?" I asked him.

"Fine." A tornado could tear through his school, killing half his classmates, and he'd say "fine." On the other hand, let him lose one Pokémon card he has 14 copies of, and the day is "terrible." So I'll take "fine."

He took his books out of his backpack and got straight to his homework. Like most kids with autism, Ethan is a creature of ritual. He does his homework as soon as he gets home. Let him wait until later, even a half-hour later, and there will be a scene resembling King Kong's rampage after the infamous flashbulb incident. Ritual can be good.

By this time, Leah had also made it home. She goes to a so-called primary school. In a year, she'll begin attending Ethan's elementary school. She gets to and from school on a bus. When the bus lets her off in the afternoon, she walks the two doors down from the corner "all by herself," since she is now, at seven, officially "a big girl."

When Leah enters a room, she takes it over through sheer force of personality. This afternoon, she slammed the door behind her, hung up her backpack on the last remaining banister hook, and smiled. "Hi, Daddy." She need do no more—that child has me wrapped around all ten of her fingers and a number of her toes. I have extracted from her a solemn agreement that she always call me "Daddy," no matter how old either one of us gets. In return, I have agreed never to call her "Pussycat" in front of her friends. I got the better end of the deal on that one.

Leah is a peanut—in the fifth percentile for height in her age group. It actually suits her beautifully, since she has raised being cute to an art form, and being small adds to the effect.

"How's my girl today?"

"Good." See previous observation re: comments on the day. I don't think she's ever said anything except "good." A couple of times she's come home in tears, and when I asked how the day had been, she said, "good."

She was already working away on her homework when I forced her to come over and give me a hug. Leah hugs are renowned in my family as the best hugs in the Western Hemisphere, and they are a highlight of any day. She certainly wasn't getting away without one today.

Once they were busily ensconced in homework, I decided I'd better get to work on what I had decided to call the Beckwirth story. Calling it "the Beckwirth *case*" would have been just too Jim Rockford. I started by calling Ladowski in his law office—not the borough office—and telling him that I was investigating. He tried, unsuccessfully, to keep the smirk out of his voice. He also filled me in on some of the details.

He said Gary Beckwirth had been a web specialist for a brokerage house in "The City" (nobody in New Jersey ever actually says "New York") until hitting on exactly the right dot com to invest in and make himself a pile of money. At the age of 46, he was handsome and rich, but I had to work for him anyway.

Madlyn, 44, had been a college student when she met young Gary and fell head over heels. Problem was, every other girl in the dorm fell head over heels for Gary, too, so she had to make herself stand out. Madlyn wasn't the most beautiful girl in the dorm, or even on that floor, but she made sure she slept with Gary first, and that had forged a certain kind of loyalty. I guess what the beer company says is true—you never forget your first girl. Gary had his flings, but he kept coming back to Madlyn. When he was 22 and in business school, he came back once too often, and Madlyn got pregnant. They knew all their options, but still chose to go the old-fashioned route, and got married. Two months later, Madlyn miscarried.

Bucking the odds, they stayed married, Ladowski continued. Gary worked, and Madlyn finished her degree in history, with an eye toward law school. But they didn't have enough money to swing the tuition during those years. And by the time they did, they had a son.

The little Nazi—pardon me, Joel—was born when Gary was just starting to earn bonuses on Wall Street, and was toilet trained roughly when his dad was getting into the computer end of the biz. By the time Joel was in second grade, his father, already a very rich man, continued to provide venture capital to online businesses and invested heavily in web-related companies. He had a good eye for a coming windfall, and generally got himself caught up in the breeze. He also had the rare ability to know when to get out before the roof caved in.

Madlyn, meanwhile, was doing the housewife thing, and happily, according to her husband. She had precipitated the move to Midland Heights five years ago, just about the time Gary had hit the online jackpot. She doted on her son, according to Milt, but couldn't have any more children because of damage done to her uterus during Joel's delivery. In the womb, the kid was already making sure nobody would have it as good as he had it.

This had gone on for 14 years, until now. Gary was rich, Joel was rigid, and Madlyn was gone.

If I'd had to guess, my instinct told me she'd tired of life with Gary and Joel and decided to move on. But who moves on at two o'clock in the morning on an entirely ordinary Monday? Nobody in town seemed to know anything about tension in the Beckwirth house, Milt concluded.

I had to start somewhere, so I decided the first order of business would be to talk to Joel. Kids see and hear more around the house than their parents give them credit for. Maybe I could grill him long enough that he'd have to sweat a trip to the bathroom. Give him a taste of his own medicine. I'd have to have Milt call Gary and make sure I could talk to everyone I needed.

First, I called Barry Dutton at borough police headquarters. Luckily, he knows my name, and took the call. Any other reporter calling the chief would have gotten the message taken, and a call-back sometime around seven, when the chief was done for the day and the reporter, in all likelihood, would be at home, covering a municipal meeting, or catching a quick dinner.

Dutton was in the middle of something, so I asked if he'd be around the next morning, and he said he would. I told him I'd bring the coffee and donuts, and he said to stop making cop jokes. I didn't tell him my coffee would be hot chocolate. Ruins the macho image.

It was just about six, and I had to start thinking about dinner. I do most of the cooking for the kids, since my wife is the commuting breadwinner and the kids get hungry early. I've learned, painstakingly, over the years, to make macaroni and cheese. Out of the blue box. She does most of the cooking for the adults, since she is a good cook.

That was another reason I couldn't be a private investigator. I know about cooking what Dr. Seuss knew about the Great American Novel—how to do it for kids. You read enough mystery books, you find that cooking is practically a pre-requisite for a gumshoe. Spenser cooks for himself and Susan Silverman, usually something involving lamb and champagne, and they invariably have sex while the lamb's in the oven, which is a suggestive image, I guess. What do you want from a guy with no first name?

Elvis Cole is always making venison for himself and Lucy Chenier, but his partner, Joe Pike, is constantly crashing the party, and that means Elvis has to switch to something vegetarian. So all your big detectives cook. Probably Sherlock Holmes could make a steak and kidney pie that would knock your eyes out.

I put a large pot of water on to boil. I wasn't sure exactly what I was making for the kids, but hot water is the basis of virtually everything they eat.

One of the problems with Asperger's kids is that they tend to have somewhat limited menus. Some will eat the same thing, at the same time, every day, just like Woody Allen and Alfred Hitchcock. Others, not being famous filmmakers, are not indulged quite this completely, and will accept two or three variations on a theme at any given meal.

That's the way Ethan is. So my creative choices here were somewhat limited.

I took out some boneless chicken breasts from the meat compartment of the refrigerator, and in a bowl, mixed matzo meal, garlic salt, bread crumbs, and onion powder. I cut the chicken into strips, dredged the strips in the coating mixture, and made sure each piece was covered completely. Then I got a piece of aluminum foil, sprayed it with cooking spray, and put it on the top rack of the oven, which in a triumph of foresight, I had previously turned on. The chicken went onto the aluminum foil.

That would be for Leah. Ethan wouldn't hear of a piece of chicken that wasn't cooked at Burger King, so I decided against having the "you've-got-to-try-new-foods" argument tonight and stuck a couple of hot dogs in the broiler. So call the child welfare people. At least he eats.

Ethan, up in his room with his Nintendo, wouldn't be coming down until called, but Leah wandered into the kitchen, bored with Nickelodeon and looking for someone to talk to.

"Daddy?" She always asked, like she wasn't really sure it was me. "I can think of six words that rhyme with 'bat.'"

"No kidding." The water was boiling, so I got out a box of Ronzoni elbow macaroni—the biggest bang for your pasta buck—and dumped the entire box into the water. Well, okay, it was just the macaroni. The box I put in the recycling bin under the sink.

"Yeah. Cat, sat, fat, rat, hat and . . . um . . ."

I stirred the pasta in the hot water to keep it from becoming one huge ball of elbow, then put the top back on the pot and lowered the flame considerably.

"'Mat'?" I asked, reflexively. Big mistake.

"Daddy! I'm supposed to do it myself!" Leah, although the most adorable child in the tri-state area, has developed a whine that could decalcify the spinal column of the strongest adult. I bent down to look her in the eye.

"I'm sorry," I said. "What word were you thinking of?"

"You used mine!" J'accuse!

Just then the front door opened with its customary creak and Abigail Stein walked into the house. Her legs still looked every bit as good after a long day.

"Mommy!" Leah yelled, and ran to the door. She did her best to take Abigail down in a flying tackle, and came damn close, but my wife managed to put down her briefcase and drape her raincoat over the railing on the stairs in time to avoid hitting the deck.

"Hello, my love," she said to Leah. "How was your day?"

"Good."

Abigail looked at me. "So. Trying to pick up women at Borough Hall again, huh?"

"I couldn't resist, Honey. She had these great legs . . ." I walked over and gave her a welcome home kiss. Any excuse will do.

"Oh, knock it off. They're not *that* good."

Trust me, they are.

# Chapter 6

The kids had eaten by the time Abby came downstairs. We long ago gave up on the idea of a nice family dinner during the week, since for Ethan, eating is merely a quick snack to be gulped down as quickly as possible between cartoon shows, and Abigail gets home on the late side for the kids, so there's no sense in delaying dinner. They're dangerous when hungry. On weekends, or the days when Abby gets home early enough, or when the kids have late snacks, we eat together.

I was cutting up salad stuff when Abigail walked into the kitchen, having changed into a pink T-shirt and gray sweatpants. She frowned, because I was cutting lettuce with a knife. I frowned, because the sweatpants prevented me from seeing her legs.

"You know you're supposed to tear lettuce." She had passed both children on the way in, and they were so deep into the umpteenth rerun of *Hey Arnold* that neither could be bothered to turn around and talk to her. The thrill of her homecoming, like every night, had been brief. For them.

"I don't see how it tastes any different torn, and this is faster." She did one of her "you're-such-a-guy" eye-rolls, and reached under the counter for a pot, which she filled with water and put on the stove. I guess she didn't know what she was going to cook yet, either.

"So this guy wants you to, what, find his wife?" Abby squeezed in between me and the countertop to reach up for some of what we call "the adult noodles." The flavored pastas we keep in an upper cabinet. I didn't make much of an effort to get out of her way, and she smiled. She knew I liked being squeezed next to her.

"Yeah, it's ridiculous. He thinks I'm Mannix or somebody."

"God, you *are* old." She went to work with some sun-dried tomatoes, olive oil, and garlic to make a pasta sauce that might once have been in a cookbook. Or not. All I know is, it involves the food processor, which means extra clean-up time for the kitchen crew, which is mostly me.

"Look on the bright side," I said. "I could have made a passing but obscure reference to C. Auguste Dupin."

"Edgar Allan Poe, right? *The Purloined Letter? Murders in the Rue Morgue?*" I started slicing two celery stalks. Abby wrinkled her nose a little. She won't admit it, but she doesn't much like celery. It's one of the few vegetables I can claim an edge on.

"Very good. Keep that up, and I'll make you stay after school." I gave her my best Groucho eyebrow-wiggle, but she was too intent on cooking to swoon.

"So, why exactly does he think that you're New Jersey's answer to Elliot Ness?"

"I haven't the faintest idea. But if it means I'll keep running into you in the middle of the day, I don't really mind." The lid on the pot was leaking steam, so Abigail put in the linguine and lowered the flame.

"Don't count on it. I'll be in the office the rest of the week." She turned back to face me, and I slipped my arms around her waist and kissed her.

"This is my favorite part of the day," I told her. I spend half my time trying to come up with new ways to tell her I love her. And we've been married 14 years. Disgusting, isn't it?

"Well then, anything that would have happened later tonight would have been a letdown, wouldn't it?"

"What's this 'would have' stuff?"

"Well, I don't want to disappoint you . . ."

I was just about to kiss her again when the phone rang. Abigail was standing right next to the kitchen wall phone, but simply stood and looked at me. She refuses to answer the phone at home, insisting that it's either a business call for me or someone she doesn't want to talk to. Luckily, I wasn't far from her, and I reached past her head to pick up the phone.

"Hello?"

The voice was muffled, as if a cloth had been placed over the mouthpiece, and the caller mumbled, just in case the cloth wasn't doing its job properly. The caller was definitely male, but that's all I could tell. In fact, I barely made out a sound before I heard the name "Madlyn Beckwirth."

"What? What did you say?"

Whoever it was spoke up just a little, as if irritated by my inability to hear him the first time. "I said you should leave Madlyn Beckwirth alone. Find her, and you'll kill her."

"Who is this?" Bright question. Like the guy's going to just give me his name, address, and social security number while perpetrating what I was relatively sure was a crime. And there are people who think I'm a detective. "Hello?"

Click.

# Chapter 7

I must have been staring at the phone, because Abby looked at me with concern. Her eyes kept moving from my face to the receiver in my hand.

"Somebody selling us something?"

I hung up the phone and walked to the kitchen table. I sat down. Abby walked over, worried now.

"What is it? Who was that?"

"I don't know. Somebody said that if I find Madlyn Beckwirth, I'll kill her."

"WHAT? What the hell does *that* mean?" She sat down in another of the kitchen chairs, which creaked. I made a mental note to tighten the screws under the chairs. Somehow, that didn't seem terribly important right now.

"I have no idea. Some guy said I should leave Madlyn Beckwirth alone, because if I found her, I would kill her."

"Jesus!" But even then, I could see the legal mind going to work. She frowned. "Who knows you're looking for Madlyn Beckwirth?"

I thought. "Nobody. Gary Beckwirth, Milt Ladowski, and Dave Harrington. I think we can eliminate Harrington from the suspects. Beckwirth is desperate for me to find Madlyn, so he wouldn't call, and Milt is the one who hired me."

"Milt Ladowski wouldn't make a call like that," said my wife. "His whole law practice could be ruined if he's found making a threatening call." One of Abby's few failings is that she thinks everyone else thinks like her. Nobody would ever do anything irrational, or not consider the consequences, because she would never do anything irrational, or not consider the consequences.

"Wait a second . . ." I got up and walked to the phone, picked it up, and punched *69. If I knew the number from which my last call had come, I'd be able to trace . . .

"This service cannot be activated, because the telephone number is not in our service area." I hung up. Abby looked at me with that same concern, as I must have looked completely baffled.

"What?"

"The call came from outside Verizon's coverage area. That means that unless Beckwirth or Ladowski got into a car and drove west at 80 miles an hour from the moment they last saw me, it wasn't either of them."

Now Abby looked baffled. "So who else knows that you're looking for Madlyn Beckwirth?"

"Apparently, somebody who doesn't want me to find her."

The sun-dried tomatoes sizzled on the stove, and Abby took a moment before walking over to deal with them.

We exchanged tense glances all through dinner. Fortunately, the kids managed not to crack under the strain, because *Catdog* was now on.

# Chapter 8

The next morning, after making lunches and breakfasts and kissing my wife good-bye and making sure all the homework was in backpacks and walking Ethan through the ritual of putting on his shoes and picking up his stuff and putting on his jacket and walking out the door, (then coming back in to say good-bye, then forgetting to close the door on the way), and after putting my daughter on the schoolbus, I walked into Barry Dutton's office carrying a Dunkin' Donuts bag.

"Morning, Chief."

"Don't call me Chief!" We laughed at the joke from the old (and I do mean *old*) *Superman* TV series. We are both George Reeves fans.

Barry is a year older than me, which would make him 44. He stands about six feet tall, and isn't fat. I stand considerably under six feet tall, and I could lose ten pounds. Okay, fifteen. But we go back a long way, and he doesn't scare me. Anymore.

He gestured to the chair in front of his metal desk (with maple woodtone top, of course), and I walked to it. Before I sat, though, I opened the bag, carefully checked the two cups, and gave him the one with the coffee. Light, no sugar. Like it changes the taste of that stuff at all.

Dutton saw me take another hot cup out of the bag, and snickered. "Is that cocoa?"

"We who have taste prefer to call it hot chocolate."

"Hot chocolate is two adjectives. You work with words, you should know that. Hot, chocolate *what?"*

I sat down and sighed. "You're a real pain in the ass, Barry. You should have been a freelance writer." He laughed. The really intelligent people laugh all the time at what I say.

"I assume you're not here just to buy me a cup of coffee, are you?" Dutton walked to his desk and sat on the edge. I shook my head "no," and then reached into the bag. I took out two donuts: a regular cruller for me, and for Dutton, a creme-filled chocolate. His eyes widened. His wife had been after him to lose weight (like he needed to) for months, and he hadn't seen a creme-filled chocolate (you'll notice they don't spell it "cream," and there's a reason) since roughly last spring.

"This *is* serious, isn't it?" He considered, almost walked away, then picked up the donut and smelled it, inhaling deeply, a man enthralled. "You know I'm on the Carbohydrate Addict's Diet, don't you? I'm not supposed to have anything like this."

"You gonna let Donna push you around? Who wears the gun in your family?"

"Oh, what the hell." He bit greedily into it, and a little of the chocolate stuff masquerading as cream squished out from the hole they put in the donut for exactly that purpose. There was a low rumble, something like a small earthquake, which I came to realize was Barry enjoying the donut. He smiled, and sat down in his swivel chair.

I took a napkin out of the Dunkin' Donuts bag and threw it at him. "Here. You got powdered sugar all over yourself, and you're going to lose the respect of your men."

"It's worth it," he said. At least, I *think* that's what he said. He could barely get a sound out through the mouthful of donut. What actually came out sounded more like "iss worf id." With the donut nearly consumed, Dutton's eyes narrowed, he swallowed one last time, sat up, and considered me. "You're plying me with a donut."

I reached into the bag for the chocolate frosted. "You want another one?"

"Oh, boy. This must be a doozy." Imagine a police chief who uses the word "doozy." Luckily, the man pumps iron every day of his life, and has a chest the size of a five-drawer dresser, so everyone is afraid to call him on it. He took a long gulp of his coffee. "What is it?"

"Madlyn Beckwirth."

Dutton's mouth tightened down to a slit in his face. His eyebrows threatened to meet in the middle. And his eyes actually closed, as if he were grimacing in pain. It startled me, and I leaned forward just a bit. Quick as a flash, Dutton reached over and grabbed the chocolate frosted out of my hand. Hell, I would have just given it to him.

"Why are you bothering me about Madlyn Beckwirth?"

"I'm writing about it."

"Why, did she take the stereo system with her when she left?" It's good to have a funny police chief. He must keep the criminals in stitches —maybe laughs them into confessions. I knew for a fact he'd never drawn his gun on anyone in his life.

"The *Press-Tribune* assigned her to me. I'm looking into her disappearance."

"You're kidding." I sat and looked at him.

"Would I have brought donuts if I were kidding?" I tried to look intense, but that's hard to do with a hot chocolate mustache.

"Aaron," Dutton said, "Madlyn Beckwirth probably ran out on her husband because he's an insufferable twit." Even the cops in Midland Heights sound like college professors. Can you imagine a cop at the 23rd Precinct in New York City saying "insufferable twit"?

"Probably. But *he* doesn't think so."

"They never think so. It's part of what makes them so insufferable," Dutton said.

I took a bite of the cruller. Dunkin' Donuts hadn't lost its touch. "Well, there's more."

"Don't talk with your mouth full. More *what?* More donuts?" He looked hopefully in the bag, but all he found were packets of artificial sweetener and about fifty-eight napkins.

"You really *are* a carbohydrate addict, aren't you? No, not more donuts. More about Madlyn Beckwirth."

"Oh yeah?"

I told him about the prior evening's threatening phone call, and I saw my friend Barry become Chief Dutton of the Midland Heights Police Department. He sat back and listened, absolutely all attention. If I could get Ethan to listen like that in fifth grade, I could start filling out his application to Princeton tomorrow. Dutton put his fingers together, like he was going to show me the church and the steeple, and put them to his nose. When I got to the end of the phone conversation, and my attempt to trace it, he stood up.

"Outside the area? Maybe I can trace it here. Let me get Verizon to send over your phone records from last night. Maybe we can find out who made that call." He looked at me, frowning. "Were you going to tell me about this?"

"I just told you, didn't I? And I made the appointment to see you before it happened. I knew I'd be here this morning."

He didn't like it, and neither did I. The only people who knew for sure that I was looking for Madlyn Beckwirth couldn't have made the call, and the idea that, by finding her, I'd be killing her just flat-out didn't make sense. I asked Dutton what the cops had been doing to locate her after Beckwirth reported his wife missing.

"Well, he hasn't exactly been forthcoming with help, you know. Won't let us talk to his son. Doesn't want to let us into his phone records. He 'doesn't see what that has to do with this.' He's convinced somebody just up and snatched the woman out of her bed at two o'clock in the morning while he slept."

I nodded. "So you sent a detective over. Westbrook?"

"It's a small town, Aaron, and a small police force. You think I'm loaded with detectives around here? Beckwirth wouldn't talk to me, so yes, I sent Westbrook."

"Is he around?"

Dutton picked up his phone and pushed a button. "Marsha, ask Gerry to come in here, would you?" He put down the phone and looked at me. "You take it easy on him." A pause. "So you come in with two donuts."

"Three." I waved the other half of my cruller at him. He had inhaled the chocolate frosted, and probably was thinking about pulling his gun on me for the rest of the cruller. I bravely stuck it out, and had it just about finished when Westbrook walked in.

Gerry Westbrook had spent twenty-five years as a Midland Heights cop. It took twenty-two of them to make detective. His shift to plain clothes was so impressive—to him—that he actually wore his shield on the outside of his jacket. And not just on the job, either—at the movies, in the supermarket, at the florist, wherever. If his I.Q. were as large as his hat size after the swelling of his head, he'd have been the greatest detective in history.

He was of average height, making him taller than me, and needed to lose fifty pounds, so at least I could feel superior in the waistline. He also had lost almost all his hair, and was doing that Larry Fine thing with what was left. I, of course, have every follicle I started out with, although some of it is not the original color. Westbrook grunted in my direction as he came in.

"What's the electronics press doing here, Chief? We installing a big-screen TV in the squad room?" The level of wit in a room always rises when Westbrook leaves.

"You have to have a squad before you can have a squad room, Westbrook," I told him. "Of course, if you gain another couple pounds, you might qualify as a squad all by yourself."

Dutton stifled a chuckle. Westbrook would have reacted to the fat joke, but he was trying to sneak a peak inside the Dunkin' Donuts bag to see if there might be some powdered sugar he could lick up.

"Gerry," Dutton said, trying to re-establish some sort of professional tone, "Aaron is working on an article about the missing persons report you took the other day."

"Bulworth?"

I groaned. *"Bulworth* is a movie with Warren Beatty, Gerry. This is *Beckwirth.* Madlyn Beckwirth."

"Yeah, yeah. Beckwirth, Bulworth . . . what's the difference?"

I looked at Dutton. "Is it any wonder the case isn't solved yet? With Inspector Clouseau here working his usual magic, it's a wonder more people aren't missing."

Westbrook's face turned red, matching his nose. *"You're* gonna be missing in another minute, pip-squeak!" I think he would have lunged at me, if he were capable of lunging, but the extra fifty pounds made it more like a lumber than a lunge. *Pip-squeak?*

Dutton said, "oh, sit down, Gerry." Westbrook lost his bluster and sat in the chair next to me. But he moved it a few inches away, so our sleeves wouldn't touch on the armrests. I was hurt, but I managed not to show it.

Dutton leaned across his desk and pointed a finger at Westbrook. "You're going to cooperate fully with Aaron on this, Gerry, or I'm gonna know about it. Is *that* clear?"

Westbrook flapped his jaw a little, but nodded. Then Dutton pointed his finger at me. "And you, Mr. Tucker, are going to be respectful of my detective at all times, or I will bring the full power of the legal system to bear on you. Is that clear?"

I blinked, but managed "sure."

"Good," said Dutton. "Now, both of you get the hell out of my office." He pointed toward the door.

Westbrook managed to extricate himself from the chair, while I contemplated how a system of pulleys and chain-hoists might be more efficient. He walked out first, and I turned at the door to face Dutton.

"*The full power of the legal system?*"

He chuckled. "That's right. I'll tell your wife on you."

You gotta love funny cops.

# Chapter 9

Gerry Westbrook knew roughly as much about Madlyn Beckwirth's disappearance as I know about Organic Chemistry, and that's a course I assiduously managed to avoid in high school.

Westbrook had faxed the State Police and the surrounding cops about Madlyn, checked the morgue and the hospitals, and then gone out to Denny's and forgotten the whole thing.

After the necessary 30-second conversation with Westbrook to find this out, I walked out of the police/fire building and inhaled as much air as my little lungs could hold. We'd been experiencing typical March weather — one day of unseasonable warmth, followed the next day by a slap in the face of late-winter chill. This was one of the warm days, so I decided to walk to Gary Beckwirth's house from the police station.

I had stuck the cell phone in my jacket pocket on the way out. Flush with a $6,000 paycheck sent me by the online service of a cable entertainment network, I had bought myself a wireless phone a couple of months before. Abby had had one for a few years already. Since I'd covered the wireless industry for years, I got a deal. I was still trying to figure out how to pay the monthly rate, but what the hell, I looked cool talking while I walked, like I was negotiating a three-picture deal with Paramount on the way to the Foodtown. On a whim, I whipped the phone out and tried Abigail's office number. Surprisingly, she answered.

"Abigail Stein."

"How dare you defile my wife's name like that?"

"I know. I feel so cheap. How are you?"

"Fat," I told her. "I just bribed the chief of police with fried dough."

"You should go to the Y."

"Can't. I have to go talk to Beckwirth. I only have until next Thursday on this, and right now I'm nowhere."

Abby was silent. She was probably in her problem-solving mode, frowning.

"I can hear you frown," I said.

"You should be here. It's quite fetching, really."

"I had a dog once who was quite fetching."

She groaned. I have that effect on women. "Was there a point to this call, or are you just trying out awful puns and figured I didn't have anything else to do but listen?"

"I'm strolling up Edison Avenue in the warm March sunshine, and the blue sky made me think of you." There was more silence on the line. "Now I can hear you smile."

"It's even better than hearing me frown."

I smiled. "I know."

I usually change topics in a conversation like a 1986 Dodge pick-up in need of a ring job. Abby shifted conversational gears smoothly, like a BMW. "What did Barry have to say about the phone call?" she asked. She was already calling it "the phone call." Eventually, it would become "The Phone Call," and then I'd really be in trouble.

"He's going to get our phone records from Verizon. He'll trace it."

"Good," she said. "I shudder to think what would have happened if one of the kids had answered the phone."

"I'd have died of a heart attack. They don't answer the phone when they're sitting right next to it. They inherited that gene from their mom."

I was now passing the supermarket. Industrious Midland Heights residents were jockeying for parking spaces in the store's woefully inadequate lot. Of course, because this is New Jersey, nobody was walking, not even the people who lived across the street from the supermarket. So naturally the parking lot was woefully inadequate. Because I was counter-culture, and walking outside to get to my destination, I might have patted myself on the back for my commitment to the environment, but then, to be a complete environmentalist, I probably would have had to jettison the cell phone I was holding next to my ear (hadn't it been linked to cancer somehow?).

"Is it possible that it was Madlyn Beckwirth herself calling you?" Again, my wife's amazing capacity to change the subject served her well.

"No, it was definitely a male voice on the phone. On the other hand, since I wouldn't be able to pick Madlyn out of a line-up, it's equally possible I wouldn't know if she had a voice like James Earl Jones." A woman in the Foodtown parking lot was wrestling with this weird gadget they have that makes you pay 25-cents for a cart, then pays you back when you leave. She shook the gadget both ways, then hit it with her purse. Clearly, it wouldn't give her back her quarter. Finally, she kicked the cart, yelled something in the store's direction, and stomped back to her minivan. Another quarter in the pockets of the Establishment. If she came back with a pair of channel locks and cut the gadget off, every citizen of the borough would have applauded.

I passed the supermarket and crossed the main drag of Midland Heights, Midland Avenue (original, huh?), against the light, trotting across the far lane. A guy in a Mercedes-Benz 4x4 honked and gave me the finger as he passed. Probably on his way to pick up his tuxedo for some mountain climbing.

"That call really worries me, Aaron," said Abigail. "Somebody knows what you're doing, and they know where you live."

"That's why I have you to protect me, Love."

"Everything's not a joke, Baby," she said. "We have two small children living in our house."

I considered pointing out that Ethan is not close to being a small child, and could in fact take me two out of three falls, but I saw her point. "I'll be careful, Honey. And if this gets out of hand, I'll tell Harrington he can have the assignment back."

Beckwirth's house was a block past the library, and I was approaching it now. "I'll talk to you later, Abby. Don't worry."

"What, me worry?" My wife—a regular Alfred E. Neuman.

I said a few loving-husband things far too mushy to record for posterity, put the phone—which was already flashing the "battery low" signal—back in my pocket, and rang the bell on Beckwirth's door. The huge house stood silent, and I half expected a thin, bald-headed butler with a British accent, to open the door. Ian Wolfe, maybe. John Gielgud, if it was going to be a big part, and he was still alive.

My luck, it was Beckwirth. At least he had shaved, and was dressed in clean clothes, but he still had that recovering-addict look in his eyes, and his skin looked like it was made out of vanilla Turkish Taffy that had melted on the sidewalk. There was an upside, though. This time he didn't hug me. You have to accentuate the positive.

"Well, Gary, you got me. I'm not sure why you wanted to so badly, but you got me."

"Come in," he said quickly. I did, and he closed the door. His mood was not nearly as welcoming as it had been the last time. Again, I wasn't complaining, because it seemed there would be no physical contact on this visit, but now that Beckwirth had gotten me involved in finding his wife, he didn't seem to want to know me anymore. Familiarity, apparently, really does breed contempt. At least in my case.

"Sit down," Beckwirth said, pointing at a loveseat in the adjoining room, which I guess was a study, or a library, or a sitting room, or some other kind of a room that people in the middle class generally don't have. Maybe if I did find Madlyn, I'd tell Beckwirth my fee required the moving of one of his mansion's extra rooms to my house. I could badly use a separate room for my office. That morning, I'd stepped on a Working Woman Barbie getting to my fax machine, and put a permanent dent in my right instep.

"What's the matter, Gary? Having me isn't as pleasing a thing as wanting me?" *Star Trek.* Sometimes you have to go with the classics.

"I want to go over your strategy. I want to know everything you're going to do before you do it." Beckwirth, I guess, was used to dealing with employees. Now that I was, indirectly, working for him, he thought I was an employee.

"I can't do that."

He stared. No doubt his minions had never said "no" to him before, and his body language said clearly, "You must have misunderstood. This was not a request." Then, with real words, he put it to me this way, "Of course you can. Just tell me what you plan to do."

"No. For one thing, I don't know that you didn't have something to do with Madlyn disappearing."

Now, Beckwirth positively sputtered. It was a good performance, though I'm no drama critic. I'm no detective, either, so any observations I make have to be taken with a shaker of salt. "Why would I be so anxious to have you investigate if I were behind Madlyn's kidnapping? That's ridiculous."

"You could be doing your best to divert suspicion," I said calmly. "Or you could be doing your best to hamper the investigation by making sure the least competent person available is working on it."

Beckwirth did his best to smile a friendly smile in a regular-guy sort of way. I'm sure most women would have ripped off their underwear and launched themselves at him after he gave them such a smile, with just enough teeth and a twinkle in his eye. Well, some women. Not Abigail, I'd like to think.

"Oh, you're just being modest," he said.

"No, I'm not. I haven't the faintest idea if I'm doing the right thing. I could be hampering the investigation myself, because I don't know what I'm doing. But I'm what you asked for, and I'm what you got. At a bargain price for an investigator, I hasten to add. And an inflated price for a freelancer."

His eyes narrowed. "Is that it? Not enough money?"

I threw my hands up, exasperated. "No, that's not it!" I, well, screamed. "I'm telling you that if you're really trying to find your wife, you're going about it in the wrong way! *You've hired the wrong man!* Is that clear enough?"

Apparently, it wasn't. Beckwirth tried the ol' regular-guy smile again. "Don't worry. I have faith in you."

There is nothing you can do with some people. Gary Beckwirth was one of them. So I proceeded. First, though, just to show him my level of irritation, I sighed.

"Ooooooooookay," I said. "The first thing I have to do is talk to your son."

The businesslike frown and impersonal tone came back to Beckwirth. He picked up a croissant from—I swear to God—a silver tray on the coffee table, and took a bite. Apparently, he could shift gears easily, too. I considered taking myself in for a tune-up. "Joel? That is your son's name, isn't it?" I said.

He ignored me. I was getting used to being ignored. "Joel is very upset by his mother's disappearance. I don't think he would be very helpful to an investigation."

"All right, we'll wait a little while on Joel."

Beckwirth stood, to better intimidate me. It wasn't working, largely due to the croissant crumbs on his shirt. "I don't think you understand. I don't want you to involve Joel at all. Besides, there's no reason to talk to Joel. This is a case of kidnapping, and it's tied to the campaign for mayor. Joel has nothing to do with it."

"You think that people would resort to abduction over a $20,000-a-year part-time job?"

"You have no idea, Aaron. The corruption in this town is rampant.

And the other side will stop at nothing to keep what they have."

*The other side?* I wasn't interested in playing this role. I wasn't interested in being in this movie. I had no response to the torrent of clichés he had just tossed at me.

"When do I get to talk to your son, Gary?"

"I just don't see the point to that," he said, his face impassive.

I stood. Two could play this standing-up game. My intention, however, was not to intimidate Beckwirth. My intention was to leave.

"Mr. Beckwirth . . ."

"Gary."

*Oy gevalt.* "*Mr. Beckwirth,*" I began. "I'm a reporter following a news story. I'm under contract to the Central New Jersey *Press-Tribune* to investigate, and write about, the disappearance of your wife. I'm under no obligation to you whatsoever. So we're either going to proceed by my rules, or I will go home, call my editor, tell him I'm unable to find out anything, and your wife will remain missing. Until such time as the police find her, which in all probability they will. Now. Am I going to get to talk to your son, or am I going to turn down the assignment and get back to something I know how to do?"

"Joel isn't here."

In retrospect, I don't know why I didn't go for his throat at that moment. I certainly *wanted* to go for his throat. It would have made me feel better. It would have been the right thing to do. Probably visions of arraignments and prison terms danced in my head. I've not been married to an attorney all these years for nothing, after all. In any event, I didn't give Beckwirth the throttling he deserved.

I didn't even ask why he hadn't mentioned his son's absence throughout this conversation. I merely stared at him a moment, hoping my eyes would convey contempt and astonishment at his behavior, and pressed on.

"Fine," I said a little too forcefully. "I'll talk to him later." I didn't give Beckwirth time to interject. "Now, may I see your last three months' worth of phone bills?"

Beckwirth put down the croissant and turned away to look out the window. I half expected him to walk to a wet bar and pour himself a brandy from a crystal decanter, like they do on all the soap operas when the director can't think of any other way to communicate tension.

"I don't see what benefit that would have," he said.

I turned and left.

*Oy gevalt.*

# Chapter 10

"So this guy wants you to find his wife, but he doesn't want you to ask questions or anything. Is that it?" Jeff Mahoney stuck another shim under the screen door we were both holding up, and tapped it in with a hammer. It stayed, and we each went to work on a hinge, screwing each into the door jamb. "What, are you supposed to throw a dart at the map and start looking, or drive up and down the Turnpike yelling her name?"

Mahoney has been my best friend ever since he wore sneakers to our senior prom. He'd lost a bet to me at the high school cafeteria lunch table (it hinged on the name Gummo Marx, but that's a whole other story), but I had never intended to hold him to it. Prom night, he showed up in a cream-colored tuxedo, light green shirt, brown bow tie, and high-top Converse tennis shoes (it was the '70s—get off my case). In admiration for his personal integrity, I took off my shoes and spent the rest of the evening in my stocking feet. Strangely, neither of us ever heard again from our prom dates. Women, we theorized, just didn't understand codes of honor.

Now, Mahoney was six-foot-three and built roughly like that big hunk of rock that confounds everybody in *2001: A Space Odyssey*. Needless to say, during our little home maintenance chore, he was concentrating on the upper hinge of the door, while I knelt down to deal with the lower one. We each had a cordless screwdriver. I found this amusing, since I've never seen a corded screwdriver.

"I'm stuck," I said.

"What, did the shims come out?"

"No. On the story." Mahoney works as a mechanic for one of the larger car rental agencies at Newark International Airport, and travels around the state fixing their broken-down junk-heaps. He is also a disciple of Bob Vila, so whenever I need to do anything more complicated than change a light bulb in the house, he gets a call. It's a ritual: I ask him how I should do it, he suggests using a tool I don't have, and the next thing I know, he's at my house, "helping" me with the repair, which means I hand him tools while he does the work. Sometimes I actually hand him the proper tools.

"Well, I don't get it," he said. "Why would the guy ask you to find his wife, and then stop you from finding her?"

"Maybe it's a love/hate relationship."

Mahoney looked down. "No, move a little bit to your left." I thought my hinge was in exactly the right place, but since he is right about these things roughly 100 percent of the time, I asked no questions, and moved it slightly to the left. "Good. Right there."

"Maybe he really *doesn't* want me to find his wife. Maybe he's glad she's gone, but doesn't want to admit it. Maybe he's just a rich guy who's used to having everybody do everything his way, and he doesn't like me insisting on doing it my way."

I pressed the button on my cordless screwdriver, but the screw didn't go in. Sheepishly, I noted that I had the machine set for "reverse." Changing it, I looked up to see that Mahoney had driven in all three of his screws already.

"Rich people suck," he said, and laughed. At a much younger age, Mahoney and I, along with three of our friends (these days, they'd be called our "posse"), used to drive around Millburn, Short Hills, and Upper Saddle River, proclaiming that very slogan ("Rich People Suck") out our car windows at an amplified volume. It was a sentiment that came straight from our hearts. One of those "posse" guys is now a state assemblyman.

"Maybe so, but this particular rich guy is indirectly paying me a grand to find his wife."

"That's all?" Mahoney started driving in the screws I wasn't working on. He wasn't showing me up. He just does everything better than I do.

"What do you mean, 'that's all?'" I said. "That's like five times what I'd usually get for a newspaper story like this."

"Hell of a lot less than V.I. Warshawski would take." Mahoney was a fan of the female detectives. He was especially fond of Kay Scarpetta, the snoopy coroner, and Kat Colorado, the L.A. detective with (surprise) a bad love life. I was more partial to Stephanie Plum, the Trenton-based bounty hunter. She readily admitted not knowing what she was doing.

We stepped back to admire his handiwork. It looked perfect. But when I opened the door to try it, it flew open and almost clocked me in the forehead. I jumped back in alarm while Mahoney practically had a seizure, doubling over in laughter. It's nice to have a best friend.

"You've ... gotta ... put on the ... spring," he managed between roars of hilarity. I snatched the spring and two O-hooks out of his hand and let him see me measure exactly where on the door jamb I intended to put them.

Mahoney stopped laughing, eventually, and watched me with the eye of a proud teacher. I must have been doing something right.

I made a pencil mark on the jamb at the level of the door's wooden divider (no sense trying to screw the spring into the screen), and used the drill to make a pilot hole in the wood. Then I attached the spring to the hook and set about screwing the hook into the pilot hole.

"Hold it," Mahoney said. I stopped immediately, and he took the hook out of my hand and removed the spring from the hook. "Put the spring on *after* you've got the hook in. It's easier."

I did just that. "Anyway," I said, trying to regain a little self-respect,

"I don't care what V.I. would have gotten for the job. I'm not a detective, and her movie was boring."

"Bad script," said Mahoney. "Kathleen Turner was good to look at, though."

"She generally is," I agreed, "but the aforementioned lack of script definitely sunk the movie."

"What do you know?" he said, with just the hint of a twinkle in his eye. "You're not a detective."

The goddam hook wouldn't get started in the hole, and I was getting frustrated. "I'm a screenwriter."

"I thought to be considered a screenwriter, you have to get paid for it." That's what the twinkle was about. He was looking for a place to stick the needle in, and he'd found my soft spot. Right where he knew it would be.

I didn't rise to the bait. "I've gotten some option money," I said. "Besides, I'm living three thousand miles away from the right place for that kind of work. And how is this helping me find Madlyn Beckwirth?"

He knelt down, taking the hook out of my hand and starting it himself. Of course, for him, it went in like it was dying to start its new life as a spring anchor. "I thought I was helping you put up a screen door. Since when am I supposed to help you find Madlyn Beckwirth?"

The hook was in, and I actually managed to attach the spring without any outside help. "Since you decided to belittle my fee," I told him. "You want to mock me, you can at least help me, too."

"I do all the work around here." He started attaching the hook to the door, and neither of us tried to perpetuate the myth that I was actually doing anything useful in this project. I sat down.

"Let's assume for the moment that I can't talk to the kid and I can't get the phone records," I said. "Where does that leave me? I have no options."

"Sure you do." Mahoney had the hook embedded in the door securely and was stretching the spring to meet it. This door would close faster than a frog's tongue going after a fly. "You can still talk to the friends of the family, you can go after this girl who's running for mayor, you can get the cops to run Madlyn's credit cards and see if she's charging up a storm in Vegas on the old man's Visa."

He attached the spring to the hook, and tried the door. Sure enough, it closed perfectly, with a satisfying SNAP! that would undoubtedly become tiresome this coming summer. "I don't want to talk to the woman who's running for mayor," I said thoughtfully.

"Why not?"

"Because the rich guy wants me to. That's what this whole maneuver has been all about. He wants to control the way I track down his wife."

Mahoney set about measuring for the doorknob. "You got any coffee?" he asked. That was it—I'd been relegated to kitchen duty. I got up. He chuckled as I walked away from the front door and toward the kitchen.

"Rich people suck," he said to himself.

# Chapter 11

Rachel Barlow sat in her kitchen, which was bright and airy and had nice white lace curtains on the windows. Plants hung from the space over the sink, where they'd be sure to get plenty of light and moisture. The wallpaper was a subdued pattern of milk pails and straw piles. The floor was ceramic tile. The chairs and table were country oak. There was absolutely nothing out of place. It was like being in the Museum of Suburban Kitchens.

Rachel herself, every inch the political candidate, subsection: female, was in a very sensible skirt and blouse, not showing anything above the knee or below the shoulder blades. Thank goodness, or my uncontrollable male urges might have moved me to throw her down on the center island and have my way with her. She was tall and blonde, and looked like she really wished she could wear a beehive hairdo, because it would have made her more comfortable.

"Can I get you some coffee?" she asked in a voice that sounded very much like that of a Barbie doll who had grown up and gotten her MBA. "We have regular and decaf."

"No, that's okay," I said. "I think we should just get going on this."

I know. I had just told Mahoney I wasn't going to talk to Rachel Barlow, and here I was, talking to Rachel Barlow. Well, there were good reasons for changing my mind. For one, I had already checked with

Dutton, who had nothing on Madlyn's credit cards, but expected word back on my telephone records by that afternoon. And I had talked to two of Madlyn and Gary's friends (actually, Madlyn's), both of whom reported no problems in the marriage and absolutely nothing unusual of late. I had decided, also, that my petty feelings about Gary shouldn't impede the investigation, so I shouldn't exclude a whole avenue of inquiry just because it came from him. Besides, I didn't have any other ideas.

Rachel Barlow had decided to run for mayor, I found out through Harrington's clip morgue, because she felt it was time for "a new voice" in Midland Heights. Seeing as how the old voice, Mayor Sam Olszowy, had been in office for more than fifteen years at the time, it was a safe bet that the town liked hearing the voice it had now.

But Olszowy had made several potentially critical errors. He had seriously underestimated Rachel Barlow, dismissing her out of hand as a credible threat in the Democratic primary. There are no more than 200 registered Republicans in town, so the Democratic primary, assuming Hitler isn't nominated, will pretty much decide the general election.

In office and in his campaign, Olszowy was ignoring the town's changing demographics, too. He continued to cater to the senior citizens, who didn't want the school budget passed, and weren't interested in bringing more businesses to the downtown, either. But ignoring young parents in Midland Heights is like running for office in New York and announcing that you're a big Atlanta Braves fan.

Next thing you know, Rachel Barlow, with her "we'll set up a committee and investigate it" platform, and her strong advocacy of a healthy school budget, despite having no children of her own, was running close to even with Olszowy in the polls (assuming one can take accurate polls in an election this insignificant). Who the mayor of Midland Park might turn out to be would have as much an impact on my life as what brand of liquid soap they chose to put in the men's room at New Jersey Turnpike rest stops. Maybe less.

"What is it you want to know?" Rachel asked, her hands folded in her lap, like the last contestant at a fifth-grade spelling bee waiting for the word "extraneous" to be called out.

"Well, to start, how well do you know Madlyn Beckwirth?"

Rachel shifted gears to that of a beauty pageant contestant asked how bikini waxing could actually help end hunger in Third World countries. Her eyes rolled up in their sockets, looking for an answer lodged tightly in her left frontal lobe.

"Madlyn is my campaign manager. We moved to town just about when she and Gary did, five years ago. I asked her to manage my campaign because she's my best friend, and I trust her. Also because she brings an impeccable record to public service, having been a past president of the PTO at Roosevelt School and treasurer of the Boy Scout troop her son used to belong to." Rachel rolled her eyes back down to look into mine, with all the charm of a department store mannequin.

"That's fine," I said, in my best reporter style, "but I'm really not looking for her resumé, and I'm not asking essay questions, either. This isn't a shadow-debate with Mayor Olszowy. Just relax and talk to me."

"I thought that was what I was doing." Rachel's eyes bored in just a bit, and widened maybe a millimeter. There was a side of her that you didn't want to cross. She was hiding it, but not well.

"You are, but you need to relax. We're just having a conversation. You're not being questioned by the grand jury." I was trying my best to smile, but the cold front that had drifted over the kitchen table was hard to get past. I was pretty sure I could see my breath. "Now. Have you noticed Madlyn acting unusual lately?"

"*Unusual?*" Rachel said the word like it would be visible coming out of her mouth, and would be ugly and hairy. Anything that wasn't usual clearly wouldn't be welcome in this kitchen.

"Not ordinary," I said. "Something she wouldn't do under normal circumstances."

"I know what 'unusual' means." Rachel didn't exactly spit the words out at me, but she would have liked to. Only her terrific political instincts prevented a harsh, adversarial tone from kicking in. Great warming up the source, Tucker. The Pulitzer committee will no doubt reward your interviewing techniques someday. "No," added the mayoral hopeful. I waited.

"That's it? No?"

"No. I didn't see anything *unusual* in the way Madlyn's been acting lately."

"She didn't seem at all anxious or nervous?"

"No."

"Excited about something?"

"No."

"Worried about anything?"

*"No."*

"Mention anything to you about trouble in her marriage?"

"Good lord, no."

I stood up. "Well," I said, reaching for my denim jacket, "I'm sorry to have taken your time."

Rachel looked surprised. "That's it? You're not going to ask me about my campaign?"

"That's not what this interview is about, Rachel. I thought Milt explained that I'm looking into Madlyn's disappearance."

"But the campaign is the reason for Madlyn's disappearance," said the I-wanna-be-the-mayor.

I stopped, midway through shrugging the jacket onto my shoulders. "You know that for sure?"

"Absolutely. Madlyn said she'd been getting phone calls, anonymous ones, threatening her if she kept managing my campaign. She didn't take them seriously at first, but when they started coming every night, she got upset."

I sat back down. "Did she call the police?"

"No. Gary doesn't trust Chief Dutton. He believes the town police force is guilty of racial profiling."

"Has Gary ever *met* Chief Dutton?"

Rachel smiled tolerantly. She was dealing with a mental midget, and she knew it. But one must keep up appearances, especially if one wants to gain high elected office. "Just because the chief is an African-American doesn't mean he wouldn't tolerate, even encourage, racial profiling if he thought his arrest rate would go up and his reputation would be enhanced."

It occurred to me to point out that racial profiling was something done to ferret out drug dealers, operating under the racist assumption that non-whites are more likely than whites to be drug dealers. But the police in Midland Heights spend roughly 98 percent of their time giving out speeding tickets in a town whose speed limit never exceeds twenty-five miles per hour. As far as I knew, even the Grand Wizard of the KKK didn't believe that being a member of a minority group made one more likely to drive forty miles per hour.

Still, I needed information from this woman, and engaging in a debate probably wouldn't help me get it. "So she didn't call the cops. Did Madlyn do anything else about the phone calls?"

"Well, she tried to 'star-sixty-nine' them, you know, but it was always out of the coverage area. And Gary wanted her to buy a gun, but she said they scared her."

"You think whoever made those calls is responsible for Madlyn's disappearance?"

Tears began to form in the corners of Rachel Barlow's eyes. They appeared to be real. "I think they killed her," she said softly.

# Chapter 12

Some expressions sound exactly like what they mean. In my case, "in over my head" was precisely what I was. This is not a height joke. I was now operating in clearly alien territory, and most probably hostile territory as well. Everything I was doing, breathing included, had become a conscious and calculated effort.

Rachel Barlow, of course, was completely obsessed with her own self-importance. That was the only explanation for her thinking that someone would kill Madlyn Beckwirth because she was doing too good a job running her campaign for mayor. In a town whose main claim to fame is the only kosher Dunkin' Donuts store in the country, even Ted Bundy wouldn't kill someone over who the next mayor would be.

Over Rachel's embarrassed blubbering, I made my apologies and left. I hadn't brought the car, since I hadn't gotten to the Y again that morning, and had decided instead to walk wherever it was necessary to go in town.

That's probably why I noticed right away the blue minivan following me. If you're in a car, it's hard to tail somebody on foot. Only in suburban New Jersey would it never occur to someone trying to properly tail a pedestrian to first park his car.

This particular motorist kept his minivan far enough back that I couldn't see into the driver's seat, so my using "his" in this sentence was strictly conjecture. And I couldn't very well turn around and take a good look, or he'd know I was on to him and peal away, leaving me with no chance at my first unambiguous clue in the case. So I kept walking, but I pulled the cell phone out of my pocket and called Barry Dutton. Marsha answered the phone, and I told her it was important. Dutton immediately picked up.

"What's going on?"

"There's a guy in a blue minivan, I think a Plymouth, following me on East Second Avenue."

"What are you driving, the minivan or the car?"

"I'm on foot."

"You're on *what?*"

"Feet. In my case, often used along with the adjective 'flat.'"

"You're telling me that you're walking through Midland Heights and somebody's following you in a car?"

"You didn't get to be chief of police just because you're handsome, did you, Barry?"

He made a sound like a balloon slowly dying. "How fast is this guy driving if he can stay behind someone on foot?"

"Maybe he's just worried about getting a ticket from the Midland Heights cops. I hear you guys are racially profiling speeders."

The sigh turned into a groan. "Rachel Barlow?"

"Just spent the morning with her. It was swell. She offered me coffee four times. By the way, she also thinks Madlyn's been murdered."

"You'll forgive me if I don't get all atwitter over Rachel Barlow's crime-fighting instincts. Let's stay focused on your, um, alleged assailant there. You sure he's following you?"

"Barry, there's nobody else on the street, and this guy is staying behind me by driving three miles an hour. Either he's thinking of buying all the property on East Second, or he's following me. What should I do?"

"Can you get a license plate?"

I tried a sideways glance. "I don't want to let on that I know he's there. Should I stop and look?"

"You don't have a mirror, do you?"

"Oh yeah, let me whip out my compact."

Barry's balloon let some more air out. He was clearly wondering if he should actually help me escape. "If you didn't know he was there, you'd be even stupider than he is. Stop and look."

So I stopped and looked. And of course, that was the moment the minivan decided to take off at 60 miles an hour in the direction of Park Street.

"Was that sound I just heard the minivan accelerating at a great rate of speed?" Barry asked.

"Lord, you *are* a great detective, Chief. It was too hard for me to get the whole plate, but I got Thomas-Victor-seven. And there can only be one minivan doing sixty through this town's streets. Maybe one of your crack officers can track down this dastardly villain."

"Maybe. But only if he's black."

"I thought you had to say African-American."

"I *am* African-American! I can say 'nigger' if I want to! Aaron, get over here as fast as your little white feet can carry you, okay?"

"Gotcha, you racist. I'm five minutes away."

"And Aaron?"

"Yeah?"

"Don't call me *Chief.*"

# Chapter 13

Gerry Westbrook was already in Dutton's office when I got there, wearing a tie that looked exactly like the Formica top of a diner table from the '50s. I'm pretty sure there was a shirt under it, of a clashing pattern, but the tie was so wide, it was hard to tell. Westbrook had last seen the inside of a clothing store when John Travolta was staging his first comeback.

I figured the best way to deal with Westbrook was to ignore him, so I spoke directly to Barry. "Did your guys find the minivan?"

"In this town, you want us to find one minivan?" Dutton smiled. Westbrook scowled, probably because I hadn't offered to polish his detective's shield when I came in.

"You're telling me you couldn't find . . ."

"We found it," Barry said. "The plates are stolen. We're tracking the ID number. And the van was empty when we got to it." Dutton sat back in his chair and every once in a while flipped his eyes toward Westbrook, trying to remind me to include him in the conversation.

"Did you find anyone suspicious walking nearby?"

"Gee, Tucker, you gonna tell us how to do our jobs now?" Westbrook decided that if I wasn't going to include him, he'd include himself. As usual, he did so with the subtlety of a tank battalion.

"Yeah, that's it, Westbrook. I'm not concerned about someone following me down the street with possible intentions of harming me. No. What I'm worried about is hurting your feelings. Always a top priority."

"When you have twenty years in on this job, Tucker . . ."

"I'll be about six grades above you, Westbrook."

"You little . . ."

Barry smacked his hands on his desk, palms down, to silence us, and it worked. He stood up, glaring at both of us.

"Do I have to separate you two, and write on your report cards that you don't play well with others?"

"Sorry, Barry," I mumbled. I thought of looking at my shoes for a while, but decided that would be too over-the-top.

"Chief," said Westbrook. It was hard to know what that meant. I considered telling Westbrook not to call Barry "Chief," but decided that might not be what Barry had in mind about getting along, and all that. I stayed quiet.

"Here's what we have," Dutton continued. "We have a missing woman who hasn't contacted her family in a week. We have a husband who's not exactly cooperative. We have speculation that the woman's disappearance might be tied to the Rachel Barlow campaign for mayor. We have a blue minivan with stolen license tags following a private citizen down the street for no apparent reason."

I interrupted. "Rachel Barlow also told me that Madlyn had been getting threatening phone calls, from outside the Verizon coverage area, for a few weeks before she disappeared. That sound familiar?"

"If you hadn't interrupted," Dutton added with the trace of a gleam in his eye, "I was about to say that we have all those things I listed, plus a call to your home the other night, Aaron, from the cellular phone of a Mr. Arthur P. MacKenzie of Emmaus, Pennsylvania."

I searched my brain, taking in the information. "Who the hell is Arthur P. MacKenzie of . . . where?"

"Emmaus, Pennsylvania."

"Emmaus? Sounds like a cyber-rodent."

"Come on, tell the truth," Dutton said. "You just needed the time to think up that joke, didn't you?"

"No, I honestly can't think of an Arthur MacKenzie. Why in God's name would he call me up and threaten me?"

"The very question we'll ask when we get the Pennsylvania State Trooper to go out and talk to him," Westbrook said.

I immediately decided that was a bad idea, but I couldn't be sure if I thought that just because it was Westbrook's. I looked at Dutton.

"Barry," I said, "could we maybe keep the Pennsylvania boys out of it for the time being? We don't really know what we're looking for, and a trooper at the door is going to scare off this MacKenzie guy before we find out anything."

Barry's eyes narrowed. "Well, I can't spare Westbrook to drive all the way out to Pennsylvania. You know, someone else might commit a crime while he was gone. Not to mention the travel voucher that the new mayor, if she's elected, might consider a waste of the taxpayer's money."

"I was thinking maybe I'd go myself," I said.

Westbrook snorted.

"What was that, Gerry?" I said. "I couldn't hear you over your tie."

Westbrook started to tell me what an ass I was making of myself, sticking my nose in police business and all those other clichés he was undoubtedly ready to trot out. But Dutton was too fast for him.

"You really want to drive all the way out there to see a man who made what could be construed as a threatening call to your house? Without a police backup?" He seemed surprised when I grinned at him.

"I don't need the police," I told Barry. "I've got a rental-car mechanic."

# Chapter 14

"I should get my head examined," Mahoney said. We were tooling down the highway in his rental car van—he calls it "The Trouble-Mobile," and refers to himself as "Chief Troubleshooter" for the rent-a-car guys. Sorry, but I'm not allowed to mention the name of the company. But remember the last time you rented a car, and they couldn't find the two-door sedan you had reserved two months in advance? It's them.

"Why a head examination now," I asked. "You getting that bad dandruff again?"

"No, because I let *you* talk me into driving out to some hick town in Pennsylvania to get shot at by a guy who likes to make phony phone calls to freelance writers."

"Yeah, if he'd just stuck with 'do you have Prince Albert in a can', we'd all be better off," I said. "But nobody said you had to come."

"Abby did. She said if I didn't protect you, she'd never let me forget it when your body was discovered."

I sighed. "Abby spent three years working in the county prosecutor's office," I told him. "She's seen too much crime."

"Well, she married you, didn't she?"

"What's that supposed to mean?"

"I don't know. I thought you'd let it go."

We drove in silence for a while because we had obviously hit a valley in the wit department. Mahoney stuck an Electric Light Orchestra eight-track into the "Trouble-Mobile's" tape-deck. He insists that eight-track is a misunderstood technological miracle, that having four program tracks makes it easier to hear your favorite song fifty-seven times during a four-hour drive, and that outweighs any acoustical inferiority. Of course, he disputes the acoustical inferiority as well, saying that "it's just numbers the guys in *Hifi Magazine* make up. You can't *hear* it." Maybe he should skip the rest of his head and get just his ears examined.

What he laments is how hard it is to get eight track cassettes of recently recorded music. Since he doggedly sticks to that ancient audio format, we are therefore stuck, when in his vehicle, with music that at best was current when we were in high school. A lot of the tapes, of course, have worn or broken, so there are what Mahoney calls "flat spots," where the music is interrupted by scotch tape and 8 millimeter movie splices (Mahoney doesn't believe in videotape, either).

So Jeff Lynne and ELO sang most of "Sweet Talkin' Woman" as we made our way west, over the "Trenton Makes—the World Takes" Bridge into Pennsylvania. It could have been worse, I guess. Mahoney could have gotten stuck on Quadraphonic sound.

By the time we passed a sign reading "Welcome to Emmaus," ELO had gotten through "Sweet Talkin' Woman" four more times, and they were currently halfway through the "Concerto for a Rainy Day," crooning out lyrics I actually claimed to understand for a week in college after my sophomore year girlfriend dumped me. Might have been the tequila, but I digress.

Being an up-to-the-minute 21st century technologist, I consulted my MapQuest directions to the home of Arthur P. MacKenzie, who all evidence suggested had called me a few nights ago and said that Madlyn Beckwirth would be dead if I kept looking for her. After a couple of wrong turns precipitated by Mahoney's refusal to turn down one of his favorite songs—"Mr. Blue Sky"—we pulled into the driveway of a rather large, lonely ranch-style house with a backyard that looked like it easily took up three acres. By Midland Heights standards, this was (the Beckwirth estate excepted) the largest piece of property in the world.

The house itself was unremarkable except for a greenhouse, attached to a back room, that jutted out from the house at a 90-degree angle. Not the kind of thing you generally see in suburban Pennsylvania, but not horribly unusual, either. MacKenzie clearly liked his flowers. The greenhouse had no broken windows, and the open skylights on either side of the structure indicated that the owner kept it active. Perhaps this was where he hatched his evil plots, cultivating orchids, while he planned to abduct helpless housewives and thereby take over the world when husbands were left to do the laundry. I dismissed this idea, since I already do the laundry at my house.

We had decided that, on this visit, Mahoney would stay back, out of the way, and observe. If I looked like I was getting into trouble, he'd advance, but otherwise, we'd make it look like I was here alone. Before I rang the doorbell, Mahoney trudged off to one side of the gravel driveway. The crunch of the gravel made me wince. I hoped MacKenzie's hearing wasn't acute.

As Mahoney ducked around the side of the house, I pushed the doorbell button and started to open the storm door. It was still too early to take out the glass and put in the screen. Could get cold again any day now. In fact, this evening was getting a bit chilly, and I was glad I had brought my jacket.

The front door took its sweet time opening, and eventually revealed a tall, thin, elderly man with enough bearing to be minor royalty. Forget Ian Wolfe or John Gielgud. If I ever needed someone to play a butler, this gentleman would be exactly the right choice. I couldn't dismiss the possibility, though, that MacKenzie could afford a butler. On the other hand, most people in this neighborhood couldn't afford a greenhouse, and I was willing to bet that the majority of them didn't threaten people's lives on the telephone. So who was I to judge?

"Hello," he said, with a question in his voice. The voice itself was a little rheumatic, but otherwise he appeared to be in perfect shape. I should look so good when I'm 103 years old.

"I'm looking for Arthur P. MacKenzie," I said, in my best gruff voice. When you're 5'5" (I was doing my intimidating stance, and my calf muscles were feeling it), a gruff voice, however incongruous, is your first line of defense.

"Yes?" he said. Maybe the old guy wasn't as healthy as he seemed. The hearing was definitely going.

I spoke up a little more, but fell down on my heels. I wasn't intimidating him anyway. I was just pissing him off. "I'm looking for Arthur P. MacKenzie," I came close to shouting.

"Yes?" Ah. Not deafness. Alzheimer's. A shame.

"Is Mr. MacKenzie home?" I just about screamed.

He looked at me with a mixture of pity and aggravation. "Yes, he is," the old man said. "I'm Arthur MacKenzie."

There was nothing else to do. I signaled for Mahoney to come out from around the corner.

# Chapter 15

Arthur P. MacKenzie was as surprised by the reason we were there
as we were at finding out he was Arthur P. MacKenzie. He offered us
hot coffee, which Mahoney accepted, and served it in the greenhouse,
where MacKenzie had been working when we arrived. Vivaldi played
on a stereo system he had set up in the large structure, with speakers sit-
uated strategically throughout the room. The plants were getting very
clear, very well amplified musical nourishment. MacKenzie was, among
other things, about six decibels off of deaf. But the sound system, it had
to be noted, was quite a step up from "Sweet Talkin' Woman" in
Mahoney's "Trouble-Mobile."

We spoke up and over "The Four Seasons" to be heard.

"This *is* your phone number, isn't it, Mr. MacKenzie?" I showed
him the police printout that Dutton had given me. Verizon clearly
showed the number of the call at exactly dinner time on the evening in
question. I hadn't received a phone call for an hour before or after, so
there wasn't any way to make a mistake.

"It might be my cellular, but I'll have to check," MacKenzie said.
"My daughters gave me the silly thing for when I'm working back here
in the greenhouse, but I never use it. You know they charge you even
when someone calls *you?*" He shook his head at the impudence of the
phone companies—probably had a nostalgic rush of warmth for the

times when Ma Bell was the only monopoly in town—and walked over to a small metal box on a table near some hothouse roses.

MacKenzie opened the box and sorted through a number of "3x5" index cards, each of which bore a phone number neatly printed in dark marker. He found one marked "CELLULAR," and compared it to the paper I'd handed him.

"Well, I'll be damned," he said in a dreamy voice. "It's my number, all right."

"And I'll bet you didn't call me that night," I offered as he stashed the card in the box and set the box back carefully in exactly the same place.

"Mr. Tucker, before your unannounced arrival here tonight, I had never heard of you, and no offense, my life didn't seem all that much emptier."

"No offense taken," I said. I was starting to like this guy.

"I'm sorry I can't help you gentlemen," he said, "but I'm sure, Mr. Tucker, I've never called you and threatened some woman I've never met."

"Are you sure nobody else could have used your phone, Mr. MacKenzie?" Okay, so I was grasping at straws, but I'd driven all that way, and was looking at another two-hour trip down the musical memory lane of my youth on the way back. I had to come home with *something*.

MacKenzie shook his head. "No, nobody ever comes in here except me and occasionally one of my daughters. Besides, I'd never leave someone alone in here. I'm very protective of my plants."

"Maybe somebody picked up the phone without your hearing..."

"I know my hearing isn't what it used to be, Mr. Tucker, but I like to think I would have noticed someone using my phone while I was in the room. And as I said, only my daughters come here to visit me. You did say the caller was male, didn't you?"

I forced a smile and shook MacKenzie's hand. "Yes, I did. And I'm sorry to have taken up so much of your time, Mr. MacKenzie."

"Not at all. And put that phone down, Mr. Mahoney."

Mahoney looked sheepish and replaced the phone in the drawer. "Sorry."

"Don't be. You needed to try. But you see, I did notice. I hope you didn't call out of the area. They charge you for that, you know—at least on my plan."

"I didn't get to call anybody, Mr. MacKenzie. You were too quick for me."

MacKenzie laughed until he started to cough. "That is the first time anybody's said that to me since Jimmy Carter was in office," he said.

Mahoney pointed at one of the flowers MacKenzie had ready to plant. His brow wrinkled, which usually means he's about to say something you wouldn't expect from a rent-a-car mechanic.

"I've never seen roses like these before, Mr. MacKenzie. The pink petals with the blue specks in a diamond shape like that." See what I mean?

"Yes," MacKenzie beamed. "I'm real proud of those. They're a hybrid I developed myself."

"But can't these roses be planted outside at this time of year?" Mahoney asked. "I'd think they'd be able to withstand even one of the colder nights this late in the season."

"You have a keen eye," MacKenzie nodded. "I actually could plant them outdoors now, but the fact is, my knees are shot. I can't bend and plant things in the ground the way I used to. It's one of the reasons I took my retirement savings and built this greenhouse six years ago."

"It's an impressive set-up," Mahoney said. He took a few steps around, nodding. If he were wearing a tuxedo, I'd have sworn the next words from MacKenzie's lips would have been, "so, Mr. Bond . . ."

Instead, Mahoney said, "I don't suppose you'd sell me some of these hybrids? I could use them in a flower bed in front of my house."

MacKenzie smiled. "I do sell some on occasion, Mr. Mahoney. But since I couldn't help you gentlemen with information tonight, and seeing how you drove all this way, you can have the rose bush for nothing."

He walked us to the front door, and as the white gravel crunched under our feet, we waved at MacKenzie like we would to a favorite old uncle. I slumped into the passenger seat of "The Trouble-Mobile" and consciously didn't put on my seat belt. Mahoney, using some coarse twine, bound together the skinny rose bush and its enormous thorns, placed them in the back of the van, and secured them between a couple of 10-gallon drums of oil.

"What's your problem?" Mahoney asked as he barely coaxed the van into ignition. I hoped the company's rental cars ran better than this vehicle, but then again, if they did, the company might not need a chief troubleshooter.

"What do *you* think is my problem? The only halfway decent lead I had turns out to be another dead end." If you're going to whine like a high schooler, it's best to do it in the company of someone who knew you when it was age-appropriate for you to do so. Mahoney grinned.

"I've got just the thing for you," he said, and pulled out an eight-track tape from a box under his seat. He slammed it home.

Billy Joel. "Turnstiles."

# Chapter 16

At midnight, after thirteen choruses of "All You Want to Do Is Dance," we arrived back at my house, and a yawning Mahoney said his quick farewells without getting out of the van. A couple of middle-aged guys who used to be able to greet the dawn with bright eyes after a night out and about. It was sad, really. I dragged my weary ass up the front steps.

The lights were on in the living room, which was unusual. I'd told Abby I'd be late, and that she shouldn't wait up. But even before I had the chance to open my newly installed screen door, the steel door inside opened, and my wife, in a T-shirt and sweatpants, stared me in the face, her eyes looking anything but pleased.

"So? What are we going to do?"

Ah. Clearly, she was speaking in anagrams tonight, and I'd have to decipher her meaning. I was up to "doot noigg" (I've never been any good at anagrams) when she spoke again, impatiently: *"Well?"*

"Well, what? What are you talking about?"

"You didn't *see* it?" Abigail walked out through the screen door and pointed at the sidewalk. My weary eyes could barely focus.

"See what?"

"Honestly, you must have walked right over it." She walked to a spot on the sidewalk and pointed straight down. Calculating how much the average mental institution cost per month, I followed her.

Something in very faint orange was scrawled on the sidewalk. In the dark, with just the porch light on and after having spent the night not finding anything I was looking for, I had a hard time working myself into a lather over it. There were two choices: I could pretend to get all bent out of shape so she'd have company, or I could be honest and risk my wife's wrath.

I'm a good husband, but I was tired and irritated.

"So?"

Abigail's teeth clamped shut so tightly I was afraid she'd drive the top ones up into her skull. Somehow, she still managed to speak.

"Well, if this doesn't bother you ..."

"Honey, I don't even see what you're talking about."

"Take a better look." Abby produced a small flashlight from the back pocket of her sweats and pointed it at the sidewalk.

The orange blotches became a little clearer as I knelt to follow her flashlight beam. And then I saw why Abby was so upset.

There on the sidewalk, in clear (however faded) block letters were the words "FUCK ETHAN."

"Oh, shit." I suppose *you* could have done better.

"I spent the whole night comforting him and then washing the sidewalk," said Abby.

"Any idea who might have done this?"

"You're the investigative reporter."

I started to feel like I'd eaten a hand grenade for dinner. "Oh, not you, too."

"Hey, you're the one who's been off all night playing detective."

I stood again, my knees cracking as I did. "Yeah, and doing a damn lousy job of it, too." I noticed something lying next to the garbage cans on the side of the house, and walked over to it. Bending down again, I found a plastic squeeze bottle.

"Well, our first clue." I examined it in the light from the porch, and probably chuckled in spite of myself.

"I don't see how this is funny," Abby sniffed.

"Well, you have to see the humor in it. Somebody just wrote 'Fuck Ethan' on our sidewalk with a squeeze bottle of barbecue sauce." I held it up to show her.

Sure enough, the bottle, which had clearly been pilfered from some restaurant counter, bore the label "Big Bob's Bar-B-Q Pit"—a picture of a large porcine creature wearing a chef's hat and standing next to a log cabin.

Abby burst out laughing, then put her hand over her mouth, upset with herself for the natural response. I stood up and took her hand.

"Could be worse," I said.

"How?"

"Could've been ketchup." We both hate ketchup, and she involuntarily made a gagging sound.

Abby turned off the flashlight and we started back up the steps to the house. I put my arm around her shoulder to prove that I'm really not that bad a guy, and she put her arm, hand still holding the flashlight, around my waist, to prove that I'm really not that bad a guy.

"Is he still up?" I asked as we made it back into the house.

"I wouldn't be surprised. He's pretty upset. He figures it means that absolutely nobody at school likes him and he's destined to live his life alone and in misery."

"It probably really means that someone in his class just learned the word 'fuck.'"

She chuckled. "You're so naive."

"How do you wash a sidewalk, anyway?"

"With Mr. Clean and a brush."

"Aha, two-timing me with this Clean guy, huh?"

I trudged up the stairs to talk to my son.

Ethan was lying in bed, his overhead light dimmed to just slightly not-off. He's working on his fear of the dark. Pokémon posters decorated the walls, and used socks decorated the floor. He'd been crying.

"Hey, Pal."

He didn't move. "Hi, Dad," came a voice from somewhere near his pillow. Two artists from Webster's came in and began sketching a picture of Ethan to put next to their definition of "dejected."

"How you doing?"

"Bad."

Uh-oh. I sat down beside him. He hadn't left me much room on the twin bed, and I had to fight to keep from falling onto the floor.

"I heard about what happened tonight," I said.

"Yeah."

"You have any idea who might've done it?"

He rolled over, so as not to be facing me. "No. It could have been anybody. Nobody likes me."

"*I* like you."

"I mean nobody young." Webster's artists now had a choice: they could take Ethan's face or mine.

"Well, let's think about it," I said, remembering a technique Ethan's therapist had offered. "How many people like you?" He didn't move.

"Let's see," I continued. "There's me, and Mom, and Leah. *She's* young."

"She's *too* young," he countered.

"Okay. How about your friend Matthew? And Andrew from camp? And Thomas from the baseball team?"

It took a long time, but he rolled back to look at me. "I guess," he said.

"And Emma from school . . ."

"Emma doesn't like me. She calls me names all the time."

"You have a lot to learn about girls, my friend."

"Girls don't count, anyway," he went on, ignoring what I'd said.

"So. We've established that a pretty decent number of people, some of whom are not even related, like you. Now. Who doesn't like you enough to write that on our sidewalk?"

His face clouded over again. He didn't turn away, but he didn't look at me, either. Ethan's dark eyes stared at the outdated posters on his wall, pictures of characters any other 11-year-old would have thrown away months, if not years, ago. But for a kid whose intellect is eleven and whose emotions are eight, there is great comfort in things that aren't quite as mature as he is.

"I dunno."

I didn't want to push it. Maybe tomorrow he'd remember a name. Or think of someone he'd especially pissed off today. Maybe by the time we woke up tomorrow, rain would have washed away the rest of the barbecue sauce that had formed the objectionable phrase. Maybe tomorrow I'd find the little bastard who wrote it and throttle him until his clavicle fell out—whatever a clavicle might be. I hadn't gotten all the way through biology class, either.

"Well, get some sleep, okay, Pal? Remember, all sorts of people with really good taste like you."

I started to stand, but Ethan, uncharacteristically, reached up suddenly and grabbed me in a tight hug. I held my son close, kissed him on the head, and felt my shirt get just a little damp where his eyes were pressed against it.

"It's okay, Ethan. It's going to be okay. It's okay. I promise." I stroked his cheek and repeated myself for a long, long time.

# Chapter 17

The next morning, the sun was shining brightly and the stain on our sidewalk was plainly visible. Figured. When you *want* bad weather, you can never get it.

Ethan was the last one down the stairs that morning, which is not unusual, but he was ten minutes later than on an average morning, and his expression was dour in a way that only an 11-year-old boy's can be. Not only was he sad, but everyone within a fifteen-mile radius of him should also be sad, and never be happy again for the rest of their lives.

Leah, of course, compensated by being so cheerful Walt Disney would have gone into insulin shock in her presence. That just served to blacken Ethan's mood another degree or two. He clomped into the kitchen, wearing the same *Star Wars* T-shirt he'd slept in, a pair of shorts that had last been washed before Keith Richards took up smoking, and a pair of white athletic socks that I felt it best not to actually look directly at.

"Good morning, Pal."

He glowered at me and sat at the kitchen table.

"What would you like for breakfast today?"

"I'm NOT HUNGRY!" he said, flashing me a look that defied me to make something of it. Clearly, it was my fault someone had written an epithet on the sidewalk in front of our house with his name on it.

"Well, have an apple or something," I said, trying to hold onto my calm. *One* of us had to speak in a normal tone for a moment.

"Daddy, I got my cereal and the bowl all by myself this morning," Leah chirped.

"Very good, Cookie."

Ethan's mocking tone mimicked me perfectly. "Very good, Cookie." Then, in his own voice, "I may puke."

"Watch yourself, Ethan."

*"Watch yourself, Ethan."*

"Look, Pal, it's not my fault that . . ."

In mid-sentence, he started aping me again. And my eyes were just a little wider, my throat a little tighter, than when I'd started speaking. Remember, I told myself, he's the one who's having the rough time. It's not his fault.

Ethan got up from the table, with a triumphant smirk on his face, and started for the living room. I walked to the cabinet where we keep his Ritalin pills and took one out.

"Hey, Ethan, you forgot your pill."

*"Hey, Ethan, you forgot your pill."*

Leah's eyes widened a bit as she watched me, sure that I'd blow up in Ethan's face. I am not the most patient man in the world, and Asperger's Syndrome is a perfect fit for someone like me (your Sarcasm Alarm should be going off about now). I'm likely to pop a blood vessel one morning.

"Ethan . . ."

*"Ethan . . ."*

I grabbed him by the forearms and forced him to look into my eyes. His hands started to flap at his sides, and his eyes rolled up in their sockets, a sign the Asperger's was in full bloom.

*"I* didn't write anything on the sidewalk," I said. *"I'm* not the one who doesn't like you. *Don't take this out on me!"* As usual, I'd tried, and failed, to hold onto my temper. A swell start to another great day.

Leah jumped up and ran to the bow window in the living room.

"Who wrote something on the sidewalk?"

Abigail walked down the stairs in her work clothes, still putting on her earrings, just in time to hear Leah ask, "Daddy, what does F-U-C-K mean?"

"Nothing, Honey."

"Then how come somebody wrote it out on the sidewalk, with Ethan's name . . ."

Ethan broke my grip on his arms, glared at me, then walked out of the room. He grabbed his backpack off the banister hook, threw it over his shoulder, and barreled his way out of the house, slamming the door behind him.

Abby looked at me.

"What happened?"

"What do you think happened? He's upset, so he's taking it out on me because you're upstairs putting on pantyhose."

"Hey, it's not my fault that . . ."

"It's not mine, either."

She looked at me and took a long breath. Then, at the least likely time, she reached over and kissed me gently on the cheek. "I know."

"I know, too." I held her in my arms, the only time of the day I truly feel right, and exhaled. "I'm sorry."

"Well, the Ritalin will kick in before he's at school."

I groaned. "No, it won't. He didn't take his pill before he left."

Abby stared at me. "Are you kidding?"

"No, and he didn't eat breakfast, either."

"Oh, shit."

"Mommy, what does 'oh, shit' mean?" Leah suddenly appeared from behind Abby.

"Nothing, Baby." She looked at me. "You want me to . . ."

"No, I'll call the nurse and tell her to get a pill into him as soon as he gets there. They know me. Besides, I think I'll be over there this morning, anyway."

Abby nodded. After she left, Leah and I had our Dad-and-daughter time, when she usually gets silly with me and plays some game like "move your arm like this." But today, she just wanted me to sit next to her on the living room couch.

"Daddy, why did somebody write something about Ethan on the sidewalk?"

"I don't know, Sweetie."

"Is it something bad?"

"Yes," I said. "It's something bad the way they used it. And as far as I can tell, they did it just to be mean."

"Is that why you and Ethan got into a fight?" Leah hated it when voices were raised in the house. I sometimes wondered how she'd gotten into this family to begin with.

"We didn't get into a fight, Leah. Ethan was upset, and I got upset with the way he showed it. A fight is where people try to hurt each other, and we never do that."

"But that's why he's upset, right?"

"Right, Baby."

She sat still for a very long time, which is not at all Leah's style. "I don't like who did that to Ethan." She rested her head on my knee and stared at the TV set, which was turned off.

"Neither do I, Honey."

After Leah got on the school bus, I got out a bottle of chlorine bleach from the basement laundry room and poured some over the sidewalk. Let it set, and I'll come back later to hose it down. Maybe that'll get rid of the stain. Then I packed a lunch for Ethan and walked over to the Buzbee School, where all Midland Heights children—those who attend public school, anyway—go from third to sixth grade. This was Ethan's third year there, and both he and I are well known in the Buzbee hallways.

I walked up the front steps of the two-story brick building, which stretches all the way across a city block. At the lobby, I made a quick right turn into the main office.

Ramona the school secretary was behind her desk, Jersey hair a foot in the air, drinking an orange soda at 8:20 in the morning. Ramona, it was rumored, had once been the receptionist at an Atlantic City brothel, and, having dealt with all sorts of juvenile behavior, was perfectly suited to her work in an elementary school.

"What's up, Mr. Tucker?"

"He forgot his lunch, Ramona." I waved the bag in front of her. Ramona nodded.

"I thought maybe Mrs. Mignano had called you," she said, taking the lunch bag out of my hand. Ramona flashed me a look, then glanced quickly into the principal's office behind her.

My lips tightened around my teeth. "Did something happen?"

"Ethan tried to choke someone."

"He tried to *what?*"

"Before school, Justin Hartman was getting on Ethan in the playground, and Ethan went for his throat." Ramona's voice lowered from its usual glass-breaking pitch to a tone that could only be heard across a football field.

"On the playground? Why wasn't he in the Before-School Club?" Joan Delbert, a teacher who's displayed more patience in a single minute than I have in an entire lifetime, runs the Before-School Club for kids who are, frankly, better off not staying on the playground when they don't have to be there. And Ethan has been in the club every morning for two and a half years.

"I don't know. He's usually there."

"Was his aide there?" I saw Anne Mignano, Buzbee's principal, approaching the office, and figured we were about to have a conference.

"Wilma hadn't gotten here yet. She's used to Ethan going to the club." Ramona spotted the principal, too, and smiled at me to pretend we were discussing her recipe for chocolate soufflé.

Anne wasn't taken in. She smiled when she saw me, but wasn't convincing. Her well-tailored gray suit gave her a starched appearance, but we'd been through a few battles together, and I knew her to be a warm-hearted administrator (if those words can be placed next to each other) who cares deeply about the students in her school.

"I was going to call you," she said, extending her hand, which I took. "I imagine Ramona has filled you in."

"Yeah. Have you got a minute?"

"No," she said. "But for this, I don't have a choice."

We walked into Anne's office. She closed the door behind us, and motioned me to a chair behind her disturbingly neat desk.

"It seems we have a problem," she said.

"We have more than one problem. One of the reasons he's on a short fuse is that somebody wrote 'Fuck Ethan' in barbecue sauce on the sidewalk outside our house last night."

She didn't flinch. "Aaron, I know that's upsetting, but it doesn't mean he can grab people by the throat."

"I know. Believe me, he's not going to be rewarded for his behavior when he gets home. But Anne, I need some help. Is this Hartman kid a particular enemy of Ethan's? Might he have written something like that in front of my house?"

Anne's face, more attractive, not less, because of the fine lines around her eyes and mouth, seemed to narrow in a frown as she thought. "No, he's not the type," she said. "You know, there's nothing I can do about that, since it happened outside the school, not during school hours." Her eyes looked right into me, and I got the impression she could make an educated guess as to who our graffiti artist might be.

"I'm not asking you to do anything, but if you have any ideas, let's just say nobody's ever going to know who my source is."

Anne Mignano nodded. She thought for a few seconds more, and reached for a sheet of blank paper in a Lucite box on her desk. She wrote a few words on the paper and put it back in the Lucite box. Then she coughed, surprisingly daintily, twice.

"Excuse me for a moment, would you, Aaron? I need a drink of water. Won't be gone a minute." Anne got up and walked out of her office, but closed the door behind her.

I reached over and took the paper from the Lucite box. On it were written three names. I pocketed the paper and waited a moment until Anne returned.

"I'm sorry I can't help you with your investigation, Aaron," she said.

"It's okay, Mrs. Mignano."

"Now. About Ethan's behavior ..."

"How is the school dealing with it?" I asked.

"He's getting three days detention and a special homework assignment."

I nodded. "Does Mrs. Turner know he needs his medication?"

"Yes," Anne said. "I think he's already had it."

"Good. Then his behavior should improve—somewhat—in a little while." I walked to the door and opened it, then turned to her. "And rest assured, Anne. He won't be seeing his Nintendo game for a good long while."

"Good luck, Aaron."

On my way out, I waved at Ramona, who was finishing her orange soda.

Ethan at home with no Nintendo, extra homework, and detention. I took the slip of paper out of my shirt pocket and looked at it. One of the names was Joel Beckwirth's.

Good luck, indeed.

# Chapter 18

When I got home, I finished up a piece on "How To Shoot Your Baby," which—honestly—was a home video article for *American Baby Magazine*, and emailed it to my editor. I took a deep breath, sat back in my prized swivel chair, closed my eyes, and tried to summarize my progress, if you could call it that, on the Beckwirth story.

Gary Beckwirth didn't want me to speak to his son, who might have been the kid who wrote epithets on my sidewalk with barbecue sauce. These two facts, of course, immediately heightened my suspicion of Joel Beckwirth, and made me wonder what it was his father was trying to hide. Probably a secret stash of plastic squeeze bottles in the basement, along with copies of "Catcher in the Rye" written entirely in condiments.

At this point, I decided that since every other single thing I could think of doing was more pressing, I'd work on my latest screenplay.

I've been writing movie and TV scripts since high school, when Mahoney and I filmed three epics: "Unseen Enemy," a war movie in which we had only enough actors for one side (Mahoney refers to it as "Unseen Enema"—I counter with the fact that if you can see an enema, they're not doing it right); "House Of Halvah," which we billed as "the world's first (and hopefully last) detective/horror/musical/comedy"; and "Marriage Contract," the story of a guy who hires a hit man to *almost* kill his girlfriend, so he can rescue her and impress her so much she'll agree to finally marry him.

I've been a movie freak since my parents took me to see *Pinocchio* when I was four. Because I knew I couldn't act, but could write, screenwriting has been a professional goal since I was roughly nine. Mahoney saw it as a hobby. I thought of it as a career path. We spent a few thousand dollars making those three movies, and were in pre-production on "Far Trek," our science fiction epic, when Mahoney had to go get married and spoil everything.

After college, I began writing screenplays with an eye towards actually selling one. I've written 22 now, and still have the same eye. Hollywood, in my opinion, is just playing incredibly hard to get.

Comedies, dramas, westerns, sci-fi's, fantasies, and romances have all come tumbling out of my printer. One actually made it as far as a three-year option from a very, very big production company (no names, but a frog's involved), but ended up being returned to its original owner (that's me) unproduced.

Writing my latest screenplay, the story of a doctor who falls in love with a woman who ages only one year for every ten she lives, was proving to be a struggle. I was aiming for romantic comedy, but the characters, those vicious little scamps, kept turning serious on me, and I was afraid I'd end up with an unhappy ending. To a writer who's "new" in Hollywood parlance (despite 20 years of experience), a dark curtain-closer would be the kiss of death. That is, unless you're selling to the New York independent film crowd, who love unhappy endings, but then everybody in the movie would have to wear black and live in converted warehouse space, and at least one of the main characters would have to be a heroin addict. I wasn't sure I could write that.

Anyway, I began as I always do, by re-reading what I'd written the day before, and had fingers poised over my keyboard when Milt Ladowski called. He was in his high-priced office, you could tell, since a secretary came on first, asking me to hold for Mr. Ladowski. Mr.

Ladowski, after all, couldn't be bothered taking sixteen seconds out of his life to talk to an answering machine, had I not been in.

"How's the Beckwirth investigation going, Aaron?"

"I'm sorry," I said, "Mr. Tucker's in the john right now. If you'll hang on a moment . . ." I took the cordless phone into the bathroom and flushed.

"Very amusing, Aaron."

"Amusing, hell. I had shredded wheat for breakfast."

Milt allowed a long silent period to destroy our fastpaced and sparkling repartée. No doubt he was trying to figure out how to bill Beckwirth for the conversation.

"Beckwirth, Aaron. What's going on with Beckwirth?"

"Milt, your client and close friend is tying my hands. He wants me to perform the ceremonial wife dance and have her fall into his arms from the sky. He won't let me talk to his son, he won't give me his phone records or his credit card bills, and he won't tell me anything about his marriage, other than it is blissful as all get-out. Now you tell me, how do you think the Beckwirth investigation is going?" I put my feet up on the desk and waited. It was fun letting somebody else worry about this thing for a while.

"This isn't good, Aaron. Gary's expecting me to call him with progress." I could picture Ladowski's pinched face frowning behind his $6,000 desk. Luckily, I could focus my mind's eye on the desk.

"What do you want me to do, Milt? Everything I've turned up so far has been a dead end. But Barry Dutton is . . ."

"I'll get you in to see Joel," said Milt.

"What?"

"I said, I'll make sure Gary lets you talk to Joel. Give me an hour."

I gave him maybe ten minutes before he called back. I was right. "It's all set. But Gary has to be in the room with him, and you only get fifteen minutes."

"For crying out loud, Milt, I'm not asking for an audience with the pope!"

He ignored me as only a man with a manicure can. "You can do it today at three."

"No, I can't," I said. "I have an 11-year-old coming home after detention and a seven-year-old getting off the bus. If Beckwirth wants, I'll come over after dinner, when Abby's home."

Ladowski grumbled a bit, but saw the logic in my reasoning. Either that, or my voice told him that I wouldn't budge. Ladowski is an experienced mediator. "I'll clear it with Gary," he said. "Be there at seven-thirty."

"Okay," I sighed. "And Milt?"

"Yeah?"

"Does Joel like barbecue sauce?"

# Chapter 19

There were pictures of professional wrestlers on Joel Beckwirth's walls, and that surprised me. In a house that had no visible TV set (and no Nintendo or Playstation in Joel's room), I didn't expect pictures of "The Rock" or "Stone Cold" Steve Austin. I expected pin-up posters of Mozart or Pierre Cardin.

The room, except for the posters, was just like the rest of the house—impeccable. No socks on the floor—no potato chip crumbs, either. The bed was tightly made. The large boy sitting on it was tightly wrapped.

Joel Beckwirth had inherited from his handsome father only his blue-green eyes. In fact, judging from the picture of Madlyn now prominently displayed on the piano downstairs, Joel didn't much resemble either of his parents. His face was mostly chin, some forehead, and not much in the middle. He looked like Humpty Dumpty in an Eminem T-shirt.

Gary ushered me into the room, speaking in hushed tones, as if we were about to enter the presence of the great Oz and should speak only when spoken to. He had informed me, through tight lips, that Milton Ladowski had "strongly recommended" he allow me to speak to his son, but that Joel was still "extremely upset" over his mother's disappearance and should be handled with great care. I believe "kid gloves" were mentioned once or twice.

I did my best to smile and fought a natural urge to ask about Joel's preference in fast-food toppings. "Hi, Joel," I said. Mr. Rogers couldn't have been less threatening.

"Uh." The boy was clearly a witty conversationalist.

"You know why I'm here?"

"Uh-huh." My God, the lacerating brilliance of it all! I considered asking Gary if the boy had been to Professor Henry Higgins for diction lessons. Once again, though, I forced myself to remember the task that had brought me to this Ozzie-and-Harriet-Meet-Goldberg place.

"You're worried about your mom, huh?" Now he had *me* saying "huh."

"I guess." Words! Who could possibly have hoped for more?

"Well, do you know why she might have gone away?"

The boy's eyes narrowed, and Gary stepped in before he could say anything. "Do you really think it's necessary to be asking . . ."

Just what I'd been waiting for. "Gary, I'm here to do a job. One which, as I recall, you were pretty set on me doing, even when I told you I didn't know how. Now, you're either going to let me do that job, or you can do it yourself. But if you leave it to me, you must stand back and be quiet." I glanced at Joel. Had challenging his father's authority at my very first opportunity produced the desired effect? It had. Joel was grinning nastily.

But Gary wasn't done. "I don't have to listen to . . ."

"That's right, you don't," I said. "In fact, I'd prefer it if you'd wait outside so I could talk to Joel privately."

Beckwirth positively gasped at the very notion, and his face took on color, making him look like a remarkably handsome strawberry. "I absolutely *forbid* it!" he shouted, and Joel snorted, trying to suppress a giggle.

"Fine," I said. "It's been nice meeting you, Joel. Good night, Gary." And I headed for the exit. Beckwirth senior was harrumphing even as I turned away from him. He came close to actually choking on his own words when I placed my hand on the bedroom doorknob and began to turn it.

"Where are you ... *going?*"

"Home. I'd like to see my daughter before she goes to bed, and there's nothing here that's holding me back."

Beckwirth's eyes were the size of silver-dollar pancakes. The irises looked like blueberries. A little maple syrup, and I'd have had one super-delicious snack right here.

"But, what about Madlyn?"

"I don't know. What about Madlyn?" Beckwirth started to point a finger at me, but I cut him off. "If you're *really* that concerned about her, and you *really* think I'm the best man to find her, then Gary, get the hell out of this room, and let me do my job." I folded my arms and looked at him.

So did Joel. He was watching his father with a look of rapt fascination. Clearly, he'd never heard *anyone* stand up to Gary Beckwirth before, and he was enjoying it as much as a body slam from Sable. Well, maybe not quite as much.

Beckwirth spoke very softly and quickly. "I'll be just outside," he managed, and walked out. I turned toward Joel after the door had closed behind me. There was no keyhole for Beckwirth to listen through—I had checked. And because the house was old, there would be no listening through the door or the walls. At that very moment, Gary Beckwirth was no doubt cursing his homebuilder's fine craftsmanship.

"So," I said to the boy on the bed, who was now lying back on his pillows and grinning. "What do you want to talk about?"

"How did you do that?" His voice, now that it was actually producing words, was that strange combination that only occurs in the newly pubescent boy—deep and light at the same time.

"Do what?"

"Make my dad go away."

"You saw," I said. "I told him I didn't want anything from him. If I don't want anything from him, he has no power over me." It occurred to me that I wouldn't be thrilled with anyone teaching Ethan this particular lesson, but what the hell, Beckwirth was no friend of mine.

"Wow. Nobody *ever* does that."

"Not even your mom? They don't ever argue?" Am I subtle, or what? The kid neither curled up into the fetal position nor began to suck his thumb at the mention of his mother. You want to talk experienced interviewer . . .

"No." Joel's face closed. He started looking past me to the poster behind my head. I regrouped. I pulled out a chair from behind the desk. As a concession to the 21st century, the boy had been allowed a desktop computer, but used it, no doubt, for nothing but homework.

"Not ever? All married couples argue once in a while."

He sputtered, a kind of laugh. "Married couples," he said. "Argue."

"Was your mom unhappy lately?"

"I dunno."

"Would she say anything to you if she was?" I sat backwards on the chair, just a friendly guy asking friendly questions. Joel's diamond-shaped face was doing its best not to look in my direction.

"Probably not."

I concentrated on what Spenser would do in this case. Probably he'd go to his office and wait for a gangster to show up and explain the whole thing to him. Or he'd go down to the gym and work out with his friend Hawk while discussing whether Jersey Joe Woolcott was really better than Felix Trinidad.

Personally, I didn't see how Spenser's approach would help me here, but then, I'm not equipped to outpunch . . . well, anybody, to be completely honest. So I guess I couldn't criticize the guy. Besides, he's fictional, and that's always an edge.

I decided on another approach. I rubbed my eyes with my thumb and forefinger, trying my best to look perplexed. Problem was, I also dislodged my left contact lens, and spent a couple of minutes blinking at Joel while he stared, mystified, at this insane man who had decided to come to his room and poke his own eyes out.

"Are you okay?" he asked, less out of concern than simple curiosity.

I stopped rubbing, and did my best to look like I was in deep despair. "I'm okay," I sniffed, "it's just that I'm ... well, never mind ..."

"You're what?" He was hoping I was going to say that I was dying of an inoperable brain tumor, or distraught because his father was so much richer than me. He leaned forward, elbow on a knee, listening intently.

"I'm just worried about your mom," I said. "I'm supposed to find her, and nothing's going right." I did my best to sound on the verge of tears, although my acting experience ended with "House of Halvah," roughly the time Ronald Reagan was first elected president. (I believe that if an actor can be president, there is no point in being an actor. But that's another story.)

"Oh," Joel said, disappointed. "Well, what have you been doing to find her?"

"Well, that's just the thing. I don't know *what* to do. I've asked everybody she knows. Nobody can think of a reason she'd leave." Maybe *he* could, went the inference.

Alas, the child was as good at reading inferences as he was at witty exchanges. "Maybe somebody kidnapped her," he said, with definite relish in his voice. The relish reminded me to ask him later about the barbecue sauce.

"Well, did you hear anything the night she, um, disappeared?"

"Yeah," he said, and then sat there, staring blankly at me.

*Yeah?* He'd heard something? There might be a way to proceed from here? Somebody, especially this kid, was going to *cooperate?* How could that be?

I waited a few seconds, nodded, and looked encouraging. Then I realized that was all he was actually going to say.

"*What* did you hear?" I asked a little too forcefully.

"This scraping noise."

"*What* scraping noise?"

"I dunno. It was late, and this noise woke me up. Sounded like some metal, or something. Kept on going. Then there was this really loud rip, and the sound stopped."

"And you went back to sleep?"

"Yeah," he said. "Right after the car's brakes stopped screeching."

It suddenly occurred to me that this interview would be much more productive if Bud Abbott were putting the questions to the kid. He'd have way more experience in dealing with answers like this: "Car's brakes? WHAT car's brakes, Lou?" "

"The ones that screeched right before the dog started barking."

"Dog? What dog?"

"Oh, you know, the one that started barking when my grand-mother fell out the window."

"What? Your grandmother fell out the window?"

"Well, she was startled when she noticed the fire."

"Fire? What fire?"

"The one that got started when my uncle hanged himself and knocked over the candle."

"What? Your uncle ..."

You get the picture. I shook my head to get back on task. "You heard a car's brakes screeching?"

"Yeah," he said. "Real loud. I almost got up to see what it was, but I went back to sleep instead. And when I got up, my dad said *she* was missing." Madlyn's disappearance didn't seem to bother him as much as having been awakened in the middle of the night. The way he said *"she,"* you'd think he was talking about the maid.

"About what time of night was this?" I asked.

"I dunno," Joel said. "Must've been around two or three in the morning. Or four. I'm not sure." He shrugged.

"Did your dad hear it?"

"My dad? He wouldn't hear it if an elephant farted in his bedroom." Joel dissolved into hysterics at the graphic word-picture he'd created. The tone of his chortling would have triggered both anger and fear in an ordinary man in his forties. I got up and opened the door.

Gary Beckwirth, to his credit, was not leaning in to listen at the door. He was in the next room—his and Madlyn's bedroom, looking through a box of photographs he had strewn all over the chenille bedspread. He had one picture in his hand, and was silently weeping over it. I stayed in the doorway, unable to decide whether to invade his privacy.

He solved the dilemma for me by looking up and guiltily wiping his eyes with the backs of his hands. "Sorry," he said softly. I walked in and saw him put behind his back a photograph in which Madlyn seemed to be wearing a wedding dress. He straightened up like a soldier being brought to attention.

"Don't be sorry," I said. "You care about your wife, and you're worried. Why shouldn't you cry?"

"I'm not being strong," he said. "Madlyn would want me to be strong." He sniffed, once, and regained his composure. Gary looked me in the eye, his bearing once more that of a long-suffering employer.

"What you did in there was unconscionable," he said.

"I need Joel to trust me, and I needed you not to be in the room, so he could be completely honest with me. If you had agreed to let me talk to him alone when I asked the first time, that scene wouldn't have been necessary."

"You undermined my authority with the boy," said Gary.

"Are you his father or his headmaster?"

He twisted his lip into something halfway between a sneer and an attack of gastroenteritis, and ignored my question. "What did he say to you?" he asked.

"I can't tell you that."

Beckwirth looked like he was going to swallow his lips. His eyes narrowed, his neck appeared to widen to twice its original size, and his veins stuck out. "Oh, *really?*" he said.

"Yes, really. Joel is a source for an article I'm writing, and I will not reveal to you what he said to me."

"He's my son!"

"I'm aware of that," I said in my most soothing "we're-both-dads-here" voice. "But you have to understand, Gary, that Joel is also a confidential source, and he needs to know that what he tells me in confidence is going to stay that way. If he doesn't trust me, I won't get any more information from him."

"I don't see where your information is making my Madlyn reappear," he said coldly.

"Neither do I," I admitted, "but then, I didn't apply for this job. I was drafted. By the way, the night Madlyn disappeared, did you hear anything?"

"I've already told you, no!" said Beckwirth, almost as if he were vibrating. "I didn't hear anything. I didn't see anything. Now, are you going to find Madlyn or not?"

"I have no idea if I'm going to find her," I said. "But I *will* keep looking. At least until Thursday."

He started scooping up the pictures and placing them back into the box, but not before sorting them for size and shape—ever the Distraught Anal-Retentive Husband. "What's Thursday?"

"My deadline," I told him. "I have to submit copy to the paper on Thursday, and so far, on this story, I don't have anything to write."

"They'll extend your deadline," Beckwirth said. "I'll make a phone call . . ."

"Gary, if I don't find anything by Thursday . . ." I didn't know how to say the rest.

"What?"

"If I can't find her after she's been gone ten days, Gary, well . . . I think maybe you'd better get used to the idea that she might not want to come back."

Beckwirth looked like I'd slapped him in the face. With a sledge-hammer. He clamped his teeth together and spoke through them in a voice more reptile than human.

"Don't ever walk through my door again unless you have something cheerful to say to me about my wife," he said. "Cheerful"—that's really the word he used. "The next time you say something like that in my presence, Mr. Tucker, I will most certainly kill you."

I pursed my lips and nodded a bit, digesting the soliloquy. I turned toward the door, then back to Beckwirth. "By the way, Gary, does Joel like barbecued ribs?"

Gary Beckwirth tried as hard as he could not to speak to me, but his pride at having raised his son correctly won out over his determination. "Joel," he said with a triumphant shake of his head, "is a vegetarian. Why?"

I walked out the door, mumbling. "Figures," I said. "It figures."

# Chapter 20

When I got home from Beckwirth's house, I checked the sidewalk carefully for further messages—there were none. The other good news of the moment was that, even though it hadn't quite shown up on my sidewalk, I finally might have a lead to work with in this Beckwirth story.

The possibility of a car driving by, loud enough to wake Joel Beckwirth, at some time after midnight, raised a number of possibilities. It could mean somebody had driven off with Madlyn against her will—the squealing tires and screeching brakes would certainly support that theory. At the very least, someone had been in a great big hurry.

But I wasn't ready to accept Beckwirth's sinister theories yet. It was equally possible that Madlyn had planned her own disappearance. Suppose she'd decided to leave in the middle of the night, knowing that Gary couldn't be roused easily. True, Beckwirth had pointed out that neither her car nor his had been moved, but that didn't mean Madlyn hadn't driven away. She could have rented a car, or reserved a taxi, and arranged to have it waiting outside for her, or—more likely—have a friend pick her up. The driver might still be in a hurry, giddy with Madlyn's new-found freedom.

It was also entirely possible that Madlyn had gone out to investigate the noise, and been eaten by a passing bear. But I wasn't going to mention that cheerful theory to Dutton, nor especially to Beckwirth. I had no bear tracks to back me up. You write something in the newspaper, you need evidence.

I opened my front door wearily and walked into the living room. Abigail hadn't been able to leave the house for her nightly run because I was out, so she was exercising on the cardio-glide contraption we have in front of the television, which I've unaffectionately nicknamed "The Thing." The look on her face—tired, pinched, beaten-down—was enough to tell me what kind of night it had been.

"Which one?" I asked.

"The boy." She rolled her eyes. "You'll hear him banging around up there in a minute."

I glanced involuntarily up the stairs, sagged onto the couch, and exhaled, rubbing my eyes. "He's been a joy since his banishment from Nintendo," I said.

"Yeah. Thanks."

I wasn't expecting that, and sat up, my eyes widening. It wasn't enough that other people's families were beating me up. Now mine had to get in on the act? "Well, what did you want me to do? He grabbed another kid by the throat."

"It would have been nice to have been consulted before you laid down the law. That's all." Abby got off "The Thing" and wiped the sweat off her face and neck with a towel she'd brought in from the bathroom. She picked up a bottle of spring water from the coffee table—pardon me, the spring water table—and opened it.

"That's the advantage of my being here, Abby, and the disadvantage. I'm the one who's here, so I have to react to stuff as it happens. We didn't have time to discuss this one."

She put down the water after a long swallow and nodded. "I know. But then you go out and leave me to handle the consequences. You haven't been home many evenings lately."

"It'll all be over by Thursday. Then I can go back to being a writer again." She sat next to me on the couch, and I couldn't resist putting my hand on her slightly moist thigh. She wears shorts when she exercises in the house and sweatpants when she goes out. There are advantages to having her stay home.

Abby nestled her head onto my chest and sighed a little. "So what's with Joel?" she asked.

I caressed the skin on her leg a little more. "He heard something. Says there was a car spinning its wheels outside the house on the night Madlyn left."

She looked up at me, interested. "So, where does that lead?"

"Well, first, I'll call Westbrook in the morning and ask if he checked the outside of the house for tire marks or anything like that."

Abigail curled her lip, and her voice took on a sarcastic tone. "And after he tells you he didn't?"

"I canvass the neighborhood. Ask the people who live around there if anybody else heard anything. See if some busybody happened to look out the window at the right time. There's a yenta on every street. Somebody's bound to have seen something."

"That's not much."

"It's a hundred percent more than I had before I talked to him."

"You've got a point there," Abby said. Her expression changed, and now she was looking at me in an altogether more agreeable manner. She snuggled closer. "Maybe you're cut out for this gumshoe stuff, after all." She gave me a kiss that was more than agreeable, and I responded with one of my own. We sank down into the couch.

And that, of course, is when my son decided to come stomping down the stairs from his room, unannounced, a look on his face that would unnerve General Patton. Luckily, Ethan is an Asperger's kid, and didn't take any notice of what his parents had almost been doing.

The kid has a great sense of timing, though—I'll give him that.

"Dad?"

I removed my hands from where they wanted to be and sat up

straight on the couch, groaning just the way my father used to when he sat up. When I was 22, I never groaned when maneuvering on, onto, or off chairs and couches.

"Whatever it is, Ethan, the answer is 'go to bed.'"

"I can't sleep."

"Read."

"There's nothing to read."

Abigail sat up now, grinding her teeth just a little. It was clear this was the same argument they'd been having before I got home.

"You have a million books up there, Ethan," she said. "Pick one out and read it."

Ethan stopped, truly thinking about what she'd said. "I don't have a million books up there. They wouldn't all fit."

Abby took a deep breath and let it out, the only technique she had retained from Lamaze class when she was pregnant with, well, Ethan. "That's right. I was exaggerating. But you have a lot of . . ."

"I don't FEEL like reading!" Ah, so it was going to be one of *those* arguments. I stood up and pointed a finger at my son.

"You're *not* playing video games tonight. You're not playing video games *tomorrow* night. And you're not playing video games the night after *that*. You choked somebody at school, and you have to pay the price for it. Now, go to your room and *shut up!*" Abby was frowning at me. She thought this was her argument and didn't want to see it degenerate into what she calls "a scene."

Ethan, despite having heard this speech before, had the nerve to look surprised. "It's not FAIR!" he bellowed, and ran back up to his room. Abby folded her arms and looked at me, a 43-year-old man pointing a menacing finger at a pre-teen no longer in the room, his eyes wide, his teeth tightly clenched. I couldn't see them, but I would have bet that the veins in my neck were sticking out about four inches. I was moments away from hyperventilating.

"Nice work, Dad," she said.

# Chapter 21

Diane Woolworth was a fifty-ish woman who clearly wished she had been born in a Jane Austin novel. Her home was awash in dark maroons, royal purples, doilies, and tea sets, and her manner was that of a woman who should have been living in England, but by accident had been set down in suburban New Jersey. If she had been able to pull it off, she would have spoken with a British accent, like Madonna.

I had spent the bulk of Wednesday morning ringing doorbells on Beckwirth's street, and being told politely by local residents that they hadn't heard a damn thing on the night in question.

Once in a while, I'd hit a house where the doorbell was not answered. These were generally the ones with no vehicle in the driveway, indicating either that some rich people in Midland Heights actually work for a living, or need two incomes to be rich.

Occasionally, the residents who answered the door were not quite so polite, like the guy who told me to "get lost" because he was "sick and tired of snooping assholes asking questions about the bitch across the street." Not Noel Coward, I'll grant you, but certainly to the point.

Diane Woolworth's doorbell was the third-from-the last one on the block, but the first whose owner had invited me in for a cup of tea (which I declined—if anything, tea actually tastes worse to me than coffee). And—I swear on all that is pure and decent—she also offered me a "crumpet." I don't mean the Tastykake kind with the butterscotch frosting on the top, either.

"You're looking into poor Mrs. Beckwirth, then, are you, Mr. Tucker?" Diane asked, stirring the fat-free milk (you can't call it "skim" anymore) into her tea. "The poor woman. I can't imagine what might have happened to her."

It occurred to me to ask why she'd invited me in if she had no information, but one thing a reporter learns is to let people talk. They'll eventually say something you can use, even if they don't intend to. Especially if they don't intend to. So I sat back and took a bite of my crumpet, which is the dirtiest sentence I've ever committed to paper. (A crumpet, by the way, is nothing more than an English muffin that has a publicist.)

"You know, I used to see her out in her garden with her gardener, telling him where to put the shrubbery," Diane continued. "You get used to seeing someone, and then just out of nowhere, they're gone. Unsettling, it is."

The lamentations went on for a few more minutes while Diane drank two cups of "very nice tea" and offered me another crumpet, which I declined. I began to wonder if my reporter's tricks would come up short this time, and I'd just walk away with a crumpet-enhanced waistline and no additional information.

Just when I was about to stand and thank Diane for her hospitality, her daughter Jane, about 22 and one tattoo short of a biker chick, stormed down the main hall stairs and into the dining room, where Diane and I were having our very nice tea and crumpets. It was as if Freddy Krueger had wandered onto the set of *The Remains of the Day.*

She was short—around five-foot-one—not slim, dressed in old, unwashed jeans, an Aerosmith T-shirt, and no bra. Her feet were bare, and had last been washed when I was still a real investigative reporter. I was willing to bet that beside her ears and her nose, there were other parts of Jane that were pierced, but I was better off not speculating about what they might be. She was vigorously chewing a piece of gum. At least I hoped it was gum. Tobacco stains the teeth, and no spittoon was visible in the room.

Clearly, her father was a Satan-worshipping, heroin-addicted, alcoholic Hell's Angel, since not one chromosome in this young woman could possibly be traced to Diane Woolworth. But then I looked on the baby grand piano and saw a picture of Diane standing next to a man in his fifties wearing a seersucker suit and bow tie, with close-cropped hair and tortoise-shell glasses.

Maybe Diane had put her wild past behind her. Maybe Jane had been adopted. Maybe she'd been raised by wolves, and Diane and her husband had been jungle missionaries who had taken her back to civilization, about, I don't know, two weeks ago, and were still teaching her about the ways of living among humans. Or maybe I was making a snap judgment based on appearance.

"Where's the car keys?" she said to her mother, not even glancing in my direction. Jane held out her hand to Diane, palm up. Give me the keys, Lady, and there won't be no trouble. She blew a bubble. Thank goodness it was gum after all.

"Jane, do you know Mr. Tucker? Mr. Tucker, this is my daughter Jane. Jane, Mr. Tucker is looking into poor Mrs. Beckwirth." Clearly, Diane was going to keep her Merchant-Ivory fantasy alive at all costs. Jane more or less turned her head in my direction and grunted, which I assumed was a sort of greeting among her people.

"Yeah. The car keys." She chewed more violently now, perhaps a subtle threat to hand over the keys and let her be on her way. I figured I had virtually nothing to lose.

"I don't suppose either one of you heard anything in the middle of the night, Monday before last?" I asked, eyes wide to show my complete non-threatening innocence.

Jane grunted again, but Diane, who had stood and walked to the adjoining kitchen so as to get the car keys off a calico-covered ring on the wall, stopped and put a finger to her chin. This was obviously a gesture she had learned by watching "Masterpiece Theatre."

"Jane, didn't you say you'd heard a motorbike or something the night before we heard that Mrs. Beckwirth had gone missing?"

"CYCLE, Mother! MotorCYCLE! How many times do I have to ..." Jane composed herself as best she could, which meant she took two steps toward Diane and stuck out her hand again. "NOW can I have the car keys?"

"You heard a motorcycle that night, Jane?" I asked in my coolest, most grownup voice.

"Nah." She turned toward me and sized me up, clearly determined I was an inferior member of the species, and curled her lip into a sneer. "I thought it was a bike, but it turned out to be a minivan with a bad muffler. I went to the window and saw it."

"Did you see Madlyn Beckwirth?"

"I dunno."

Diane brought Jane the keys, which she pocketed without a word to her mother. Jane headed for the door, and I stood.

"You don't know?"

Jane stopped, and the sneer became a look of impatience and disgust I didn't think was possible in a girl over the age of seventeen. "I saw *something*, you know. I'm not sure it was *her.* This minivan peals out, you know, like ninety miles an hour, and I see something fall over the railing, backwards, you know, down the hill over there next to that great big house. Coulda been her, you know. Coulda been a sack of shit too."

"Jane! Really!" I thought Diane might actually put her hands to her ears, but she managed to avoid the urge.

"Did you tell the cops what you saw?" I asked.

"What, that fat guy with the tie from 1972? Nah. He didn't ask, you know." I knew. She turned and walked out the side door without so much as a backward glance. Diane sat back down at the dining room table and took a sip of tea.

"You sure you won't have another crumpet, Mr. Tucker?"

That was odd, in a way. I'd heard what Jane had said, and that would seem to be the only useful information available in the Woolworth home today. Would Diane continue the conversation just to have someone to talk to, or did she have something eating away at her that she wanted to spill? I didn't want another crumpet, but I sat down.

"Did *you* hear anything that night, Mrs. Woolworth?" What the hell, you never know what you might hit. Diane could have seen Madlyn flying over the side of the low railing next to her house. She could have seen Madlyn hop on a broom and fly off into the dark night. She might express her observations in terms that would do justice to Emily Brontë, but it was possible she'd seen something.

"Oh, no, Mr. Tucker. I sleep very peacefully. But I did hear ... and you understand, I'm not one to gossip ..."

Finally! The busybody I'd been looking for!

"Of course not, Mrs. Woolworth. This is a strictly confidential investigation."

"Exactly. So my name will not appear in print?" Diane eyed me carefully for signs of non-British behavior, but I was having none of it. In a moment, I'd be saying "lift" instead of "elevator."

"Not at all." I thought that sounded like something Inspector Morse would say.

"Well then." Diane seemed to compose herself, trying to devise exactly the proper way to impart the information and still seem like everything she said belonged on an embroidered sampler. "There was talk around the department that Mrs. Beckwirth and a certain gentleman were ... friendly."

"The department? What department?"

"The English department. I teach 19th century English literature at the university." Midland Heights has a large population of professorial types who don't want to live in the small city across the river that the state university calls home. It's one thing to teach people, another to live near them, you know.

"And you'd heard that Madlyn might be having an affair?" The hell with being polite about it.

"Well, Mr. Tucker, that was the talk around the department." Diane was flustered that I wasn't being British anymore, and she nervously sipped from her cup, eyes watching me over the rim.

"Why would this be the talk of the university English department?"

Diane looked away. We were clearly in an area she didn't want to explore. But she had opened this particular can of kippers, if you will, and she'd have to deal with the consequences. "Well," she said, "the gentleman in question is also ... employed at the department."

"He teaches English at the university."

"Yes." She wiped the corner of her mouth with a cloth napkin, again looking away. Maybe she was considering adjusting the small photograph of Queen Elizabeth she had framed on the wall. It was crooked by maybe a half-inch.

But I was getting impatient with all the cute little games. "What's his name, Mrs. Woolworth?" I asked in my best Humphrey Bogart-without-the-lisp voice.

"Oh, I can't decide if I should ... it's all idle gossip, you know," she twittered.

"Mrs. Woolworth?" I practically snarled. She lowered her head a bit and spoke very softly.

"Martin Barlow."

For a moment, I couldn't make the connection. My head for names isn't great under normal circumstances. But in this case, my head was now overloaded. The rush of information that came from that name was almost too much to handle all at one time.

"Rachel Barlow's husband? The guy whose wife is running for mayor? The one who had Madlyn Beckwirth as her campaign manager?

*That* Martin Barlow?" I had risen out of my chair at some point in this discussion, but couldn't remember when.

Diane Woolworth nodded, just perceptibly.

"Well, why didn't you say anything before this?"

She looked up at me, offended, and her eyes widened.

"Well, Mr. Tucker," she huffed, "I wouldn't want people to think that I'm a busybody!"

# Chapter 22

I couldn't depart Diane Woolworth's home fast enough. After thanking her for the crumpet—and getting an unsolicited recipe I threw away immediately after leaving—I all but ran for the door, and headed out on foot across Midland Heights.

Olszowy and Barlow campaign signs were already littering lawns about town, as the academics and the relatively new parents took up arms against the old fogies and the traditionalists. You could tell a lot about a family by whether a red Olszowy or a blue Barlow sign, each with understated stars and stripes, was displayed on its lawn.

I was walking at about twice my usual pace, and keeping my eye out for any unusually slow-moving minivans, as I decided which new information I would act upon first. Should it be Jane's witnessing a blue minivan possibly knocking someone or something over the guard rail to the side of McThemePark? Or should I immediately work the sex angle, and question Rachel Barlow's husband Martin about his alleged hot affair with, of all people, Madlyn Beckwirth?

It wasn't a difficult decision to make. Jane's information was more easily and efficiently dealt with by the cops. I lit out for the Barlow home. Removing my cell phone from my jacket pocket, I dialed police headquarters, where Marsha the dispatcher answered on the second ring.

"Midland Heights Police Headquarters. Sergeant Ames."

"Hi, Marsha, it's Aaron Tucker."

"This is getting to be a habit, Aaron."

"I know. I'm gonna have to join Cops Anonymous. Is Barry there?"

I picked up the pace just as a male bicyclist, a dog on his leash, passed me. The poor mutt was probably as winded as I was.

"No, he's out of the office meeting with the county freeholders. Aaron, are you okay? You sound like you're running."

The guy on the bike made a left turn, nearly julienning his dog with the rear wheel. "I'm all right, Marsha. I'm just in a hurry. When's Barry coming back?"

"Not until after two." Shit. It wasn't even eleven yet. "You want to talk to Gerry?"

"No, I don't *want* to talk to Gerry, but what choice do I have?"

Marsha chuckled in her deep-throated way, a guttural guffaw that indicated real amusement. "I'll put you through," she said.

I walked half a block while Westbrook made it all the way across his cubicle to the telephone, a distance of maybe three feet.

"Westbrook."

"You don't have to be so proud of it."

There was genuine consternation in his voice. "Who is this?"

"It's an obscene phone call, you dimwit. Gerry, it's Aaron Tucker."

I was getting used to people groaning when they heard my name on the phone, but with Westbrook, I actually took some pleasure in it. Getting groaned at by Gerry Westbrook was practically a red badge of courage. "What do you want, Tucker?" he said when he was done grimacing out loud.

"I *want* Bob Zemeckis' private phone line so I can pitch him a script," I said. "But I'll settle for some information on the Beckwirth case."

"And why should I even bother telling you anything I know?" He did his best to sneer.

"Because, in the extremely unlikely event that you do know something, your chief has made it very clear he will not be pleased if you withhold it from me," I explained patiently. "And because, in the extremely unlikely event that you do know something, you probably don't understand it, and I can explain it to you in terms you might be able to absorb. I have a seven-year-old, and she used to have the same trouble you do."

I made a left turn onto North Seventh Street and tried to remember which house was Barlow's. It was brown, I was pretty sure.

"You're a real riot, Tucker," Westbrook said, in his imitation of wit. Jackie Gleason could have taught him a couple of things about delivery, if he didn't have the disadvantage of being dead. And he was still funnier than Westbrook. "How about you tell me what you know, and then maybe we can trade."

"You're eating an eggplant parm sandwich right at this moment— that's what I know," I said. "Now, tell me if you searched the area of undeveloped land to the north of Beckwirth's house the morning you got the call."

"Why would we do that?"

I'd figured as much. "Because you're the police, Westbrook, and you're supposed to investigate possibilities. I have a witness who saw a minivan tear-assing around that bend at the time Beckwirth supposedly went missing, and the witness may have seen this minivan hit something, or someone, that fell down that embankment. So how about you get somebody over there to look?"

Westbrook rumbled like an oncoming thunderstorm. "You want to tell me who this *witness* is, Tucker?"

"No, I really don't. This person may need protection at some point, and I'd just as soon you didn't know the name. You might trip over your tie on the way into the safe house and set off the alarm."

"Very funny."

"Oh, and while you're at it, get somebody to check the front bumper of that minivan that was tailing me. If it's the same one, there may still be some blood or cloth or something from Madlyn Beckwirth on it."

"Anything else, *Boss?*"

"Nah, that oughta do it for this shift. Afterward, you can go out to the Salvation Army Thrift Shop and buy yourself a new sports jacket and tie. See ya, Westbrook."

As I approached Barlow's house (which was, in fact, green), I started to close the cell phone, but heard Westbrook call my name again, and reopened it before the connection could be broken.

"Hey, Tucker!"

"Yeah, what is it, Gerry?"

"How'd you know about the eggplant parm sandwich?"

I hung up on him.

# Chapter 23

When nobody answered the doorbell at the Barlows', I spotted some movement around the side of the house, so I walked by a perfect white picket fence and through an impeccable trellis arch into the backyard.

The Barlow home was something of an anomaly for Midland Heights. It was new construction, for one thing—a variation on the Epcot mini-mansions—with skylights coming out its ears. It also had a backyard that would be medium-sized for a normal suburb, meaning it was an enormous one for Midland Heights. You had to wonder how a college professor and his non-working wife afforded it. There was, of course, a "Barlow for Mayor" sign very tastefully adorning the lawn.

Martin Barlow was wrist-deep in soil, although the gardening gloves he had on his hands were probably keeping the wrists clean, too. Barlow appeared to be the kind of man who would wear Audrey Hepburn evening gloves while gardening if he didn't think people would laugh at him. He was wearing a salmon-colored T-shirt that once had a logo of some kind on its back, but had been washed so many times it was no longer legible, a pair of khaki carpenter's shorts that showed off his knobby knees, and a painter's hat that read "Midland Paint and Hardware." Gotta show support for your local businesses when your wife is running for mayor.

He was planting, or digging a hole in which to plant, a bush whose buds one day would become stunning pink roses. On a fine late March day, when his students were no doubt cramming like mad to read five complete Dickens novels in three days in preparation for Barlow's midterm exam, it was good to be the professor.

Martin looked up when he saw me walk toward him. Since we'd never met (at least not that I could recall), he looked tentative, wondering if I was going to try to sell him an encyclopedia on CD-ROM or convert him to Christian Science.

"Is there something with which I can help you?" English professors—man, you gotta love 'em. Such great grammar! His voice was as reedy as he was. Slim to the point of skinny, Barlow had the body of a marathon runner. He had the face of a beached haddock—pockmarked, with deep eye sockets and a nose that could have sucked in the whole backyard if he'd inhaled hard enough. If Madlyn Beckwirth had indeed forsaken her pretty-boy husband Gary for this guy, she had a perverse sense of irony. Somehow, that possibility elevated Madlyn in my estimation.

I stuck out my hand and identified myself, adding the *Press-Tribune's* name for added credibility. I didn't notice any eye-widening or any other register of apprehension at being questioned about Madlyn Beckwirth. He suggested that I might really want to talk to Rachel, since she was Madlyn's closest friend, but I informed him, to his apparent surprise, that I'd already interviewed his wife.

"Would it be acceptable if we were to talk while I plant this bush?" he asked. "I really prefer not to leave it out of the earth much longer."

"Be my guest," I told him. "No skin off my nose." I'd been staring at his, and the comment just came out. Sue me. He didn't appear to notice.

Using a spade, he widened the hole he was digging, then got down on his right knee and began deepening it with a hand tool. Martin wasn't perfectly neat, but his backyard certainly was. The lawn and the garden were so well-kept you'd think Mike and Carol Brady lived here. Maybe they did. After all, Mike was gay and Carol went out on a date with her son Greg. You never know what goes on in some households.

"How well do you know Madlyn Beckwirth?" I began with the standard opener. Again, there was no guilty flinch, no tic in Barlow's lip, no raising of the eyebrows. He was a better actor than Mike Brady, too.

"Well, as I have indicated, she is Rachel's closest friend. I see her quite often when she and Rachel are planning the campaign, and socially when Madlyn and Gary come by for dinner." Barlow picked up the small, and measured it in the hole, determined an imperfect fit, and removed the bush. An imperfect planting simply would not do. He began digging again, hard, working up a sweat.

"So then you don't know of any reason why she'd decide to run away from her husband and son?"

Barlow stood up and smiled a wry smile. "You realize, of course, that 'reason why' is redundant. The word 'reason' implies that you are asking 'why.'" He placed the bush in the hole again, and this time it fit exactly.

"Fine. Then tell me the reason *that* you decided not to answer my last question."

He started to fill the hole with top soil, and frowned at being scolded. You'd think Rachel Barlow's husband would be used to getting scolded. "In answer to your query, no, I know of no reason Madlyn would want to be away from her family."

"No trouble in her marriage, then?"

"Martin!"

Rachel Barlow, a grocery bag in hand, stood in the archway, gate open, looking impatient. She was wearing a very neat L.L. Bean denim shirt and Banana Republic khakis, and looked like as if she were about to cover supermarket shopping for *Yuppie Life* magazine.

Her husband straightened up at the sound of her voice, and seeing her holding the bag, literally ran to her side and relieved her of her terrible burden, which appeared to be an entire loaf of white bread.

"There are more packages in the car," she said. He nodded, ever the humble manservant, and went off to unload the victuals from the late model Volvo station wagon, parked next to the even later model Ford Explorer minivan in their side-by-side driveway.

Rachel, relieved of the tedious task she had been facing, noticed me. She walked over, trying to find her political candidate smile and coming up, instead, with something that looked like Joan Collins in *Dynasty.*

"Something I can help you with, Mr. Tucker?"

I tsk-tsk'ed her. "Ending a sentence on a preposition, Mrs. Barlow." I shook my head. "I can't imagine your husband would approve."

"Martin's grammar is an excellent example for his students, Mr. Tucker. I wish more people would pay as much attention to syntax."

I considered punning on the idea of "sin tax," but gave it up as too obvious. "In answer to your question, Rachel, I'm actually here to talk to Mr. Barlow."

*"Doctor* Barlow. He has a Ph.D. in English Literature."

I glanced over at *Doctor* Barlow, who was now attempting to navigate a two-liter bottle of Diet Dr. Pepper into his home without taking a five-minute time-out to catch his breath.

"I hoped he might be able to shed some light on Madlyn Beckwirth's disappearance. Does he know her well?"

Rachel's veneer of pleasantness—thin though it was—disappeared entirely. She positively scowled, and put an impatient hand to her hip. "I'm sure Martin has already *told* you that he and Madlyn know each other chiefly through me, and that I would be the best person to talk to about her state of mind. I told you, Mr. Tucker, I'm afraid the poor woman is lying dead somewhere, and you're doing nothing . . ."

Martin, having restocked the kitchen (and for all I know, repainted it as well), reappeared at his wife's side. There was no outward sign of affection between the two of them, but they made heavy eye contact, and the bond was unmistakable. Also obvious, at least to me, was that he was scared to death of her. He picked up the spade and stood at her side. She put an arm on his shoulder. "Suburban Gothic."

More out of annoyance than strategy, I looked Rachel Barlow in the eye and said, "then I suppose there is no truth to the rumor that Martin and Madlyn are having an extramarital affair."

Their reaction was the last thing I expected. Each got the identical smug smile, just a little tinge of amusement, around the lips. Martin Barlow looked me straight in the face. "I can assure you, Mr. Tucker, that is not happening." He seemed to find the notion of sex with Madlyn hilarious. I'd seen pictures of her, and while it wouldn't exactly rate as highly as a romp with Salma Hayek, it wasn't hilarious either. "It is, indeed, absolutely impossible," he added.

For a woman who believed one of her closest friends was a murder victim, Rachel Barlow was having an equally hard time masking her repressed humor. It was the first sincere smile I'd ever seen on her face.

"I can't imagine Martin having an affair with Madlyn," Rachel said. "I can't imagine Martin having an affair with *anybody*. But especially Madlyn!"

I left the two of them like that, grinning like a couple of Jack-O-Lanterns. Whatever it was that was tickling them, I didn't want to be around when they decided to act on it.

Something was bothering me, though—that smile on Martin Barlow's face. It looked the same as his wife's, of course, but on closer examination, his eyes were maybe a fraction wider, his lips just a hair tighter.

Either he was a man with something to hide, or I was a paranoid conspiracy theorist who would make Oliver Stone's eyes roll in disbelief. But there was something going on with one of us, and I didn't think it was me.

I was feeling more stymied than ever on the Beckwirth story, but at least I knew who I'd be voting for in the mayoral primary.

Sorry. That should be "I knew *for whom* I'd be voting."

# Chapter 24

Clearly, what I needed was a break. I mean, paranoid fantasies about Martin Barlow's smile were the limit for a man whose most serious deductive reasoning usually involved sorting white athletic socks out of the laundry for a family of four, all of whom at some time in the day wore white athletic socks.

The best kind of mental vacation, of course, would have been an afternoon in a secluded spot alone with someone as attractive as, say, Abigail Stein. But since that wasn't going to happen, at least not today, and since I still had another mystery to solve, I left the Barlow house and went to Big Bob's Bar-B-Q Pit.

It was a small store front on Edison Avenue, catercorner to the Buzbee School, and a favorite afterschool hang-out for the kids, especially since two arcade video games had been installed a few months ago.

Big Bob's was a small place for a fast-food restaurant. It consisted mainly of a counter, with four stools in front of it and a blackboard suspended from the ceiling behind it. The blackboard held the menu, which didn't seem to have been changed since Big Bob had moved in. Ribs, burgers, hot dogs, and chicken "fingers" were the staples. A side dish was generally french fries, and your beverage was of the carbonated variety. Big Bob could have named the place "Seventh Level of

Cholesterol Hell," and it would have been just as accurate.

I decided that my investigative reporter mode had not been doing wonders for me in this matter, so I gave in to all my detective impulses. I walked into Big Bob's with enough attitude for ten men, or at least one man a few inches taller than me. I considered turning the collar of my denim jacket up, but decided that would have been too much. And there just wasn't enough time to take up smoking.

No one was in the place except Big Bob himself, a man of about 40 with a crew cut, and a tattoo on either forearm—one of an eagle, the other reading "Big Bob." That second tattoo was pointed up, at Bob's eyes, in case he ever forgot his own name.

I sat on the stool nearest the cash register and stared up at the blackboard like there might actually be a surprise on the menu. Big Bob walked over and stood in front of me for a few seconds before curiosity got the better of him.

"Can I help you?"

"Burger, fries, Diet Coke," I said, wincing inwardly at the "Diet." It's hard to be macho when you're avoiding unnecessary carbohydrates. After finishing this story tomorrow, I'd have to get serious about my diet—tomorrow. "And make the burger well-done."

Bob nodded and turned to prepare the food on the grill that was maybe three feet behind him, visible to all who sat on the stools. He put the beef patty on the grill and got to work on the deep fryer, and barely turned when I spoke to him.

"This look familiar?" I asked, pulling the barbecue sauce squeeze container out of my jacket's inside pocket. I held it up for him to see.

Bob finished his potato preparations and turned to look. "Yeah, it's one of my squeeze bottles. So?"

"So, you missing one of these lately?" I asked in my best Bogart, which wasn't too good, even with the recent practice. "Had a little shrinkage on the condiment containers in the last few days?"

Big Bob turned the burger over, despite my request for well-done, and chuckled. "You're kidding, right? You think I know every time one of the little punks steals a ketchup bottle? I'd be out of business in a week if I worried about little stuff like that!"

Okay, so I felt foolish, but when had that ever stopped me? "Well, take a look at this one. Maybe it's different. Maybe it's special."

"How?" asked Bob, taking the spuds out of the deep fryer and shaking off the oil—well, some of it, anyway. "Has it got a naked picture of Buffy the Vampire Slayer on it?" He laughed at his own Shavian wit.

"Just take a look, will you?"

Big Bob gave me a very skeptical look, took the burger off the grill, and brought me my lunch. The burger was still bleeding onto the roll. I handed Bob the bottle.

"So?" I asked.

"You're right!" he marveled. "It *is* different! It's ... it's ... it's barbecue sauce!"

Bob laughed so hard, he practically suffered the heart attack his food had been promising everyone else. He doubled over behind the counter and guffawed himself into a quivering mass.

"All right, all right," I mumbled. "You don't have to rub it in."

When he could finally straighten up again, he leaned on the counter in front of me. "What do you think I do, specially mark each one in case it gets robbed?" he said, still grinning.

I took out the slip of paper with Anne Mignano's handwriting on it. "Well, how about this, then?" I said. "You recognize any of these kids? They might come in here after school."

Bob didn't even bother to look at the paper. "What, you think I know their *names?*" he said, starting to chuckle again. "You think I'm, like, the local malt shop owner, and when Archie and Jughead and Veronica come in, I call out their names, and they say, 'hi, Pops!'? Is *that* what you think?" He started laughing again, and I tried a french fry. It was still cold on the inside.

Bob composed himself again while I contemplated sending my lunch back to the chef with a negative review. "Geez, Mister, you made my day, I gotta tell you," he said. "Think I'd recognize a squeeze bottle." Chuckle. I was thrilled to bring a little levity into what must obviously be a drab and dreary life. "What do you want to know for, anyway? You a cop or something?"

"No," I told him. "I'm not a cop. Or anything."

I picked up the burger and took a bite. It was barely cooked, and juice dripped down my chin.

"How's the burger?" Bob asked.

"Perfect," I said. "Now, where's the Diet Coke?"

# Chapter 25

After eating maybe a third of Big Bob's elegant repast, I retreated to my office and spent the afternoon wrestling with a love scene, which is the hardest thing to write for a movie. There have been so many such scenes that it's nearly impossible not to repeat something that's been done before, and virtually every line of dialogue you can think of sounds like a cliché. But this is the kind of work I desperately want to do, and so I toiled away at it for a couple of hours, writing all of a page and a half, which I'd probably delete tomorrow. Nobody ever accused writers of being rational.

Maybe I wasn't up to snuff because it was a tad early. Under normal circumstances, I can't write a word of screenplay before three in the afternoon. I don't know why. I can know exactly what I'm trying to accomplish as early as ten in the morning, but I can't bear to bring myself to the keyboard and create something new before that clock hits three. Then, of course, I am wildly inspired, clear in my vision, unbridled in my enthusiasm. And that's when my kids get home from school. So I periodically try to force myself to write earlier in the day, but it's never much of a success.

Today, however, I didn't think that was the problem. The Beckwirth story was invading my mind, and it was hard to concentrate on the fiction I was trying to create. There was something vaguely spooky about the look on Martin and Rachel Barlow's faces, that eerie laugh when I'd suggested that what Diane Woolworth had heard was true. There was more to it than simple amusement. They were *enjoying* Madlyn's predicament. And that didn't jive, at least for one of them.

I gave up on the love scene because my characters just wouldn't cooperate. Ungrateful little bastards. You give them life, you name them, you point them toward each other and make their lives interesting, and they repay you by going off on their own and screwing up your plans to exploit them. At least you don't have to pay their college tuition bills.

Why hadn't Westbrook called yet? If he'd found something, would he deliberately hold back? If he hadn't found something, would he deliberately take the rest of the day off to visit Pizza Hut?

I checked the Bullwinkle clock. Almost two-thirty. The kids would be home soon. But it was possible Barry Dutton would be back in his office by now. Should I call?

Call and say what? That a crazy lady who thinks she's British heard that maybe Martin Barlow was having an affair with a woman whose husband was about fifteen times better looking and fifty times richer than him? That someone saw a minivan driving away from Madlyn Beckwirth's house during the night she left, but not necessarily at the time she left? That Martin Barlow had a guilty smile on his face? That I had to write something for the newspaper by tomorrow? And that the question I *really* wanted to answer was: who's been writing nasty things about my kid on the sidewalk with a zesty beef topping?

I'd had enough of this Beckwirth thing. It was taking up too much time, leading to too many dead ends, and causing me to come into contact with people I'd prefer to avoid at all costs. I'd received a threatening phone call and been followed by a threatening minivan. All this to make a measly thousand dollars.

Okay, so I could use the thousand dollars. But it wasn't like the sheriff was at the door evicting us. Abby makes a nice living, and even if I don't, I did have other work. And I was sure Spielberg would be calling directory assistance for my number any minute now.

Did I really need this story? Couldn't my time be better spent finding out who hated my son, so I could beat that child to a bloody pulp and feel better?

That did it. I picked up the phone and called Dave Harrington. He sounded relieved when he heard it was me. "You got the missing woman story, Aaron? Tell me you're a day early."

Swell. He was going to make this easy. "Well, to tell you the truth, Dave, I was just calling to say, well, that is . . ."

"Aaron, this doesn't sound good . . ."

There was a *beep* in my ear, my call waiting device indicating another call on the line. We home office workers are so high-tech!

"Can you hang on a second, Dave? I've got another call." I hit the "flash" button on my phone, and immediately found myself voice-to-voice with my agent, Margot Stakowski, of the Stakowski Agency of Cleveland, Ohio.

"Aaron!" That's Margot's way of saying "hello." And she always sounds surprised, as if she were calling Francis Ford Coppola and got me by accident.

I rolled my eyes, and managed to stifle a sigh at the sound of her voice. "How you doing, Margot?"

"This business sucks," she said. "I'm just checking in to see what's going on."

This took a moment to sink in, just like it always does. "You're calling *me* to find out what's going on? Isn't it supposed to work the other way around? Aren't you supposed to know what's going on, and then let me know?"

"Don't get testy. I had to drive my mother to her rehab today, and I'm buried under a pile of scripts." Margot's chief function as an agent is to read other people's scripts. She read mine once, and since she was the only agent to offer me representation, I was thrilled to sign on. But nothing had happened since then. And now she called every week to find out if I'd managed to make myself a deal she could siphon ten percent from.

"Is anything up, Margot? I've got an editor on the other line."

"Oh! No, go ahead. Let me know if you get a book." Margot always thought the mere mention of the word "editor" meant "book." In fact, "publisher" means "book." "Editor," at least in my world, means "cheap newspaper or magazine work."

"Okay. Talk to you next week."

I clicked the flash button again, and got Dave in mid-cupcake. "I'm not taking up too much of your time, am I, Aaron?"

"I'm sorry, Dave. It was my agent. She calls every Wednesday, and never has anything to tell me. I don't know why I still . . ."

"Aaron! The missing lady? What have you got?"

"Dave, I've got to level with you. This story . . ."

"Don't tell me you need more time, Aaron. I've got a hole in the local section Friday that I was counting on filling with the juicy details of a missing woman from Midland Park."

"Midland Heights."

"Wherever. Where's the story?"

"Well, that's just it, Dave." I started staring at each of the sixteen pictures Leah had drawn for my last birthday. They all had rainbows, and a girl with long brown hair. The girl's hair usually was longer than her body, which was composed of sticks. Everything was relatively in proportion except the fingers, which were tremendously long. It looked like a girl with huge spiders on each hand . . .

"What's just it?"

"The story. See, I've been at it a week now, and . . ."

"That sentence doesn't end well, does it, Aaron?"

The man had keen instincts. "Well, no. See . . ."

There was another beep in the headset. "Dave, hang on. I'll get rid of this one faster, I promise."

"Great. I'll hold my breath this time."

I clicked on the flash button once again, steeling myself for a call from either my mother or Anne Mignano. "Hello?"

A woman's high-pitched voice—with a nervous chuckle after almost every word. "Mr. Tucker? Aaron Tucker?"

Terrific. Now somebody's going to try and sell me a subscription to *Newsweek* while I'm trying to wriggle out of a cheap newspaper assignment. "Yes, this is Aaron Tucker. But I'm not ..."

"This is Madlyn Beckwirth," she said. "I hear you've been looking for me."

# Chapter 26

There was a very long pause. It might have lasted hours. I'm not sure. They say when you go into shock, time really doesn't register all that well on your brain.

"Hello?" the woman said.

"Um ..." I stood up. When I'm having really important, or tense, conversations, I stand up. It's a reflex. I paced around the room as far as the 25-foot phone cord would allow. "You're Madlyn Beckwirth?" Stall. Find the functioning area of your brain while you keep her on the line with the other 90 percent.

"That's right. They tell me you're looking for me. I just wanted you to know that I'm okay, and there's no reason to look for me anymore." The voice certainly matched the photograph I'd seen—tentative, a touch naive—and yet not at all a voice to dismiss out of hand. A woman who probably sat in her perfectly appointed family room eating ladyfingers off a silver tray while watching a hockey game on TV.

"Who? Who tells you I'm looking for you?"

"I'm just calling to let you know I'm fine, and I'll be back in a few days. This is really no big deal." She didn't seem to be reading from a script, and there wasn't the kind of tension in her voice that would indicate anyone standing nearby with a gun trained on her.

"So you haven't been kidnapped?"

Madlyn—if it *was* Madlyn—laughed, one of those explosions from pursed lips that Carol Burnett used to be so good at. A sound like "Pahhhh!" She composed herself quickly and said, "no, I'm not kidnapped. I'm fine. Really. There's no reason to write about me in the paper."

Ah-hah. So *that* was it. "If nothing's wrong, why don't you want your family and friends to know that?" I asked. "Your husband is very worried, and your son ..." You need to know, I'm not a good liar.

"My son is ... what? Worried I'll come back?" The voice was sarcastic. Well, she knew her kid well, assuming it was Madlyn. An assumption that was getting harder and harder to avoid.

"He's worried," I said, very unconvincingly. "He wants to know where you are. Where *are* you?"

There was another stretch of silence in the conversation, this time coming from the other end of the phone. Damn! I wished Barry Dutton was listening in on my phone. He could have traced this call to its source. First time I'd ever wanted somebody to tap my phone.

The one thing I could remember to do was pull the little phone-to-recorder wire I keep for telephone interviews down from the shelf over my desk. I plugged one end into the phone line, for the briefest of seconds cutting off Madlyn, and pressed the exposed phone cord into the other, female, end. I could hear the caller again.

She said, "hello? Are you still there?"

"Yeah, I'm here," I replied. I found the portable cassette recorder behind my computer monitor, and plugged the other end of the phone line into the microphone jack. "I was asking where you are." Damn! No blank cassette!

"I don't think I want to tell you," the woman replied. I crept into the living room, adjacent to my office, and tried to reach the blank cassettes, which we keep on the mantle of the non-operational fireplace. Must get that thing repaired one of these days, when I have $5,000 I'm not doing anything with.

"Why not?" Got to keep her talking. If I could just reach that box of cassettes . . . got one!

"I don't want to be found . . . just yet," the voice said. I raced back to the desk, trying desperately to take the wrapping off the blank tape package. Finding a corner on one of these things was like finding a compassionate literary agent in Hollywood. You could do it, but it took a hundred times more work than it should.

"Don't you want everyone to see you're all right?" I asked as I finally slammed an unwrapped cassette into the recorder. I pushed the button and thanked all the spirits in the room that at least the batteries in the recorder were functional. The tape started to turn.

"That's why I called you," she said.

And then she hung up.

# *Intermission*

Madlyn hung up the phone and lay back on the king-size bed, sighing contentedly. Now maybe this reporter guy would stop bothering everybody, and she could enjoy her vacation a while longer. Maybe for good.

In retrospect, almost getting killed by a minivan had been exactly what she'd needed. When she fell back to avoid a collision, over the little metal divider and down the hill, she'd thought she was going to die. But she hadn't even been badly injured—just a couple of cuts and bruises.

It had made her think, though. You don't have any guarantees. You can't put off your own happiness and expect to pick it up again when you have the time. What if you don't have the time?

She had gotten herself up from the base of the ridge beside her house, right next to the creek that ran to the river. She'd inspected her bumps and cuts, decided they were unimportant, and started walking.

Madlyn had no intention whatsoever of returning to the house that night. Keeping that place together and keeping the boy in line was more than a 24-hour-a-day job. It was a career she hadn't studied for in college. So given this unexpected opportunity, she turned her back on the house.

By morning, she had reached the highway, and a little before noon, drawing stares because of her outfit (and obvious lack of underwear), she'd found a convenience store and called her husband, collect.

He pretended to be distraught, but she'd done this before, and he knew the drill. She expected a number of things from him, beginning with a limo to pick her up and take her wherever she wanted to go, a credit card in her name on Gary's account, and his presence as soon as possible.

When he arrived on the second day, everything was the way she wanted it. The sex was amazing, and if a married couple can't get away and remember what their dating days were like, then what was left of the American Dream?

She had stayed here the whole time, but they couldn't always be together. The pretense that she was missing had to be preserved to save everyone a lot of embarrassment.

The very thought of it made her feel lightheaded. She was watching the door closely now. Gary had called about 20 minutes ago from the car with the update. She should expect to see that door open any minute, and to feel again the things she'd dreamt about all week long.

# Part Two: Finding

## Chapter 1

I had spent a good portion of the past week staring at the phone-set in my hand, and here I was, doing it again. Only one sentence uttered by the "Mystery Woman" on the phone, and then silence. Hell, Westbrook could have done that well. At least Gary Beckwirth would be able to tell from that short clip if it was his wife's voice. That would be the "cheerful news" he had requested—Madlyn was still alive.

I was supposed to find Madlyn Beckwirth, but she had found me. "They" had told her I was looking for her, and she had called me to put an end to my search, and to get me to leave her alone. And she had done a hell of a job, too. She'd managed to get her message across without directly answering a single question. Madlyn should have been running for office herself, not getting someone else elected.

Feeling stupid, I was about to hang up the phone when a nagging little feeling in the back of my mind leapt to the front, and instead, I hit the flash button.

"Dave?"

"Well waddaya know," came back my editor's voice. "He *did* remember there was another human being waiting on the line."

"Jesus, I'm sorry," I blabbered. "It was . . ."

What was I going to tell him? That I was about to resign from the story he'd given me—which meant I'd probably never get any work from Dave or his paper again—but decided against it when the woman I was supposed to locate had located me instead? In that case, he'd hire Madlyn to write the story, and cut me out of it entirely. She called me—it was embarrassing. Did Richard Nixon call Bob Woodward and let him in on the whole Watergate thing? Well, they never *did* find out who "Deep Throat" was . . .

"Spare me the details," Harrington said. "You were about to explain to me why this *thousand-dollar* story you're working on isn't going to be in my computer by tomorrow."

Wait a second. That was the point, exactly. Madlyn had called *me*, not the other way around. And that meant . . .

"Dave," I told him, "forget everything I was about to tell you. You'll have a story on your screen tomorrow, and it's going to be much better than you have any reason to expect."

"Well, how hard is that to do?"

"I'll talk to you later," I said, and hung up on him before he could commit another atrocity of wit. Immediately afterward, I pressed the line button for incoming calls on the phone and dialed *69.

"This is—your return-call service," the automated voice said. I held my breath. If the number was out of the area, like MacKenzie's, I was completely screwed, and would have to call Harrington back and offer to wax his car by hand every week until Leah got out of graduate school. "The number of your last incoming call is: Six-zero-nine . . ." A sigh of relief was heard in houses up and down my street.

So there it was, I thought, jotting down the entire ten digit phone number on the back of yesterday's sheet-a-day calendar, the official Aaron Tucker Editorial Services scratch paper. A six-zero-nine area code meant South Jersey, and this exchange sounded like Atlantic City, which was easily a two-hour drive away. But I couldn't just call Madlyn back. She might flee. I needed to see her, bring her back, show everyone that I could, in fact, do the job I was asked, however mistakenly, to do.

The phone number I'd gotten ended in a hundred, so it had to be a business, and, if Madlyn was holed-up in Atlantic City, probably a hotel. I dialed the number.

"Bally's Casino Hotel."

It's hard to talk when you're holding your breath, but I managed. "What room is Madlyn Beckwirth in?" I asked. "Don't connect me," I added quickly.

"There's no Madlyn Beckwirth registered here, sir, and even if there were, it's our policy not to give out room numbers over the phone."

"Well, I just received an abusive phone call from your hotel, and I'd like very much to know who might have called and threatened the lives of my children," I scolded. The operator, if I was lucky, wouldn't know it was against the law to make such calls and immediately insist the cops be brought in.

"Oh, my!" she said. "Well, I can access the phone records to see which room called your number, sir." Once in a while, I get lucky.

"That's better," I said, and gave her my number. It took a few seconds.

"I have it. A call made about eight minutes ago," said the operator proudly. Way to get around the hotel rules, Tucker. "That's room twenty-two-oh-three, but there's no Madlyn Beckwirth registered there, sir."

"Who is registered in that room? Maybe there's been a mistake."

"That room is registered to Mrs. Milton Ladowski." I almost dropped the phone, but managed to thank the operator, and hung up.

I ran across the street and asked Miriam to watch the kids until Abby got home. She said her daughter Melissa would be glad to play with Leah. Ethan, I informed her, would do his homework and then disappear into the land of Nintendo, emerging only for sustenance. In other words, Miriam said it was no problem. I was in the car before I really knew what I was doing.

Once on the road, I plugged the cell phone into the cigarette lighter and called Abby in her office. She was on the phone, but I told her assistant Lorraine it was important, and gave her the cell phone

number to call back. I'd barely gotten two miles before the phone rang.
I pushed the "hands-off" button.

"Hi, Sweetie," I said.

"Is everybody okay?" The mother lion was in no mood to be called
"Sweetie."

"As far as I know. They're not home yet."

"Then what are you doing in the car?"

"If you'll shut up for a minute, I'll tell you!" She did, and I did.

"Wow," Abby said when I was done.

"Yeah, wow," I agreed. "So, can you get home a little early? Miriam
doesn't mind watching the kids for awhile, but you know how Ethan's
been ... and I forgot to tell Miriam he can't play Nintendo, so if you
find him up there ..."

"We'll let it go until I get home," she said. "I'm out of here at four."

"Real four, or Abby-four?"

"Don't be funny, Aaron, or I'll be forced to withhold sex. And you
know how cranky you get when that happens."

"Yeah, like you could."

"Let me know what you find out." And she hung up. Probably
someone walked into her office and asked her why she was having erot-
ic conversations on company time.

Motoring along on the Garden State Parkway, an hour and a half
from Atlantic City, it occurred to me that I might call Westbrook and
let him know what I'd found out. But since I'd gotten such a prompt
response to my similar request, I decided he could wait.

He could wait until I found out what was on the other end of this
highway, on a peninsula where there's gambling, cheap buffets, high-
class entertainment, and the Miss America Pageant. And, it would
seem, Madlyn Beckwirth.

# Chapter 2

Atlantic City, New Jersey is a town badly in need of a lithium pre-scription. Its manic side features all the same thrilling high spots found in Las Vegas—gambling, drinking, all-you-can-eat buffets, elaborate productions with topless women, prostitution—without the class, if you can believe that.

Its depressed side, which is where the actual residents of Atlantic City live, has abject poverty, violence, domestic desperation, and drugs. So when you're visiting, stay close to the water, which is manic, and away from the land, which is depressed. Unless you happen to like abject poverty, violence, domestic desperation, and drugs.

At about 4:15 that afternoon, I was sticking close to the water. I had driven like a madman on the way here, forcing myself to stay below 85 mph in the '97 Saturn we had bought (used) the year before. The sun wasn't even beginning to set yet, as the days were beginning to lengthen some, so my view of the Atlantic Ocean was clear. I realized somewhere around Camden that I'd forgotten to MapQuest myself into Bally's itself, but that proved not to be much of a problem. Once you're in Atlantic City itself, the casinos all make a very strong effort to ensure that you can't miss them, and Bally's was no exception. There were signs about every eight feet.

So I drove into the parking lot, which like most of the casino lots was large and underused. On my way to the hotel's main lobby, I first had to pass through the casino, and since I had all of $14 in my pocket, did my best to resist the lure of the slot machines, blackjack tables, and $4 Diet Cokes.

I also wanted to avoid the front desk, which is where they ask questions and alert guests to unexpected visitors, so I adopted my patented "I-Know-Where-I'm-Going" face and marched at an accelerated clip toward the elevators. This led to some confusion, since there are several banks of elevators at the casino, and they go to several separate banks of floors. I rode up and down to the ninth floor before I figured out exactly where I was going and how to get there.

A mere fifteen minutes later, I was on the twenty-second floor, trying to decipher the signs posted to help mentally challenged visitors like myself find the room they're looking for. These are, of course, the same rooms in which most room searchers would actually be staying, but after an active night in the casino with all the complimentary drinks, it can be hard to remember where you're going.

The carpet, although thick, was a bit squishy, and of course red, since red appears to be the official color of gambling casinos worldwide. I've never been to the casino at Monte Carlo, but I'll bet you it's heavily decorated in red. That's how you can tell the casinos are in the black.

There were a number of things to be thankful for in this hotel. For one, there was no enormous oil portrait of Donald Trump, alongside similar ones of Benjamin Franklin and George Washington, like in one of Trump's many high-class buildings here in Atlantic City. This hotel also had not been designed with one of those fabulous space-wasting configurations that allows for a guard rail about chest high overlooking a drop of several hundred feet to the casino floor, presumably to take in all the grandeur of the surroundings, but enough to turn anyone into Jimmy Stewart in *Vertigo*.

Instead, there were aisles and aisles of nondescript hotel room doors, and they didn't seem to be numbered in any recognizable pattern, or maybe it was just my level of anticipation. My heart was racing a bit, I was sweating (despite the air conditioning, which brought the hallway to a comfortable Antarctic level), and my mind was reeling. All the way down here in the car, my only thought was to get to Madlyn Beckwirth's door. Now I was practically there (if I could ever figure out the pattern), and I had absolutely no idea how to proceed beyond knocking.

In my mind's eye was a picture of me walking into Gary Beckwirth's living room, more or less carrying his errant wife by the scruff of the neck like a truant child, and depositing her on his incredibly expensive Persian rug. But first I had to persuade the elusive Mrs. Beckwirth to return, since I had no intention (nor, in all likelihood, ability) to force her physically. And Madlyn had sounded on the phone very much like someone who was not in any hurry to come home.

If I were Elvis Cole, I could just get Joe Pike to stand guard at the door, and if Madlyn got past me and tried to run out, he could give her a casual forearm to the forehead and we'd both carry her (or Joe could sling her over his shoulder) to the car and drive her home, all the while philosophizing about how a woman's place is with her husband and child, and how we sometimes had to bend the rules a little to suit our own unique moral code.

But I wasn't Elvis Cole. I wasn't even Nat "King" Cole, and I'll bet *he* would have had a better plan to get Madlyn out of the room, even if he has been dead since the 1960s. Anyone who could sing "The Ballad Of Cat Ballou," "Those Lazy Hazy Crazy Days of Summer," and "Mona Lisa" all in one career was clearly a man of broad and varied talents.

Lost in these deep and helpful thoughts, I flinched a bit when I looked up and saw the number "2203" to my immediate left. Through sheer chance, I had found the correct room. Great. Now all I had to do was formulate a plan, convince Madlyn Beckwirth to come with me, and then figure out how in the name of Ferdinand Magellan to get back to the elevators. Maybe I should have stopped at the $6.99 all-you-can-eat buffet for some bread crumbs to drop.

I had gotten this far without a plan, so I decided to proceed with-out a plan, and raised my hand to knock on the door. But I froze. Suppose someone else was in there with Madlyn. I mean, suppose someone else was in there, you know, *with* Madlyn. I guess that's why God invented knocking, so he'd have time to find his pants. The guy with Madlyn, I mean, not God.

On the second try, I managed to get my knuckle to make physical contact with the door. What I didn't expect was that the door would actually open inward, and that made me take a step back in surprise. It had been left open a crack, like Cary Grant used to do when he was expecting room service and couldn't be bothered to walk across the room to answer the door. Maybe there *was* somebody in there with Madlyn.

I knocked on the open door again, which is not terribly easy to do—you have to reach. It's especially hard to knock loudly, but that's exactly what I did, bruising a knuckle or two in the process.

"Um . . . Mrs. Beckwirth?" I called inside.

It had that feel to it. A room in which there are no people. I don't know how you can tell, but you can. I took a step inside. It wasn't dark—the room-darkening curtains were open. There was a very nice view of the Boardwalk, and the beach and ocean beyond. Must have cost a considerable amount, this room.

Another few steps inside and I could see the whole suite. It was extremely well appointed, with understated carpeting, and real wood furniture. In addition, there was a sitting room, where a TV armoire was open, a coffee table in front of the overstuffed sofa and two arm-chairs, and French doors leading out to a veranda, where there was a table and two wire chairs.

In the bedroom was a walk-in closet, whose door was also open. There was virtually nothing inside—just empty hangers. Even in this high-priced suite, they were the kind of hangers you can't take off the closet bar. Some companies don't trust *anybody*. A table and two chairs sat next to the other set of French doors, and brilliant sunshine was streaming into the room and onto the huge king-size bed.

On the bed was Madlyn Beckwirth. She was dressed in a very short black lace teddy that I would have recognized from the Victoria's Secret catalogue, had I been the type who reads such things. Under different circumstances, she might have looked quite appealing in it, but it was hard for me to summon that mental image right now.

From what I could tell, she had been shot twice—once in the stomach, which had bled considerably, and then once in the head. Whoever shot her had been aiming for her forehead and missed. The wound was through her left cheek, and had taken a considerable amount of the back of her head off. I'm no detective, but I could tell from all the way across the room that she was dead.

There are times in your life when your mind reacts to events in ways totally opposite to the way you would hope. These are times you bury in the back of your memory, but they resurface periodically, just to remind you that you are a dreadful, shameless creature barely worthy of the name "human."

For me, this was one of those times. My first thought on seeing Madlyn laid out on the bed, gut-shot, murdered, her young life wasted, was, "this is going to make one helluva great screenplay."

# Chapter 3

After a few seconds, I was able to regain my senses, and that's when reality set in. My hands started to shake, and a cold sweat appeared on my forehead. I forced myself to look away from the bed to avoid vomiting on a crime scene.

The first thing that always occurs to me when I'm in a difficult situation is to call Abigail. Luckily, that made superb sense in this case, since my wife is an attorney, and a former criminal attorney at that. I reached into my inside jacket pocket and pulled out the cell phone, hit "redial," and prayed she hadn't left the office yet.

Abby has caller ID on her office phone, so she could see the number of my cell phone before she picked up the phone. "I swear, I'm on my way out the door," she said in lieu of a greeting.

"Actually I'm glad you're still there," I told her. "I have a situation."

The smile left her voice. "Where are you?"

"I'm in Room 2203 of Bally's Casino Hotel, and Madlyn Beckwirth is here. She's dead."

Abby had once told me, in another context, that a lot of people go to hotels to commit suicide. "Suicide?" she asked.

"Not unless she found a way to shoot herself in the belly and the head and then throw the gun out the window before she died."

"Jesus," my wife offered.

"So, what do I do now?" I asked her.

Lawyer-Mode clicked in—even though she hadn't done criminal work in years—and Abby's voice dropped an octave. "Have you called the Atlantic City police?"

"I haven't called anybody yet. I called you. The police may think my behavior a bit suspicious. The door to her room was slightly open, but I did push my way in. And I didn't let Barry or Westbrook know in advance I was coming here to get her. I don't think they would have approved."

Abby sucked in on her front teeth, her way of indicating to me that I was being a moron. "You've seen too many Hitchcock movies, Aaron. Don't worry about what seems suspicious. Nobody's going to think you killed Madlyn. You don't have a motive. But think about everything you've done since you entered the room. Did you move anything, touch anything, do *anything* that would disturb the scene?"

I had already replayed the past two minutes in my head about fifteen times. "I pushed the door open. My hand might have brushed the table, you know a side . . . what's the word?"

"A sideboard."

"Right. Sideboard, in the hall, on my way in. Besides that, I haven't touched anything."

"Look down," Abby said. "Did you step in, you know, anything?"

That hadn't occurred to me. If there had been blood on the rug, would I have seen it? I didn't want to look, but now I had no choice. I examined the carpet from the door to the spot in which I was standing.

"No. I didn't step in anything." There was a faint "beep" in the phone. "I'm going to lose you in a second, Abby. The battery's running out. . ."

"Don't worry. Go down into the lobby and get casino security. The state has troopers who work in the casinos, and they'll deal with this.

I'll call Barry Dutton and let him know what's going on. Tell the troopers everything you know. And Aaron ..."

"Yeah, Baby?"

"It's okay. I love ..."

The battery on the goddam phone died.

# Chapter 4

The state troopers assigned to casino security were, as Abby had predicted, completely uninterested in me after confirming a few things with Barry Dutton. Their lack of interest, however, didn't stop them from keeping me for three hours. They took me to a bare office in the bowels of the hotel and did the usual checks on my driver's license to make sure I was who I said I was (who else would want to be me?), questioned me a couple of hundred times about how I'd come to be there, went over my phone conversation with Madlyn to the point where I could recite it in my sleep, and determined beyond a shadow of a doubt (never mind how) that I didn't have a firearm in my possession.

Unfortunately, all this took time, and they had called Gary Beckwirth almost immediately upon my reporting the murder. So by the time they were done talking to me, Gary was sitting in the security waiting room, waiting his turn to be questioned. He was on a metal folding chair—the hotel, which had blown its budget on wallpaper and crystal chandeliers in the casino, had spared considerable expense in its security section. It had the curious effect of reminding me how Jews, when we are mourning, sit on the least comfortable things we can find to remind us of our loss.

I had to walk right past Gary to get to the door. But he didn't cause the scene I was expecting. He didn't leap out of his chair, burst into tears, and accuse me of killing his wife. He didn't scream that I had botched my job and led violent criminals to his defenseless spouse's bed. He didn't even take a swing at me. What he did was worse.

Gary Beckwirth watched me walk through that room, never taking his dead, expressionless eyes off me. Milt Ladowski was sitting next to him, and Milt stood when he saw me. But Gary never acknowledged my presence other than to stare unblinking into my face the whole time we were in the same room. I wondered where Joel was, and whether he cared that his mother was dead.

I walked over to Milt, who offered me his hand.

"Aaron."

I gently shook Milt's hand, and tried to avoid looking at Gary. "We need to talk," I said, with an exaggerated sense of urgency in my voice.

Milt nodded. "I'll call you when we're . . . through here."

I couldn't avoid it. I had to talk to Gary, too. I stepped to the side, in the square-dance move you make when you're proceeding down a receiving line. Gary did not stand up, but he kept staring at me.

"Gary, I'm so sorry." For once, I wouldn't have minded if he'd stood up and hugged me.

Instead, he stared. That's all. Just those big matinee-idol eyes, devoid of any feeling, only beginning to understand the hole left in his life, staring. At me.

"Don't be," he rasped, and then turned away. He sat with his chin resting on his fist, like Rodin's "Thinker," but it wasn't a comical pose. It was the position of a man who literally couldn't hold his own head up without assistance.

I nodded back at Milt, and walked out of the casino as quickly as I could without running.

Facing a two-hour drive in the dark, I plugged the cell phone into the cigarette lighter in the car, but I didn't need to talk at this point. I needed to think. I'd just spent hours talking to the police, and that hadn't gotten anybody anywhere.

I can't listen to music while I'm thinking, so I kept the cassette player turned off. A.J. Croce would have to wait until I was in a less stressful situation. He plays a nice piano, but he couldn't help me figure out what had happened.

The facts were easy to recite. The hard part was discerning what they meant. Madlyn Beckwirth had left her house in the middle of the night a week and a half ago, apparently of her own accord. Her neighbor may or may not have seen her hit by a minivan, but she certainly wasn't injured seriously, since she was able to call me and ask me to leave her alone a mere ten days later.

Somehow, she had made it to Atlantic City, checked into an expensive hotel room, and charged the whole thing to Milt Ladowski. Where she'd gotten clothes or money, if she had indeed left with just the T-shirt and shorts she slept in, as Gary had said, was anybody's guess. All I knew for sure was that she had called me this afternoon, sounding quite healthy, and asking to be left alone. But I hadn't left her alone. I had come looking for her, and now she was dead.

It was just like the guy on the phone had said: I found Madlyn, but I found her dead. In some way, I must have contributed.

Guilt is instilled in my people pretty much at the start of our lives—probably through cells or DNA or something like that. If we can figure out some, even far-fetched, way we're responsible for the bad stuff that happens in life, we root it out, or die trying. But in this case, I didn't have to look very hard. I had taken on an investigation I knew I was ill-equipped to conduct. Oh sure, I'd protested myself blue in the face, but I'd agreed to do it, for the money and for the personal challenge. I had dismally failed the test.

Having worked myself into this state, it was now easy to wallow in it. Before I made it into Mercer County, I had convinced myself I was responsible for Madlyn's death, Joel's future psychotherapy bills, Gary's inevitable lonely life, Ethan's alienation from his classmates, Abby's having to live in an income level beneath that of most of her friends, and Leah's inability to rhyme more than four words with "cat." If the ride got any longer, I might throw in the Johnstown Flood and the Bombay Bread Riots.

What was missing from this internal soliloquy was any concern for Madlyn Beckwirth. By all reports a decent and loving woman of less than 45, she was lying on a cold slab in the Atlantic County medical examiner's office, awaiting transport back to Midland Heights for burial, after some pretty extensive cosmetic work was done or a closed casket was ordered.

Once I realized I was worried more about my own role than Madlyn's death, I made a point of feeling guilty about that, too.

But, wait a second! I hadn't pulled the trigger. If, as I suspected, somebody had been playing me for a fool the whole time, and I had played the role perfectly, I had to find out who was doing the manipulating. There was an awfully good chance it was the same person— or people—who had killed Madlyn Beckwirth.

And there were plenty of suspects. Why was Milt Ladowski's name on Madlyn's hotel bill? If Madlyn *was* having an affair in that hotel with someone, and Gary found out about it, could it have driven Gary crazy enough to do this to her? Wouldn't he more likely go after the other guy? What about my mysterious phone caller? Madlyn had been receiving calls similar to the one I had gotten, threatening her life if she continued to manage Rachel Barlow's campaign. Suppose the caller *hadn't* just been some prankster who got his kicks from phoning the local bar and asking the bartender for "Amanda Hugandkiss."

But more than anything else, there was the tight-lipped, teeth-clenched amusement of Martin Barlow when I'd suggested that he and Madlyn were sneaking around behind Rachel and Gary's backs. And the cold-hearted stare of Rachel Barlow, mayoral candidate and high-school cheerleader gone bad, as she alternately suggested Madlyn was already dead, or laughed at the idea that Madlyn might be sleeping with Rachel's husband.

My grip on the steering wheel got a little tighter, and I felt my jaw clench involuntarily. Finally, I had a story to investigate. And this time, I thought I knew just how to go about doing it. It wouldn't make me feel better about what had happened to Madlyn, but maybe it could set one-tenth of this whole mess right again, and certainly would be worth accomplishing.

When I reached the end of the long drive, my front door opened and Abigail Stein was standing in the doorway, a concerned expression on her face. It is what makes the most difficult of days worth getting through.

I had barely made it out of the car before she had run down the porch steps and into my arms, hugging me tighter than I could remember for quite some time. I stroked her hair and found time to exhale. Abby sniffed a little.

"You could've called," she finally said.

"No, I couldn't," I told her. "I had some thinking to do."

# Chapter 5

It was after nine, and I hadn't eaten since noon. Abby, who made a pasta salad for me, actually sat me down and served it to me while I gave her the rundown on my late afternoon and evening. She gave me her undivided attention, asked very few questions, and nodded at several points. I didn't tell her about my brainstorming in the car. Abby doesn't embrace self-pity the way artists like myself do.

"How'd I do?" I asked when the story was finished.

"Perfectly," she said. "You couldn't have handled it better if I were there to guide you every step of the way. By the way, Barry Dutton wants you to call him when you get home."

"I am home."

"Yeah, but only technically. You haven't eaten yet," she said.

She wouldn't let me call Barry until I'd eaten. Frankly, I was more interested in the pasta than the salad, but Abby was sitting there with me, and it was hard to avoid the tomatoes. I hate raw tomatoes—they don't look finished. So I went after the romaine, green and red peppers, scallions, and other greens (Abby had even included celery, since this was for me and not for her) until I declared myself full. I wasn't completely full—nothing the odd package of Yodels couldn't fix later.

"I've been sitting here all night wondering," Abby said. "That is, when I wasn't worried sick about some stupid man who wouldn't call from the car."

I let it pass. "Wondering what?"

"Who do you think did it?" she said, the smile of a ruthless criminal lawyer spreading across on her face. Abby, never the literary snob, has been known to pick up one or two of my mystery novels after I'm finished reading them. She enjoys the mental exercise required, and admires the work of Robert B. Parker, particularly his Spenser novels, though she thinks Susan Silverman (the girlfriend) is a pain in the ass.

"I've been giving that a lot of thought," I told her. "All I'm sure of right now is that I didn't do it."

"Good. I didn't take you in the office pool."

"The way I see it," I said, "it all hinges on whether Madlyn was really having an affair, and if so, whether it was with Martin Barlow. Because that means either Gary was so jealous he went nuts and shot her himself..."

Abigail frowned. "That doesn't seem logical," she said. "He's more the type who would kill the male offender."

I was so grateful to her for having dinner waiting that I didn't mention I'd already considered that. *"Or,"* I said, "it could mean that Martin killed Madlyn so Rachel wouldn't find out, or that Rachel *did* find out her campaign manager was screwing her husband and decided to eliminate the competition."

"Say *screwing* again," Abby said in an exaggeratedly deep voice. "You know how it makes me crazy."

"There are any number of other expressions I could have chosen," I said. "If you have a preference, I'd certainly like to know about it, for future use."

"I've always liked ..." and she stopped, of course, because Ethan, in his undying quest for snacks, chose that moment to wander into the room. He marched directly to the snack cabinet and began rummaging.

"Hello to you, too," I said sarcastically. "You know, I haven't seen you all day."

"Uh-huh. Mom, where are the Nutter Butters?" Nutter Butter cookies are Ethan's snack of choice, and he will eat them day in and day out an hour before bed, until he inexplicably decides they are inedible and moves on to some other calorie-laden goodie. This will happen with no warning at all, but by rule of thumb, it's usually a day or two after we break down and buy the super-humongous size box of Nutter Butters. Leah is a chocolate fiend and will not touch the Nutter Butters. All the remaining stock will be left to the only other person who has 24-hour access to the kitchen (that is, the only resident who doesn't leave for work or school every day). His task is to eliminate all traces of the current snack of choice. It's a dirty rotten job, but somebody's got to do it.

"Um, actually, I think we're out of Nutter Butters, Ethan," Abby said, and we both braced ourselves.

His brow furrowed for a moment. "Oh. Okay," he said, and walked away from the cabinet. I never would have predicted anything less than a raging tantrum and an emergency trip to the supermarket. Abby and I exchanged an incredulous stare. Ethan started for the living room (after all, *Spongebob Square Pants* wasn't getting any younger), but I grabbed him by the arm playfully as he passed.

"Okay, who are you, and what have you done with my son?" The phone rang. Abby, sitting next to it, stared at me.

"What do you mean? I *am* your son." It rang again. Not a muscle moved on my wife. I sighed and stood up. The break must be over.

"I was just kidding, Ethan." I walked to the phone and picked it up, as my wife grinned her cat-with-canary grin. As I suspected, the call was from Milton Ladowski, Juris Doctor.

"We just left the casino, Aaron," he told me. "I put Gary in his car and sent him home."

"Why didn't you drive him there? Didn't they call you after they called Gary?"

"Yes, but I was out," said Milt. "I was in a conference with another client, and my secretary didn't let me know until after I came out. By then, Gary was already on his way to A.C."

"So, what's the story?" I asked him, wondering silently what would be a big enough emergency for Ladowski's secretary to call him out of a meeting. "Godzilla laying waste to Midland Heights? Hope the lot's still there. He'll get back to you after the real estate closing. Try and keep Mr. Zilla away from North Seventh."

"They questioned Gary for a good few hours," Milt said. "I tried to get them to wait until tomorrow, you know, give him some time to absorb his loss, but they plowed ahead immediately. Said they wanted it while it was still 'fresh in his mind.'"

"Wanted *what?* Do they think Gary killed her?"

I could practically hear Milt's mustache bristling—it was that hard for him to contain his irritation. "Of *course* they think he killed her. It's the easiest theory, and the cops always go for the easiest theory. Their problem is, he didn't do it, so they have no evidence. Otherwise, he'd be behind bars already."

"So what did he tell them?"

"The truth. He was at his office, he has witnesses by the dozens, and he has no reason to want Madlyn dead. But does that slow them down, even one bit? Of course not!"

I considered explaining to Milt that the conduct of the Atlantic City police wasn't necessarily my responsibility, but he was on a roll. "They don't even bother looking into the matter enough to find the *real* killers, so they'll probably get away scot free."

"Easy, Milt. You're starting to sound like O.J."

He cleared his throat. I knew he had his car phone on hands-off, because the noise in the car was almost too loud to hear Milt. "Listen. Aaron. I'd appreciate it if you could keep this out of the papers for the time being."

Okay, I admit it. This caught me off guard. "What?" I practically screamed. "The man who dragged me kicking and screaming onto this story is asking me to keep it out of the papers now? Tell me you're kidding, Milton, please, or I may be forced to tell the cops about the rumors that Madlyn was having an affair."

"That's horseshit, Aaron," Milt said, clearly annoyed. Good. "Madlyn never slept with anyone outside her marriage. That's just preposterous. But think of the boy for a moment. Reading in the papers about what happened to his mom . . ."

"Oh come on, Milt, you can do better than that. The kid never picked up a newspaper in his life other than to read the TV listings. Besides, the police report is going to be all over the place by the morning. I'm surprised my editor hasn't called me already. I couldn't keep it quiet if I wanted to. And I don't want to."

Milt cleared his throat for so long it would have been quicker to just send the Roto Rooter guy down there to see what the problem was. "I'm asking you as a friend, Aaron. Please."

I wondered when Ladowski and I had become friends. "Does this have anything to do with your name being on Madlyn's hotel bill?" I asked. What the hell, maybe Diane Woolworth had gotten the headline right and the details wrong. Maybe Madlyn had been having an affair with Milt Ladowski.

"Oh, for Chrissakes, Aaron!" he shouted. "This is a simple matter of human kindness. I don't want to read the gruesome details of Madlyn Beckwirth's death in the paper tomorrow morning. Is that so much to ask?"

Maybe I could get something out of him another way. "Okay," I told him. "Okay. I'll see what I can do. But you have to tell me, *can* you explain your name on Madlyn's hotel register?"

Milt didn't talk for a long time. I knew I hadn't been disconnected, because the car sounds were still there. There was a click when he picked the phone up to hold it next to his face.

"Honest to God, Aaron," he nearly whispered. "I haven't got a clue how that happened."

Well, that didn't help much, but I told Milt I'd call him in the morning.

When I put down the phone, Abby and the kids were nowhere to be seen. She had to be upstairs getting them into bed. I could call Barry Dutton, or . . .

I went upstairs. Abby was watching Ethan floss his teeth—something I hadn't seen since the days of *Mighty Morphin Power Rangers*—and everything seemed under control. I walked into Leah's room. The light was out, but I could see the mountain made in her blanket by her fully bent knees, and it was moving around. When she heard me come in, Leah sat up.

"Daddy?"

I didn't say anything. I just walked over and held out my arms. Leah sat up and reached out, and I got my first Leah hug of the day. I held it for a very long time.

It had been, after all, a very long and unsettling day.

# Chapter 6

Once the kids were officially "in bed" (meaning Leah was in bed and Ethan was playing games on his computer), Abby and I went downstairs. Without a word, she walked to the dining room, reached down and opened the door on our sideboard (I had recalled the word since this afternoon), the one we use as a liquor cabinet, and started rummaging through the bottles. I went into the kitchen, took out two glasses, and got a tray of ice from the freezer. I cracked the ice tray, causing cubes to fly all around the room, and corralled enough to almost fill the glasses. The rest went into the sink. What the hell, I'm decadent.

Abby walked in, carrying a bottle of vodka. She knows I don't care much for the taste of alcohol, so she also carried a bottle of Kahlua. She mixed a Black Russian for me and poured herself a vodka on the rocks. During law school, my wife supported herself as a bartender in Chicago. She learned every drink ever invented, but says she never had to pour anything except Jack Daniels for boilermakers. This was before the Wrigley Field area was gentrified.

We adjourned to the living room, glasses in hand. Each of us took our traditional seat on the couch. I put my drink on the coffee table (okay, the Black Russian table) for a moment, put my arm around Abby, and pulled her close to me. She stayed that way for a sublime moment.

And then the phone rang.

I sighed, but took my drink with me. I already knew it was Barry Dutton, and he had waited as long as his patience would tolerate, hoping that I had developed enough sense to check in with him after having spent much of the day at the scene of a murder. He should have known better.

"Where the hell have you been?"

"Atlantic City. It's lovely there this time of year. And you?"

"This is the worst possible time to be funny, Aaron. Now, I want to hear the whole thing, from the beginning."

I glanced across the room at my wife, who was plying herself with alcohol and stretching out on the couch, not turning on the television. Strangely, I didn't want to spend time on the phone with Dutton. I forced myself to look away from Abigail and opened a reporter's notebook sitting on my desk.

"Can't it wait until the morning, Barry? I've been ..."

"No, it can't wait until the goddam morning! This isn't a woman running out on her husband anymore, Aaron. This is a murder! I'm going to have the Atlantic County prosecutor's people here in the morning, and I have to be able to tell them something."

I hate it when Dutton is right. There wasn't any way around it. I gave him the shortest possible version of the facts while Abby continued to lounge, finished her drink, and picked up the *TV Guide*.

"That's it," I said when I finished. "Now, what have *you* found out?" I took out a legal pad and pen to take notes.

"Well, the autopsy won't be available for a couple of days, but I don't think there's any doubt she died of gunshot wounds."

"I was there. There isn't any doubt."

"And Gary's identification confirms that it was Madlyn," Dutton added. The thought had occurred to me during the long ride home that, given my great memory for faces, I might have looked at someone of Madlyn's general physical type and wrongly assumed it was her. So that was that.

"Do the state troopers really think Beckwirth did it?"

"Aaron, almost every time someone is killed, it's done by someone they knew, usually a family member. When a married woman is killed, the first logical suspect, given no obvious outside motive, is the husband." Barry didn't sound especially convinced himself. Out of the corner of my eye, I saw Abby reach for the remote control.

"Well, let me come in tomorrow morning, and we'll talk about it," I suggested.

"Okay," Dutton sighed. "But I want you here first thing, as soon as the kids ..."

"I'll be there," I said, and hung up. I practically flew across the room, spilling a little of my now watered-down drink (the ice had melted) on the musty carpet in my office.

"Hold it right there," I said to Abby. I slithered in next to her on the couch and grabbed the remote out of her hand. "Don't touch that dial." She grinned, and I gave her the kiss I had been waiting for all day.

And what happened after that is, quite frankly, none of your business.

# Chapter 7

Later that night, I called the *Press-Tribune*, got the night editor, and told her about Madlyn Beckwirth's death. The night editor, maybe two years out of college and still struggling not to say "y'know" after every phrase, got very excited and insisted I write the story myself and email it to her immediately. I told her the writing would take me about an hour, and she promised to find space for the story on the front page.

Life is funny. There once was a time when writing a front-page story would have been a great professional thrill for me, but that time had come and gone, along with the beard I wore in my twenties. Now, the only thing that would have gotten my professional blood flowing rapidly would be a call from a two-bit producer promising to turn one of my 120-page fantasies into a bad movie that some director straight out of film school would hack up, with maybe three lines of my original dialogue intact. And I'd get paid maybe ten grand.

I again promised the nice night editor that I would send the story as quickly as possible, so I sent Abigail up to bed to minimize her ability to distract me and sat down at the Macintosh to turn what I knew into what I hoped would be a coherent news story.

The next day, with minimal editing, the front page of the *Central Jersey Press-Tribune* featured (above the fold) the following article whose headline, I hasten to interject, I didn't write.

### Local Woman Found Murdered
### Killing May Be Tied To
### Midland Heights Mayor Election

By Aaron Tucker

Madlyn Beckwirth, 44, was found shot to death yesterday at an Atlantic City hotel. Beckwirth, a resident of Midland Heights, had been reported missing by her husband, Gary Beckwirth, last week.

She had been campaign manager for the Middle Heights mayoral campaign of Rachel Barlow. Barlow is attempting to unseat long-time mayor Sam Olszowy in a Democratic primary election less than two weeks away.

Beckwirth was shot in the stomach and the head, and an autopsy confirmed that the shots were the cause of death. Gary Beckwirth, president of Beckwirth Investments, identified his wife's body late last night.

Madlyn Beckwirth had been missing since last Monday, when her husband filed a report with Midland Heights Police Chief Barry Dutton. An investigation into the disappearance by Detective Gerald Westbrook had proved fruitless until yesterday, when a *Press-Tribune* reporter received a phone call from Mrs. Beckwirth and traced her to Bally's Casino Hotel in Atlantic City.

There is still no explanation for Madlyn Beckwirth's disappearance, and no arrest was made in connection with her murder. Her husband was questioned last night, but was not held or charged.

"When a woman is killed, the first logical suspect, given no obvious outside motive, is the husband," Dutton said last night. He added, however, that he knew of no evidence tying Gary Beckwirth to his wife's death.

Prior to her disappearance, Madlyn Beckwirth had been

receiving threatening phone calls tied to the mayoral campaign, according to Rachel Barlow.

Questioned about her disappearance yesterday hours before her body was discovered, Madlyn Beckwirth said only that she was "fine," and would "be back in a few days."

"This really isn't a big deal," she said.

Gary and Madlyn Beckwirth have a son, Joel, who is 14. According to Milton Ladowski, the Beckwirth family attorney, the investigation into Madlyn's murder will be conducted by New Jersey State Troopers, the Atlantic County Prosecutor's Office, and the Midland Heights police.

The story went on to detail the political infighting in Midland Heights and the tension between Barlow and Olszowy, strictly because the night editor had asked me to include it. I thought the odds that Madlyn Beckwirth had been killed because of the mayor's race in Midland Heights to be awfully long.

Of course, I had also thought Madlyn was a simple runaway wife who'd charge up the credit cards and be back in a few days. What I thought didn't seem terribly relevant right at the moment.

The next morning, I got the kids out to school and myself out of the house as quickly as I could, successfully avoiding the inevitable phone call that would result when Milt Ladowski, the morning paper in hand, choked on his egg white omelet and decaffeinated coffee. I walked over to police headquarters and Marsha immediately pointed me toward Barry's office.

"He's in there," she said. "He's not happy."

"You think I should have brought donuts?" I asked.

She shook her head. "You could bring the whole Drake's bakery in there today," she said. "Wouldn't help you."

I took a deep breath and knocked on Barry's door. The guttural grunt from within indicated that I should enter, and against my better judgment, I did.

The first thing I saw in the office was the *Press-Tribune* on Dutton's desk. It was turned to the inside page that my story on Madlyn had jumped to. Barry, reading half-glasses in his hand, was behind the desk, doing an imitation of a college professor in the body of an angry grizzly bear. His eyes were wide, and his hands were clenched. I wouldn't have been surprised to see him chewing through a two-by-four.

Westbrook, modeling the latest from the Andy Sipowicz Collection, sat to the left of the door. I couldn't be sure, but I thought I saw the vestiges of a shit-eating grin on his face. He looked at me when I opened the door, but didn't say anything. Barry barely got "shut the door" through his clenched teeth. I did as he said. I would have liked to have shut the door from the outside, but that didn't appear to be an option.

I immediately saw a woman sitting on the table behind the door. She was in her thirties, attractive, and dressed in a very conservative suit—the kind Abigail wears to her office. Had to be from the county prosecutor's office.

"Barry ..." I started, but he shook his head vigorously and pointed toward the other chair in front of his desk.

"You don't get to talk right now," Dutton said slowly. "Right now, *I* get to talk."

I nodded and sat.

"What exactly do you think you're doing," Dutton began, "printing information about an ongoing investigation in the newspaper?"

"I'm a reporter ..." I began, but Barry shook his head again.

"I said *I* get to talk now," he said more forcefully. "Not you. Aaron, I'm always open to you, and I don't play the kind of games other cops do with the press. You *know* that."

He left a pause, and I wasn't sure what to do.

"Well? Don't you know that?"

I nodded.

"So why are you making me look bad in the paper, printing information I told you in the course of a private conversation? Don't the words 'off the record' hold any meaning for you?"

My face tightened a bit at that one. "Oh come on, Barry," I said, and this time I didn't stop when he shook his head. "I'm happy to speak to folks off the record, and I respect that whenever someone asks me for that arrangement. But you never said a word about our conversation being on background, and you know it."

Barry stole an embarrassed glance at the woman, and pointed at the newspaper. "When we spoke last night," he said more quietly, "you never said this was an interview for the newspaper. I didn't know I was talking to you as a reporter."

"What did you think—that I'd had a sudden change of heart and went into the upholstery business? Come on, Barry, admit it. You assigned Inspector Gadget here to the Beckwirth case because you didn't think it was a big deal, and frankly, neither did I. But I beat you to her, and when it turned out to be a murder, you felt foolish. Now, you want to take it out on me because I reported all that in the newspaper." I turned on a dime and extended my hand to the woman, who clasped it professionally. "He's never going to introduce us," I said, nodding in Dutton's direction. "I'm Aaron Tucker."

"Colette Jackson," she said. "Atlantic County Prosecutor's office."

"I figured," I told her. I gestured to Barry. "He doesn't usually get anybody that well dressed here."

Westbrook cleared his throat, which I guess was his subtle little way of saying he was about to speak. It sounded like he was going to spit, and I involuntarily ducked.

"What're you gonna do to him, Chief?" he asked, the impatient child waiting to see what punishment the older sibling is going to get for pinching.

"What can he do?" I answered. "I haven't broken any laws."

"You didn't call me when you heard from Madlyn Beckwirth,"

Gerry said. "That could be considered obstruction."

I shot a glance at Colette Jackson, who was pursing her lips like a librarian getting ready to shush someone. "You didn't call me with the information about the minivan or the area outside the Beckwirth house," I told Westbrook. "Did you find out anything, or did you spend your whole shift at the all-you-can-eat buffet again?"

Before Westbrook could even begin to react, Barry Dutton sat down, rearranged his face into a peaceful expression, and said, "tell him, Gerry."

Westbrook wanted to slug me, but his arms probably couldn't reach past his own belt, and besides, all us alpha males in the room were showing off for the lady visitor. So he cleared his throat again and folded his hands on what would have been his lap, if he'd had one.

"There was no debris of any kind on the bumper of the minivan you *say* was following you," said Westbrook. "As for the undeveloped property next to the Great Big House, which by the way also belongs to the Beckwirths, it's impossible to say. It's been almost two weeks, and it's usually just broken sticks and garbage, anyway."

"Now," Dutton interrupted, "you tell us what *you* know."

I sighed. "Oh come on, Barry," I said. "I told you everything last night. I told it to the troopers about sixty-eight times last night. I've said it so many times I could recite it by rote, like I did at my bar mitzvah. I'm thinking of putting it out on CD."

"But Ms. Jackson hasn't heard it yet."

Colette, to her everlasting credit, stood up and said, "I've seen the reports of the state troopers, Chief. I don't need to hear Mr. Tucker tell the whole story again." When she saw me smiling, though, she added, "Still, I do have a few questions." I believe I saw Barry Dutton grin a little as my face tightened. I nodded.

"Mrs. Beckwirth was probably dead a little less than two hours when you found her. She was wearing, according to the troopers and your report, a black lace teddy and garter belt. Is that correct?"

I nodded. I think Westbrook wiped a little drool from the corner of his mouth, but he might have been thinking that lunch was coming in only three and a half hours.

"So we can assume that she was anticipating a lover, don't you think?" Colette Jackson asked.

"I guess so," I said. "She might have just worn that kind of stuff..." Colette's face told me to shut up.

"No woman wears that kind of stuff for the hell of it, Mr. Tucker. She wears it only if she thinks it's going to be seen." The three of us—Barry, Westbrook and I—picked out three spots in the room to look at, so as not to be discovered wondering what it was Ms. Jackson had on under her suit.

"You also said that the door was ajar when you walked up to the hotel room, is that right?" I nodded again, still looking at the picture of Barry Dutton, framed on the wall, shaking hands with former New Jersey Governor Christine Todd Whitman. "Did you knock first?"

"When I knocked, the door swung open. I called inside, and then walked in when I got no answer. Madlyn was on the bed, and she had clearly been shot dead."

"Have you ever seen a murder victim before, Mr. Tucker?"

"No, but ..."

"Okay. So, how did you react? Did you gasp? Cry out? Throw up? What was the first thing that ran through your mind?"

The last thing I wanted to say was that I considered Madlyn Beckwirth's death to be a superior plot point for one of my forthcoming screenplays. "Why are you asking me this?" I said. "Am I a suspect? Do I need to call my lawyer?"

"Leave your wife alone," Dutton said. "Nobody thinks you killed Madlyn Beckwirth."

"Then what is this about?"

"We're trying to determine what your interest in this case is going to be now that you've written your story," said Colette, smiling.

So that was it. They felt I had shown them up, and now they were going to freeze me out of the rest of the story. I stared at Dutton.

"I would have believed it of Westbrook, and Ms. Jackson I've never met, but you, Barry. I thought you'd be fairer than this."

Dutton's eyes widened. He knew what I was saying, and as much as he hated it, he knew I was right, too.

"I think we're done here," said Colette Jackson. "Why don't you go home now, Mr. Tucker?"

# Chapter 8

When I went home, things weren't any better. The answering machine was just bursting with thrilling phone messages: one from Milt Ladowski, one from Abigail, one from Gary Beckwirth, another from Ladowski, one from Ethan's aide, Wilma, *another* from Ladowski, one from my mother, who had discovered that one of the pills she was taking to lower her blood pressure had caused impotence in rats, and one from Harrington. I called Wilma first, but she was in class with Ethan, and would call back. So I called Harrington.

"You see the story?" I said.

Harrington's voice sounded, I don't know, formal. Like he was being listened to by people who intimidated him. Or maybe I was being paranoid. "Yes, it was very good, Aaron," Harrington said. "A fine job of reporting."

"You okay, Dave?"

"Sure. It's just ... I'm afraid this isn't the story we had discussed initially."

I stood up and started pacing. "I know that," I said. "But this is the way the story developed. It's actually a better ..."

"I'm afraid we'll only be able to pay you the usual two hundred," he blurted out. "That's all that's in the budget for a news story like this."

I stopped pacing and my jaw hit the carpet. "Are you serious?"

"I'm sorry."

"But what about the follow-up? There's got to be a follow-up on a story like this . . ."

"We're going to have our staff writer in your town handle it."

"Sheila Warren? Sheila Warren's great for the library benefit, Dave, but crime reporting . . ."

He started talking very quickly. That's never a good sign, unless the person giggles a lot between sentences and is blonde. Sometimes, not even then. "Aaron, there have been . . . changes in the way we're budgeting the desk these days. So . . ."

I'd heard this one before. "So you'll be cutting back on freelance, right?"

There was a long silence. "That's right. I'm sorry. Believe me, if it were up to me . . ."

"Dave, is someone there with you? Listening to this conversation?"

"No. I'm sorry Aaron, I have someone on my other line. We'll mail the check." And he hung up.

I absorbed that for a few minutes, and it turned out to be a few minutes too long. This time, Ladowski found me in.

"Didn't you promise me that you'd keep this story out of the papers, Aaron?!"

"I said I'd do what I could. It turned out I couldn't do anything."

"Your name is on the article! You didn't even try!"

"And your client saw to it that I'd get screwed out of the $1,000 fee the paper promised to pay. I'd say we're about even, Milt."

"Any contract between you and the newspaper is completely outside this conversation, Tucker. We never offered you any money to write this trash in the press."

Somebody once said that when they call it "trash," you know you've gotten it right. Maybe I'd said it, now that I think of it.

"Is there a reason you called, Milt, or are you just a week behind on your pomposity orders?"

"I'm calling to tell you that my client will no longer cooperate with you in any way regarding the investigation of his wife's death. He will not accept your phone calls nor allow you to enter his home. He is considering petitioning for a restraining order to ensure that you will not approach his son. You are allowed no access to Gary Beckwirth or his family again. Is that clear?"

"Geez, Milt, how long have you been rehearsing that one? You said it almost without taking a breath."

"Goodbye, Mr. Tucker." And he hung up. It was obviously my day to be hung up on, so I called my mother. She wasn't home. That's a mother's equivalent of hanging up on you.

I called my wife. "Are they all after you yet?" she asked.

"Pretty much," I said. "What you'd expect?"

"Stay away from the Beckwirth story, and all that," Abby said. She has always been fascinated by my work, or more specifically, by the press. She studied journalism in college, and would have made an excellent reporter if she'd had a less logical mind.

"Yeah, but with a new twist, Abby. *The Press-Tribune* isn't going to use me anymore."

She absorbed that a moment. "You mean they got to your editor?"

I had to laugh. "They certainly have listened pretty hard to either Beckwirth or Ladowski, or they're just plain paranoid."

"Oh, Baby, I'm sorry," she said sympathetically. There just wasn't anything else to say.

"Do you get the feeling there's something they don't want me to find out?"

"*Now* who's being paranoid? Besides, Madlyn's dead. It's the county prosecutors' case now. Just report on what they find out."

"Report for whom, exactly?"

"That's your job, Sweetie."

"I met the assistant county prosecutor who's working the case. And

I have to tell you, when she started asking me underwear questions . . ."

"You're trying to make me jealous, aren't you?" said Abby in an upper-crust accent. "How quaint."

"Well, if that's the way you're gonna be about it . . ."

"I'll see you later," she said. "Don't make dinner."

"Words of support if ever I heard them." I hung up just as the phone rang. It was Wilma, Ethan's aide, with a long story about how something had *almost* gone wrong between Ethan and his friend Jon that morning, but Wilma had managed to snuff it out. Wilma's stories are always about how she handled something efficiently. Makes you wonder why she bothers to call in the first place.

That reminded me: I still had the barbecue sauce mystery to solve. I made a mental note to call the remaining two sets of parents on Mrs. Mignano's list after I got off the phone with Wilma.

But I didn't have the chance. In the middle of the conversation, call waiting beeped, and I clicked off gratefully. Wilma's a very nice woman, but I had an appointment the following Tuesday, and had to find a way to get her off the phone.

"Hello?" I began eloquently.

"Aaron," he said, "this is Gary Beckwirth."

# Chapter 9

What do you say to a man whose wife was used for target practice in a gambling casino's hotel room the night before? After the standard, "I'm sorry," which I had used up in the casino security office, there isn't a hell of a lot to fall back on.

"Gary, I'm so . . ."

"I don't blame you, Aaron. I wanted you to know that. I know you tried the best you could."

"I never guessed it would be this bad, Gary, believe me," I said, even then realizing how blubbery I sounded. "I was always playing over my head."

Beckwirth didn't appear to be listening. It was like he was reading from a script—a variation on the way Madlyn had sounded when she called from Atlantic City. "I just didn't want you to feel that I blamed you. I don't," he said again. "What happened to Madlyn . . . would have happened with you or without you."

"Gary, are you okay?" Then, taking note of how stupid that sounded, I added, "I mean, considering."

"Oh, I'm all right," he said, operating on auto-pilot. "I'll be okay. I'm just worried about Joel, that's all."

Oops. I wondered if Beckwirth knew that Milt had told me not to talk to him. "Gary, should we be talking right now?"

"Why, are you busy?" He sounded worried that he was interrupting me.

"No, it's just that I talked to Milt Ladowski ..."

"Oh, Milt." Now I recognized that tone. Beckwirth wasn't reading from a script. He was talking through a haze of tranquilizers. "Milt worries too much. I just worry about Joel."

"Gary, you don't have to worry about Joel." I wondered if Joel had emerged from his room long enough to find out his mother was dead. "Joel will survive just fine."

"I hope so," he said. "Well, nice talking to you, Aaron." I suddenly panicked, thinking that Beckwirth might do something to himself if I left him alone with his thoughts long enough.

"Gary," I said, "can I come over and see you?"

"Oh, no," Beckwirth sing-songed. "You can't come here anymore. You can't ask any more questions. No more, Aaron, please, no more. No more."

He hung up.

Well, that did it. Barry Dutton, Colette Jackson, and Gerry Westbrook had all told me not to investigate any further. Milt Ladowski had told me not to investigate any further. My editor had fired me and told me specifically not to investigate Madlyn Beckwirth's murder. My own wife was assuming I should stop, since I no longer had a paying client. And now Beckwirth himself was telling me that I was no longer allowed to ask questions about what had happened to his wife.

There was only one thing left to do. And I was just stupid enough to do it. I went to the sporting goods store, and bought myself a softball.

# Chapter 10

Christine Micelli looked concerned. I expected that. What I hadn't suspected was that she'd also look shocked.

"He wrote *what* on your sidewalk?" Her eyes, which were black, were wide, and not pleased.

We were sitting in Christine's kitchen, which was the very antithesis of Rachel Barlow's. There were dishes in the sink. There were crumbs on the floor. There were pieces of opened and unopened mail on the countertops. A box of cereal, left over from breakfast, was still open on the kitchen table. I felt very much at home.

"I don't know for sure that Vinnie wrote anything, Ms. Micelli," I said. "I just know somebody wrote something . . . inappropriate . . . on my sidewalk, clearly directed at my son, and I know that he and Vincent have had arguments in the past. I'm asking you if you think it's possible. I don't want to accuse anybody of anything."

If there's something in this world more uncomfortable than going to the mother of a 10-year-old and suggesting that her son writes dirty words with barbecue sauce, I sincerely don't want to know what it might be. This was the first of two such scenes I was planning for today, and already, I knew I'd have to change my shirt between them.

None of this was helped by the use of the word "fuck," which I'm not terribly comfortable saying in front of people I've just met, particularly when they're offering me brownies.

"Well, Vinnie *did* mention your son, once," she said uncomfortably. Christine got up and walked to a coffee maker on the counter, but I noticed her cup was still half full. She was doing what I had done at Gary Beckwirth's house, just using the coffee as a prop to kill time.

"I take it he mentioned Ethan in a negative way."

She filled up the coffee cup again, and was about to ask me if I wanted more, but remembered I had declined the offer to begin with. Christine put the pot back in place and sat down.

"Well, you know what kids say about each other ..."

"Christine—may I call you Christine?"

"Sure. Chris, really."

"Chris, let me tell you something that may make you feel better. My son can be a colossal pain in the ass sometimes. He annoys me on a daily basis, and I love him dearly. So whatever Vincent said, believe me, is in all probability true. He may even have watered it down for you."

It worked. She visibly relaxed. Some parents think their children are incapable of anything other than good intentions, and it disarms other adults when you prove to them you're not like that. Besides, Ethan really *can* be a pain in the ass if he puts his mind to it.

"Well, then I can tell you," Chris said. "Vinnie said Ethan called him an asshole, and tried to pull out some of Vinnie's hair."

"That sounds like Ethan," I told her, "except the 'asshole' part. Why didn't you call me when this happened?"

Chris blushed just a bit. She had a round face, and looking at it was like looking at one of the Campbell's soup twins. But in a nice way.

"Tell the truth, I was afraid to. I thought maybe *you* were an asshole, too."

We both laughed over that one, and I took a bite of the brownie in front of me. Dammit, it was really good. Of course, a bad brownie is like a bad orgasm—still better than a normal day of existence.

"Well, now that I'm here, I'll tell you that Ethan will be warned against doing anything like that again. But my question stands: do you think Vinnie held enough of a grudge against Ethan to write that on the sidewalk?"

She frowned, and seemed to be thinking deeply. "No. No, I really don't. It'd be more Vinnie's style to beat Ethan up in the schoolyard or yell ... that ... to his face. He wouldn't go to the trouble of stealing barbecue sauce and writing it on the sidewalk. For one thing, he'd want to see Ethan's face when he found it."

I finished the brownie, considered asking for another, and decided I'd best flee this place as quickly as possible. I thanked Chris for her candor, and for the brownie. As she walked me to the door, she shook her head and chuckled.

"You know, it sounds like we have two sons who act out in the same inappropriate ways," she said.

"Yeah. It's a wonder they don't get along better." I said my good-byes and left.

Outside, it was cool, but with a whiff of spring in the air. I stepped out of the house and stood on the sidewalk a moment, appreciating the breeze.

I'd still need to change my shirt before the next parent, though. This one was soaked clean through.

# Chapter 11

Let's just say that the next interview didn't go as well. For one thing, David Meckeroff, the father of the boy in question, had no brownies on hand. And if he had, he probably wouldn't have offered them to the likes of me.

What he did suggest, in no uncertain terms, was that I had a son who was "a menace" to the school, and who should never have been included in a "normal" class. Apparently, Ethan even went so far as to suggest that Meckeroff's son, Warren (you think I make these names up, don't you?), was, and I'm quoting now, "a moron."

There were about fourteen photographs of Warren, all in the same pose, on a table in Meckeroff's living room. I recognized the envelope they were sitting on. It was from the school's photographer. Meckeroff had actually been cutting the one large sheet into individual photographs. Not that this is so unusual, but he was cutting up the tiniest photographs—the ones that come about thirty-two to an 8"x10" sheet and that nobody ever uses.

Warren Meckeroff's school picture looked like that of, well, a moron. He had the most vacant eyes imaginable in a living person, and had a haircut that was reminiscent of that intellectual giant, Alfalfa Switzer. That can be cute when you're six, but doesn't work nearly so well when you're twelve.

Come to think of it, his father looked roughly the same, but he was at least thirty-eight. And considerably rounder. Still, the biceps bulging in his T-shirt were impressive enough for me not to argue the point too strenuously with him. Clearly, his son was incapable of writing such a vile thing with something intended for human consumption.

I would have gotten into a heated argument with the man, but it was obviously fruitless to try. And there were those biceps to consider. Besides, I wanted to get out the door as quickly as possible with the photograph of Warren that I'd palmed while listening to his father's lecture.

My next stop was back at Big Bob's, where once again the proprietor was the only human present. This place was clearly a front for the mob, or it would be out of business by the end of the week.

Bob took one look and started laughing when I walked in. If my screenplays were as funny as my face, I'd be a wealthy man today.

"Well, look who's here," he said. "What is it this time, pal? You got a salt shaker you want me to identify? Somebody steal a pack of Sweet'N Low, and you want me to dust it for fingerprints?" He was clearly warming up for a gig at the local comedy club and wanted to try out his new material. But I maintained my Cary Grant-like cool.

"Good," I said, "you recognize me."

He managed to suppress his hilarity long enough to bark out, "how could I forget?"

"So maybe you'll remember this face, too," I said, and whipped out the picture of Warren Meckeroff. Big Bob stopped laughing for a moment and considered the tiny image.

"Geez, did you bring a ..." I produced a magnifying glass I had picked up at home. Okay, so this wasn't exactly the next stop after Meckeroff's. I had gone home and changed shirts again. Looked like tomorrow was going to be a big laundry day.

"Mm-hmmm ..." said Big Bob, and he used the sleuth's best friend to examine the picture.

"He a regular customer of yours?" I asked.

"See, now, bringing a picture was definitely the way to go," he said. "I don't get to know their names, but I never forget a face. No sir, when somebody comes in here for the second time, a year could go by, and I'll remember him—might even remember what he ordered . . ."

It occurred to me that Big Bob being in business for a full year would merit miracle status, but I held my tongue. He did not hold his.

"Yessir, always remember a face. Every face. Big, small, men, women. Some guys remember a woman's tits. Not me. The face. That I'll remember every time. Now, names . . ."

"Bob," I came close to hollering. "Do you know this kid or not?"

He took another long look, and shook his head up and down.

"Nope," he said. "Never seen him before in my life."

This was not turning out to be a good day.

# Chapter 12

When I whipped the softball across the long, spacious family room, Mahoney just barely managed to stick his hand out and snare it from his armchair. "Watch it," he said. "You could have knocked out a window or something."

We began this softball thing in high school. I don't remember exactly how. Mahoney used to live in the attic of his parents' house, in a room roughly three times the size of mine. And whenever we needed to solve the problems of the world—which usually involved the seventeen-year-olds we described as "women"—I'd climb up the three flights of stairs to his lair, and we'd toss this old softball back and forth. We never solved any problems, but our hands got surer, and my fielding percentage went up in our after-school pickup games—of softball.

Our first high school softball, Mahoney says, is in a box in his present attic, where, as far as we know, nobody actually lives. It shares that space with our old tripod, some movie lights, a Super 8 sound movie camera for which nobody on this planet makes film anymore, and a deer skull Mahoney found in the woods in 1974, which he named "Elmo." Don't ask.

I can't explain it, but throwing the softball around gets our brains into problem-solving mode, and that is exactly what I needed today. After Big Bob's, where I ordered a black-and-white milk shake and received a black-and-white ice cream soda, I called Mahoney on the cell phone, intending to leave a message asking if we could meet later. Instead, I got the man himself, since he'd finished his last job of the day a couple of hours early ("the power of being the best at what you do") and had come home. I said I needed to throw the softball. He said come on over. And here I was. But it wasn't like the old days. Now Jeff Mahoney, of all people, was worried that I'd break some household item or fixture with an errant throw.

"You afraid Susan will yell at me if I knock over a vase?" (I used the flat "a" pronunciation to show how classy I am.)

"My wife actually likes you," he countered. "You knock something over, she'll give you a hug and blame me for the broken glass."

"Can I help it if I'm irresistible?" I grinned.

"That's not what Janet Marsden thought," Mahoney shot back. A painful memory. Old friends know the most about you. They remember how you got all your scars.

"ANYWAY," I moved on, "I don't understand anything that's happened on this story. I have nothing to go on, and everybody's telling me to quit, so I feel like I have to keep at it."

"And you don't have anybody paying you for it, right?" he said, not needling now, just clarifying.

"Right."

"Well, it's obvious you have to investigate further. They're trying to keep you from finding out *something*."

He pitched the ball back at me, and of course it landed right in my unmoving hand, chest high. And I was easily ten feet away on a low sofa. That's what I hate about Mahoney. He never loses his touch.

"Who? Who's trying to keep me from something? And what? I don't have any clues. I have nowhere to go." I tried tossing him a curve ball, and it bounced, but Mahoney still managed to scoop it up.

"Before you get the answers, you have to figure out what the questions are," he said, and tossed another one that swerved directly into my hands. The swine.

"Oh thank you, Grasshopper, but I think I know what the question is. The question is, who killed Madlyn Beckwirth?" Now I managed one he could catch without moving too much. He nodded encouragement.

"No, you're looking at too big a picture," Mahoney said. "Look at the little things. Check out the pieces of the puzzle, not the whole puzzle. What things that you have found out don't add up?"

I caught his next throw and held it, thinking. "That's just it—*nothing* adds up. Somebody killed Madlyn after she left her bed and her house in the middle of the night and went to Atlantic City. What doesn't add up? I could give you a laundry list of what doesn't add up."

He sat and looked at me, patiently. Like Master Yoda, he has the patience of the ages.

I let out a long breath. "Okay. In no particular order: Who called me to warn me off looking for Madlyn? Why do that? Why does the phone number match the cell phone of a little old man in a greenhouse in Emmaus, Pennsylvania? Who sent somebody to follow me in a minivan, and why? How come Madlyn decides to call me out of the blue, and why is she killed immediately thereafter?"

Mahoney closed his eyes. I considered smoking him one at that very moment, but he'd probably just put up his hand and catch it out of reflex, and I'd be even more outclassed. Then he wrinkled his brow, and I sat back. Here it came.

"What's interesting," he said, "is that all the clues in this story seem to center around an outside party."

"Who?"

"You. Whoever killed Madlyn spent an awful lot of energy trying to keep you away. What does that tell you?" I tried a new gambit, and rolled the softball across the hardwood floor Mahoney had sanded and refinished. The ball rolled straight, with no bumps. Naturally.

"That I have an inflated sense of my own importance," I suggested.

Mahoney smiled because he is smarter than me. "No. What's interesting is that the *biggest* concern of the person—or people—who killed Madlyn Beckwirth is that you don't find out about it," he said. "Every move they made since she disappeared seemed to be designed to keep *you* away—not to keep the cops or her husband away—but *you*."

I waited, but nothing more came. "So, what does that tell us?" I said.

He picked up the softball and examined it. "This one isn't as good as the old one," he said. "Too rubbery."

"Jeff," I said, "what does all that tell us? Am I in danger from these people, too?"

"Only if you get close to finding something out," he said.

"Well, then I have nothing to worry about." He added zip to his throw this time, and my hand stung when I caught it.

"People kill other people for two reasons," Mahoney offered. "Sex or money."

"Kay Scarpetta teach you that?" I asked.

"Nah. She just deals with the dead body. She'd tell you what was in the intestines. I'm telling you. Sex or money."

"Either one of which could apply here," I said. "Madlyn was expecting something more than croissants from her room service, if you know what I mean. And Gary has piles of cash." I threw the ball back, harder, and he caught it as if it were a Nerf ball.

Mahoney grumbled. He stood up and walked toward the kitchen. "I want some potato chips," he said. "You?"

I shook my head. The ice cream soda had been bad enough. But there had also been a brownie in the morning. I would have to do six thousand sit-ups to burn it all off—tomorrow.

Mahoney opened one of the kitchen cabinets he had hung from the cathedral ceiling he raised in the kitchen. You had to be as tall as a tree to get any food in this house, but luckily Mahoney's wife was close to six feet tall herself. I had to rely on the kindness of strangers.

"But nobody ever called Beckwirth to ask for his money," he said, grabbing a family-sized bag of Ruffles from the cabinet and tearing it open carefully. "Madlyn wasn't kidnapped. She went away on her own."

"So we focus on the sex?" I suggested.

"Nah," Mahoney said through a mouthful of Ruffles. "That's just what they want us to do. Remember what Woodward and Bernstein said."

"Follow the money." I gave him back what he wanted to hear.

"Exactly. Follow the money." Suddenly grabbing the softball again, he rifled it toward me, and I caught it neatly and without pain. "Now you're getting it," Mahoney said.

# Chapter 13

I got home just in time to receive a lecture from my son about the continued necessity of being inside the family residence whenever he got home from school in the afternoon. He'd actually had to use his key to get in the door, and had been watching television himself for an entire eight minutes. For crying out loud, what kind of father was I, anyway?

It got worse when I turned off the TV and reminded him that he had homework to do. He leapt at the remote control, switched the set back on, and screamed, "I was WATCHING that!" just as Ren and Stimpy appeared to sing "Happy, Happy, Joy, Joy." This was what happens whenever you throw him off his routine. His discipline collapses like a house of cards.

"I don't *care* what you were watching," I said. "It's time to do your homework." And, because I was born towards the middle of the twentieth century, walked over to the TV and actually knew how to turn the set "off" manually—by pressing the power button.

He stood, dramatically, knowing that the remote's infrared beam couldn't reach the TV through the all-too solid body of a father. And he was about to wail when he saw my face, which must have resembled that of the Devil, and my hand, which was in the perennial parent pose—forefinger pointing directly upward, at God, since he/she/it is the one who created this whole parenting system in the first place, and therefore deserves all the blame.

Ethan stopped, considered his options, and in a rare display of common sense, decided against trying to knock me over and turn the television back on. He made a screeching noise, then stomped over to his backpack and began getting his books out.

It was going to be another great day at the old homestead, and Abigail had already let me know she'd be home late tonight. One of the partners in her firm was retiring, and there was a dinner that night, attendance mandatory.

While Ethan slammed his books down and started working, talking to himself all the while, Leah walked in the door, gave me the customary hug and kiss, and started in immediately on that most odious of tasks, penmanship. Today's assignment was to write about 154 "R"s on a page for no particular reason. She smiled through it, on the opposite side of the coffee table (excuse me, the homework table) from her brother, who was working himself into a lather over having to read a chapter from a book that he actually liked. A study in contrasts, from the same set of parents. Go figure.

I decided to start following the money, but I couldn't go out and do that just now, so I'd have to follow it from my office. This was difficult, since I didn't know where the money had gone, or indeed what money we were discussing. It's very hard to follow something when you haven't a clue what it is or where it started. They don't teach you that in journalism school—I'm pretty sure—but it's still true.

Since I am not, never have been, and never will be a business reporter, I didn't have a prayer of deciphering Gary Beckwirth's finances. And since Beckwirth was the only person involved in this whole mess who seemed to have an inordinate amount of money, he would be the logical jumping-off point. So instead of rooting around in his business and its dealings, which could have been swindling every person in the entire state of California for all I'd know, I decided to start with what I could understand.

I searched web sites with local real estate connections until I found a record of Gary Beckwirth's purchase of the old "White House" site. I recalled that at the time (Abby and I had moved to Midland Heights about four years before Gary and Madlyn), there had been considerable talk about the great deal the new owners had gotten on the property. The "Mean Old Man" had no heirs, and the estate had been directed to dispose of the property as quickly as possible.

But it was still something of a shock to come across the purchase price of $1.2 million. Five years ago, that was a tremendous amount of money. It wasn't exactly pocket change to me now. I looked around at the crumbling shell of my $140,000 house, and marveled at how I was still able to keep up with the mortgage payments.

Even more interesting was the fact that the transaction appeared to be solely in Gary Beckwirth's name. Even though he was clearly supplying the money, most married couples (and even those who aren't married) will opt to put a house in both spouses' names, just in case . . . well, in case one of them dies, so the other will have a clear title to the home.

Could it have been that Gary *knew* Madlyn was going to die first? Might he have cooked up this whole kidnap subplot to put everybody off the scent? I really *wanted* to assume the Barlows were to blame, but I was lacking anything resembling motive, evidence, or even the suggestion of hostility from either one of them toward Madlyn.

Ethan and Leah know that even when I'm working, so long as I'm not on the phone, they are to bring completed homework to my desk so I can look at it. I'm not the teacher, but I do need to see what they are having trouble with, and in Ethan's case especially, it had become such a routine that it wasn't questioned anymore. I could set my pants on fire, and be leaping around the room looking for a bucket of water, and he'd bring over his math homework.

In fifth grade, Ethan was bringing home math problems I had trouble with in my sophomore year of high school. My father was very strong in math, and probably should have pursued engineering instead of house-painting, but the math gene had skipped my generation and gone right to Ethan.

He walked over, still sulking, and tossed the sheet with geometry problems onto my desk with disgust. He had, as usual, written "Math — Ethan" on the top of the paper, despite the fact that the math teacher would know it was math, what with all the numbers and the fact that she had assigned it and all, but that's Ethan. You put the sub-ject and your name on each assignment, and that's that.

"There. Can I watch TV now?" he mumbled, sneering out of one side of his mouth. Despite my complete inability to decipher what this sheet might cover, I made a show of examining it for a long time, just to prove to him that homework was important and shouldn't be rushed through, and, I admit it, to piss him off, since he was pissing me off. So withdraw the nomination for "Father of the Year."

I handed him back the sheet and nodded, and he tromped up the stairs to his room, where I'd be sure not to set eyes on him for another two hours. Leah, deep into her "R"s, was leaning on the table, tongue sticking out the right side of her mouth, the most adorable child of the millennium.

A groan was audible in the room, and it wasn't until Leah looked up that I realized it had come from me. "Are you okay, Daddy?" she asked.

"Sure, Puss. I'm fine."

But there was no disputing it: I wasn't being a great father to her brother, and I knew it. So I dragged my weary butt out of the chair and up the stairs to Ethan's room.

It was its usual maelstrom of used socks, videocassette boxes with no cassettes, cassettes with no boxes, and video games. The unmade bed at least still had its sheet on, which was a welcome sight. There were crumbs on the floor, and a peeled apple from the night before had turned pectin brown in a bowl on his nightstand. I remembered I was here to make up with the boy, so I ignored virtually everything my eyes were taking in.

Ethan was sitting on the edge of his bed, Nintendo controller next to his mouth, and tongue pressed against it. He took it away long enough to growl, "aren't you supposed to knock?"

"The door was open. Ethan. Please pause the game." He scowled, but did as I asked.

I sat next to him on the twin bed. He didn't like that, because he knew that meant I was going to try and be reasonable, and that would make it harder to be mad at me, which was his goal at this moment.

"Ethan, I'm sorry."

His eyebrows raised a bit. A parent who apologizes? This must be some devious ploy, designed to lull him into a false sense of security. Besides, even if he knew that I had done a hundred things to wrong him that day alone, it was just as true that I probably hadn't noticed them. Which of the offenses had put me over the line?

"Yeah? For what?"

"For only telling you about the things you've been doing wrong. For not pointing out that you're probably the nicest boy I know when you're not mad. And for passing on to you my temper, which I feel I should point out, I got from your grandmother."

That really got him. "Grandma? But she's . . ."

"You're a grandchild. You could burn her house down, and she'd talk about how resourceful you were to find gasoline in the garage. That same woman would have put me through a wall if I so much as wore socks that didn't match."

"She'd really put you through a wall?"

"Well, not really, no. It's kind of an expression I just made up." I put my hand out. "Can we start again? Pretend you just got home, and we didn't grumble at each other?"

He liked shaking hands. It seemed grown-up to him. "Sure," he said, and took my hand. He gave it the exaggerated kind of shake you'd see in a Bugs Bunny cartoon, and I laughed and put my arm around him.

"I do love you, you know," I said. "And Ethan, I'm sorry about the sign on the sidewalk. I'm doing my best to find out who ..."

He pulled away. "Uh, Dad? I'd rather not talk about that, okay?"

That made sense. "Sure."

"Can I go back to the game now?" We had made progress, and he didn't want to undo it. But hey, Nintendo must take precedence.

"Okay." I heard the phone ringing. "You go ahead. And let me know if you do want to talk ..."

"I don't." He was already putting the controller back to his mouth again. How he could move the controls with his fingers while sucking on the controller at the same time is beyond me, but there it was.

I ran to get the phone before the machine got it. Of all people, Barry Dutton was on the other end of the line, and he sounded like he was calling from Beirut.

"Barry? Where the hell are you? I can barely hear you."

"I'm in the car. Look, Aaron, I didn't want to call from the office. Colette Jackson and the troopers are all over me there."

"So I take it you still love me?"

"As much as I ever did," he said sourly. "But I can't give you special privileges in front of all them. Look, I'm coming up on a tunnel, and I haven't got much time. But you should know that the prosecutor thinks there's enough evidence to arrest Gary Beckwirth for the murder."

"What? One day of investigation and they're already making an arrest?"

"Shut up and listen! They found a gun in Beckwirth's house, and it matched the ..." Static overwhelmed the line.

Once again, modern technology at its best.

# Chapter 14

Sure enough, when I got to the Beckwirth compound the next morning, two Midland Heights police cars and one county police car were positioned out front. Next to them were two state trooper cruisers and an unmarked car. Nobody was taking Gary Beckwirth lightly, which under normal circumstances would probably have made him feel great. A uniformed cop was at the front door, which was open. Clearly, the arrest was going down. And Madlyn Beckwirth's body wasn't even in the ground yet.

I don't have a press card. The state of New Jersey requires that you get one from a publisher. All the newspapers and magazines in the state are allotted a certain number, every last one of which goes to one of their staff members. So freelancers are, in effect, frozen out of press cards.

New Jersey driver's licenses don't necessarily have photographs of the driver in question attached. So I went into my wallet, took out my only photo ID, which happened to be my membership card for the local YM/YWHA, and held it up in front of the cop at the door. "Press," I said. He stepped aside, and I walked in.

The place was in shambles. Police call the process of going through a residence for evidence "tossing," and that is exactly what it is. Every drawer, every cabinet, every closet door in Beckwith's mansion, was open. Items of clothing were strewn about the floor, next to tennis rackets, books, umbrellas, videocassettes (I knew Beckwirth had a VCR some-where!), towels, and all the packaged food in the kitchen. But for the fact that the videocassettes were all ballet and opera performances, it looked like my house.

The only other difference was the police. I didn't see Barry Dutton, but I knew he had to be there somewhere. Westbrook was probably in the house, too, wedging the uniformed cops into corners and stum-bling over valuable evidence, rendering it unusable.

I saw at least four uniforms, not counting the one at the door. State troopers were, well, trooping through, and a couple of plainclothes detectives I hadn't seen before were loitering in the living room, talking to each other.

Colette Jackson was in the room off the living room, downstairs from where Gary Beckwirth had "advised" me to return to his house only if I had cheerful news to report. This was not a day for cheerful news. Gary hadn't had many of those days lately.

I walked over to Colette and waited while she told one of the uni-forms to make sure to dust the master bathroom for prints and to tag and inventory the contents of the medicine cabinet. The trooper nod-ded, suppressed the urge to salute, and headed for the stairs, double-time.

"There must be some serious evidence for all this to be going on less than forty-eight hours after the crime itself," I said by way of a greeting.

Colette smiled the smile that will one day get her a state judgeship, and said, "we believe we have sufficient evidence to get an indictment, and a conviction, Mr. Tucker."

"And that evidence would be . . ."

"I see absolutely no reason to release that information to the press right now," Colette said. "Besides, if I recall correctly, you have no media affiliation as of this moment, do you?"

A low blow, calling me a freelancer like that. "I understand a weapon was found. Was it here in the house?"

She didn't like at all that I knew about the gun. And she didn't like not knowing that I knew. That meant someone had told me something, and now she had to determine who that might be. To protect my source, I'd have to make sure to let Barry Dutton show his natural contempt for me when he was in Colette's presence.

"I don't recall saying anything about a weapon, Mr. Tucker."

"I didn't say you said it. I asked if it was found here."

"I can't confirm or deny any information at this point. You can call my office tomorrow morning if you like."

"I'm sure you'll be happy to tell me all about it, if you're actually in the office when I call," I said.

"Count on it," she answered, and walked toward the main staircase, where a group of men was descending from the second floor.

In a cluster were three troopers, Dutton, Milt Ladowski, and Dan Crawford, a uniformed Midland Heights cop I recognized. In the center of the cluster was Gary Beckwirth, wearing the scariest expression I had ever seen on a human face.

He was smiling.

Beckwirth had the wide, satisfied grin of a child who has just mastered "Chopsticks" on the piano. With all the law enforcement personnel gathered around him, each saying something at the same time, all wearing tense expressions and stealing glances at the front door, Beckwirth was resplendent in handcuffs and a beatific smile. It was a chilling look—something you see imprinted on the insides of your eyelids for days afterward.

"Gary," Ladowski was saying, "I'll have you out in two hours. Just stay quiet and calm, and we'll make sure that you ..."

"Watch your step, Mr. Beckwirth," one of the uniforms said, and Gary paid him as much attention as he seemed to be paying to Ladowski. It was a wonder he didn't trip over the bottom step.

Colette Jackson tried to stand in front of me and block me, but I managed to nudge my way toward the stairs and the still-moving group. It was almost funny, the way they all moved like a hive, like the whole cast of the "Mary Tyler Moore Show" in the final episode, taking tiny steps toward a box of Kleenex.

"Milt, is Gary confessing to his wife's murder?" I shouted as they neared us.

"Who the hell let him in?" Dutton yelled at the cops. Good move, Barry.

"Shut up, Barry, I'm press." Why not give Colette the whole show? But I'd better be careful not to go over the top and protest too much. She'd get suspicious.

Barry, knowing when to quit, gestured to the cops, who walked over and stood intimidatingly over my shoulder, making sure I couldn't reach Beckwirth.

"Milt, did you hear my question? Is Gary confessing?"

Ladowski didn't answer, but Gary Beckwirth seemed to wake up on hearing my voice. He looked over at me, still wearing his Rod Serling smile.

"Aaron," he said. "Aaron's here."

"Gary, are you . . ."

"Don't talk to him!" Ladowski yelled. "Don't say a thing!"

They'd almost made it to the door, when Beckwirth turned to talk to me, as calm and peaceful as I'd ever seen a man.

"It's all right, Aaron," he said. "It's really better this way. Madlyn will understand. Don't worry. She'll understand."

They practically pushed him out the door. Colette Jackson gave me one last sneer before leaving the house. I stood rooted to the spot.

I just couldn't move until I knew Gary Beckwirth had been driven away. The sight of that smile again would have been more than I could bear.

# Chapter 15

"The murder weapon?" Abby asked. "To arrest him that fast, they must have Gary's fingerprints all over it and a match on the bullet."

The kids were in bed and I was having a bowl of cereal, the finest nighttime snack ever invented. How this whole breakfast thing got started is anybody's guess. Abby, meanwhile, was eating a piece of melon with a spoon. A visitor to our kitchen would have assumed that there had been a total eclipse of the sun and it was actually seven o'clock in the morning.

"Barry Dutton called me after he got home," I told her. "They have a match on the bullet, a .38-caliber Smith & Wesson police special, which they said is probably the most popular gun on the planet. They found this particular gun under a bush in the backyard, where he'd thrown it. Registered legally to Gary Beckwirth three months ago."

"I thought Madlyn wouldn't let him have a gun," Abby said, wiping some melon juice from the corner of her mouth. "I thought they scared her."

"As well they might," I said. "Maybe Gary just didn't tell Madlyn he had one."

"So did Gary confess?"

"No, not according to Barry. But he's not exactly saying he *didn't* do it, either. He just keeps smiling that psychotic smile of his and saying 'it's all for the best.' I'm telling you, he looked like Tony Perkins at the end of *Psycho*, sitting there in the hallway with that weird grin on his face."

"At least Gary hadn't dressed up like his dead mother."

"Not that we know of," I said.

"Well, they have the gun, they have the bullet, they have Gary acting nuts. That might be enough, but I can't see them moving on it that fast unless they had something else," Abby said, in full attorney mode.

"Like what?"

"A witness, maybe. Someone willing to testify they saw Gary shoot Madlyn, or heard him say he was going to shoot Madlyn." She looked at the kitchen ceiling for a moment, apparently in deep and sober thought. "We could use a dropped ceiling in here to cover the water damage," Abby said.

I laughed in spite of myself. She gave me a glance, realized how quickly, and without notice, she'd moved from one subject to the other, smiled guiltily, and shrugged. If she got any more adorable, I might have to throw myself on the kitchen floor and let her take advantage of me.

"I'd like to talk to Lawyer Abby now, please," I said.

"Wait," she said, doing her best imitation of Joanne Woodward in *The Three Faces of Eve*. She rolled her eyes back in her head, allowing her head to fall back. Then, Abby "came to," and looked me in the face, dropping her voice a full key lower on the musical scale.

"Ask your question."

"What advantage is there for a couple to buy a very expensive property and only put one name on the mortgage and the title?"

She got up to throw out the melon rind. I pinched her on the butt as she passed, and Abby said, "hey," involuntarily, not even really thinking about anything but my question. It's my gift of irresistibility. Don't ask me to explain it.

"Well, if they weren't married, or thought they wouldn't stay married, the one with more money might not want the house to revert back to the partner in case ..."

"Exactly. In case one died prematurely."

"But Madlyn wasn't the one with the money," said Abigail.

"That's the confusing part. Are there any other reasons, legal reasons, to do it that way?"

"Well, the only thing I can think of is that one of the people might not want their name to show up on a legal document."

Something about that made me sit up and ignore my Golden Grahams for a moment. "Why wouldn't they want that?"

"If they own a business, they wouldn't want the property in their name because it could be claimed in a suit against the business. Or maybe they're using an alias, they have outstanding warrants, they don't want their name to show up in a computer somewhere," Abby said, completely in hypothetical mode now. "If the other one can afford to assume the debt all alone, why risk putting up a red flag?"

I got up and kissed my wife with a passion I usually reserve only for ... well, my wife, actually. But this time, it took even her by surprise.

"What was *that* for? Not that I didn't like it, but ..."

"You may have just given me my first actual, bona fide idea in this story."

"What story? You don't have an assignment."

"Don't sweat the details. There's only one thing that bothers me, though."

Abby's eyebrows crinkled. "Only one thing? I'd have thought there'd be hundreds."

"Yeah. If you were going by an alias, would you *choose* to be called Madlyn Beckwirth?"

# Chapter 16

The Middlesex County Courthouse in New Brunswick is tall, white, and old, and looks like it should house the National Widget Corporation. One summer, when I was a student at Rutgers University, a friend clerking in the building got us up to the roof to watch Fourth of July fireworks from six neighboring towns simultaneously. That's the best use I can think of for that courthouse.

Strangely, it has the look of a building in which nothing much happens. And for the most part, that's true. Criminals come and go, jurors are shown the "welcome film" daily in the basement, then spend their day reading paperback novels and the local newspapers until three o'clock comes around and they can go home.

If you walk into the County Courthouse, you have to make a choice in the lobby. To the right is the court system, and to the left, the county government's offices. The birth certificates for those born in the city's two major hospitals or anywhere in Middlesex County are kept there, along with death certificates, marriage licenses, some automobile records, and other governmental dross. Much of it is on paper, since the county is still hoping that this whole computer thing will just blow over, and everybody can get back to work.

The County Building side, specifically the county clerk's office, is where I found myself late the next morning. I had already fielded a call from Barry Dutton, who was making it a point to keep me informed whenever he was not in his office, and treating me like the political leper I am while he was in his office. Dutton said Gary Beckwirth had made bail after an arraignment (big surprise), and was now at home.

Madlyn Beckwirth's funeral was scheduled for the next morning. At one o'clock this afternoon, however, the Barlow campaign was still going ahead with its scheduled fundraising "coffee" (nobody wants to go to a tea anymore, apparently) in Martin and Rachel Barlow's backyard. All the best Democrats would make an appearance, but there would be no music, out of respect for poor departed Madlyn. Matters of life and death come and go, but the race for mayor in Midland Heights must go on, you know.

Standing in front of the clerk's window, I was patiently explaining for the third time why I was not the person whose records I was requesting.

"I'm a member of the press," I said. "This is a matter of public record. I don't want a copy of anything. I just want to see the public record. It's very simple."

Apparently, not that simple. The very large lady behind the window scowled at me as if I had requested her underwear size, so I could publish it in the newspaper the next morning.

"This isn't your marriage license," she said. "Right?"

Eye-rolling wouldn't be sufficient here to make my point. I would have to do a dramatic double-take. Lucky for her, no glass of water was handy, or she would have gotten a spit-take that would have made Mel Brooks jealous.

"Look, I've explained this three times. Is there a problem, or is there someone else back there I can talk to? Is the great Oz behind the curtain? One of his minions? Somebody?"

Somehow, my natural charm was eluding this woman, and she made a sound very much like a growl before saying, "I'll check." Then she turned and walked away, probably to check the job postings on the bulletin board so she'd *never* have to come back. The three people

behind me in line grumbled—that's New Jersey for you. If you stand
in a line long enough, somebody will stand behind you, figuring there
must be something good at the front of the line, or you wouldn't be
bothering. But the real pleasure in lines is complaining about their
length and the amount of time you waste standing in them.

I turned to the one woman and two men standing behind me and
let a frustrated sound out between my lips. "Civil service," I said.

"I'm civil service," said the burlier of the two men. "If it wasn't for
you, I'd be back at my desk." The woman didn't look especially pleased,
either. I turned back toward the window, properly chastised.

After several eternities, the large window woman returned with
another, older woman dressed in a suit from J.C. Penney. "I'm the
supervisor," she said. "What's the problem?"

I moaned and explained the situation to her again. "You want the
county archives," she said. "Not the clerk's office. That's upstairs on
Three." She pointed at the ceiling, so I'd know which way was up.

I thought the two men and the woman, now joined in line by two
other women, would break into applause as I left. I considered coming
back to do an encore, but humility prevented me.

Upstairs on Three, amazingly, was a room marked "County
Archives," in which a very helpful woman named Louise listened to my
spiel, showed me the proper computer, and explained its operation in
words designed for a backward nine-year-old. Within minutes, I was
deep into the records of other people's lives (okay, so I looked up Leah
and Ethan's birth certificates to see my name listed as father).

Turning my attention to the task at hand and not my own personal history, I very quickly located the title on the property. Sure enough,
Gary Beckwirth's was the only name listed under "purchaser." Current
ownership records on the property showed the owner (or lien holder)
as the Summit Bank Corporation, and Beckwirth again as the sole
mortgagee.

That much I had known. But when I dug back further, I

found a marriage certificate for Gary Beckwirth and Madlyn Rossi from February 2, 1978, from a ceremony performed right across the street in New Brunswick City Hall by Judge H. Raymond Jones. The couple listed their address as Middlesex Borough.

What's scary, looking back on it, is how close I came to missing what was important. After checking the marriage license, I started to search for the next milestone in Gary and Madlyn's lives. And that meant Joel's birth, fourteen years ago. So I scanned through a considerable amount of material, and was gaining speed when something in the back of my brain noticed the name "Beckwirth" go by. I almost didn't go back, thinking I'd only imagined seeing it, but a good reporter doesn't take anything for granted, and neither, in this case, did I.

And there it was: on June 1, 1978, less than four months after they were married, there appeared in the court of Judge Roger C. Lienhart a petition for the annulment of the marriage of Gary Beckwirth and Madlyn Beckwirth, née Rossi. The petition had been granted the same day.

That's why Madlyn Beckwirth's name didn't appear on the title to Gary Beckwirth's home. She wasn't his wife, and hadn't been for more than 20 years.

# Chapter 17

Stunned, I started searching for more bombshells, but there was no record of other marriages for either Gary or Madlyn. Oddly, I couldn't find a birth certificate for Joel Beckwirth, either. That meant that Joel was not Beckwirth's son, and therefore didn't really share his last name, or that Joel was born in another county, or something else I hadn't thought of. I'd have to examine some statewide records to find that out. Of course, if Joel had been born in New York City, for example, it might be more difficult to find his birth certificate. For all I knew, he had been born on a kibbutz in Haifa. Or maybe he hadn't been born at all, but was actually the product of a laboratory experiment gone horribly wrong.

It led to a whole slew of new questions: if Madlyn and Gary's marriage had been annulled so soon after they were married, more than twenty years ago, who was Joel's father? Why were they still living together? Was that even Madlyn who had been killed in the hotel in Atlantic City?

I was getting tired of every lead producing more questions than answers. And I was more tired of the feeling, growing since I first talked to Milt Ladowski, that the whole kidnapping scenario had been staged for my personal benefit, that someone decided it would look suspicious if nobody cared that Madlyn ran off, so a patsy had to be found. A credible one, but one who wasn't a good enough investigator to actually find anything out. The more I protested, the better I must have seemed for the job.

They hadn't wanted somebody good. They had wanted somebody gullible.

I knew I should have been devastated by this conclusion. It should have bothered me that I couldn't rise above the dismal expectations of my manipulator (or manipulators), that I had played directly into unseen hands. But for some reason, it was a liberating epiphany. I had been walking around with the weight of Madlyn's death on my shoulders. The idea had been holding me back —the idea that somehow her death was my fault, that I should have done something to prevent it, and hadn't thought of it in time.

Now, I didn't have to worry about that anymore. There had been no expectations. I didn't owe anybody anything.

That freed me up to act in any way I saw fit. I had my assignment now, and it came from me.

When I got home, I called the main number at the *Press-Tribune* and asked for the obit desk. Rory Anderson picked up, and I smiled, although he couldn't see. Rory is maybe twenty-three, has hair that looks like he's trying out for N'Sync, and knows me from his days at the *Rutgers Daily Targum*. The *Targum* was, technically, my first employer, back in the days I was an undergraduate and "employer" didn't necessarily translate into "paycheck."

I had done a little advising for the *Targum* a few years back, hadn't reveled in my return to campus, and left by mutual agreement. But I'd met Rory, and actually written a letter of recommendation for him to the *Press-Tribune*. He was a good reporter who, in true *Press-Tribune* fashion, was being wasted on the obituary desk.

We had a brief verbal reunion, and I asked him to look up Madlyn Beckwirth's obit.

"Why don't you just pick up the paper, Dude?" he asked.

"Didn't 'Dude' go out with, like, Pauly Shore?" I asked. "And, for your information, I don't get your rag. I subscribe to the *New York Times.*"

"Snob." I could hear him clicking on his keys to call up the obit. "You know, you could probably get this off the web site."

"You don't keep obits more than a day."

He stopped typing. "How come you're not getting this yourself, Aaron? You work for us, don't you?"

"Hell, no. They fired me two days ago. I'm working for the enemy now."

"Cool!" Like all obit writers, Rory deeply and truly detested his employer. Anything that could conceivably hurt the paper would give him nothing but pleasure. "Got it," he said.

"I need a little information. Survivors?"

"Husband Gary, son Joel ..."

"Yeah ..."

"Mother, Mrs. Charlotte Rossi of Westfield. A sister, Mrs. Angela Cantucci of Toms River. That's it."

"You got where she went to high school?"

"No, but I'll bet it was St. Joe's."

"Why?" I asked, startled that he'd come up with a guess so quickly.

"That," he said, "is where all the good Italian girls go in Westfield, man." I thanked him profusely, and hung up. After gathering my courage, I called Mrs. Rossi in Westfield, told her who I was, and asked if I could come over to talk about Madlyn. She was unexpectedly calm, and agreed to see me the next day, which was Saturday. It wasn't until later that I remembered Madlyn's funeral would be Saturday morning. Mrs. Rossi was very brave.

And, yes, I know our interview was set for a weekend, when I should be spending time with my kids, but hey, if you can go talk to a woman about her dead daughter, what better way to spend a Saturday? I asked where Madlyn went to high school, and after a startled pause, Mrs. Rossi said, "St. Joe's." Score one for Rory.

Right then, though, I realized I was out of ideas, and there's no better place to go for someone with no ideas than a political rally.

That is how I came to walk again through the perfect white trellis behind the perfect white picket fence and into the perfect backyard of Martin and Rachel Barlow. "Barlow for Mayor" signs were hung all over the house, the trellis, the fence, the trees, and the sturdier of Martin Barlow's hedges and bushes he had installed all around the backyard.

There were maybe fifty people milling around, eating Portobello mushroom canapés and drinking coffee from insulated, specially print-ed "Barlow For Mayor" paper cups. The plates had the same imprint. The forks and spoons managed to avoid the logo, but were red, white, and blue, just in case anybody thought that Rachel was anti-American and would try to subvert the system from the great seat of power known as the Midland Heights mayor's office.

There was, as advertised, no music, which meant we were not being subjected to the string quartet that had obviously been intended for one corner of the yard. A bandstand of sorts had been set up, comprised of two pallets underneath the tops of two discarded Ping-Pong tables. It was ringed in red, white, and blue bunting and emblazoned with—you guessed it—"Barlow For Mayor" signs, in case you'd wandered back here and thought it was just a boring neighborhood cook-out.

Barry Dutton was not there, which was not a surprise, and most of the borough council members had also avoided the event, since they were still betting on Sam Olszowy to pull this thing out of the fire with a last-minute miracle. Besides, Rachel had managed to piss off enough of them throughout the campaign that even if she won, they might not attend any council meetings at which she appeared.

Other reporters were present, some of whom I recognized. Others were identifiable as press strictly by their reporter's notebooks or micro-phones. Local radio stations had sent their reporters to get some news on the murder, not the campaign event, and there was even a satellite truck outside from News 12 New Jersey, the system set up by the local cable provider and two area newspapers. Rachel Barlow was getting the coverage she so sincerely craved, but not for the reason she would have preferred.

The candidate herself was quite the vision in a blue pants suit from about 1988, reconstituted for the new millennium by cutting the pants a couple of inches above the ankle. Either that, or Rachel Barlow had grown since the last time she'd worn these pants. If she wore her blonde hair in a flip, it evoked flips from circa 1966. In sum, here was a mayoral candidate projecting herself as a complete throwback in time, as an object of nostalgia, in effect.

She was standing at the far end of the yard, near a perfectly bloomed rose bush (Martin was clearly a very accomplished gardener), answering questions for the News 12 reporter, and wearing an expression of concern and seriousness, despite the fact that, since the murder, she'd probably jumped seven sympathy-and-name-recognition points in the polls.

Martin was standing near Rachel, but not too near, dressed in a Ralph Lauren polo shirt and a pair of khakis pressed to the point where the pleats could probably cause a deep cut in anyone unfortunate enough to brush against him. He was one of the few men I'd ever met who actually would have looked more comfortable in a suit and tie. (They said the same thing about Richard Nixon, but I never met him.)

I hadn't been to the Y that morning, and I was trying to watch what I ate, so I bravely avoided the canapés. It was quite a trial, but I managed. On one table near the bandstand were bagels, slices of marble cake, and blueberry muffins (no doubt low-fat ones). That table was harder to avoid, so I decided to concentrate on the task at hand, and approached the Barlows.

When Martin saw me closing in, he put on a face like he'd smelled something bad, and I don't think it was the Portobello mushrooms. Rachel caught me out of the corner of her eye as she was saying to the TV reporter, "Well you know, Juanita, the saddest part is that she died so needlessly, just when she was about to share in the great victory we're going to accomplish here in Midland Heights." Martin caught me before I could get to Rachel, and steered me to one side, which made me mad. If he got me too close to that marble cake, there was no telling what could happen.

"What are you doing here?" he hissed. "After all you've done . . ."

"I'm a voter in Midland Heights, Martin," I said, a mocking smile on my face. It was nice to be the one wearing the smug expression for a change. "I came to hear the candidate speak on the issues."

"It's speak *to* the issues." He couldn't resist.

Neither could I. "You're wrong this time, Marty. The issues are not here listening to Rachel. She can speak *about* the issues, or she can speak *on* the issues, but speaking *to* the issues is incorrect. You're slipping. Have you gotten enough sleep lately?"

He recoiled as if I'd slapped him. "What do you mean by that?" he demanded.

I didn't know what he thought I meant, but it clearly worried him. I upped my vocal volume from the stage whispers Barlow and I had been exchanging. "I mean there's more to this murder than meets the eye," I said, and then, louder, "and you know it!"

Heads turned. Reporters pulled notebooks out of their pockets. Rachel's head turned, too.

"I know what happened to Madlyn Beckwirth," I said, coming within a single decibel of shouting, "and you know more than you're telling, Martin! So does Rachel!"

Juanita the TV reporter widened her eyes to roughly the size of garbage-can lids. And then the worst thing that could have happened to Rachel Barlow followed: the microphone was pulled from her face.

"What did you say? Who are you?" said Juanita.

"I've been investigating Madlyn Beckwirth's murder, and I'm saying Rachel and Martin Barlow know more than they're telling!" I had, of course, nothing more than a suspicion, but what the hell, this was, as they say, "great television."

Meantime, I watched Martin and Rachel Barlow. They weren't surprised or shocked. They weren't even unnerved. Their eyes narrowed, their mouths tightened, their nostrils flared.

The Barlows were good and angry.

But that wasn't what caught my eye. Just at that moment, I had one of those moments of acute observation that Sherlock Holmes himself would have treasured. I looked past the Barlows, past the reporters, who were now clamoring for my name and shouting questions at me, past the other voters who thought they were coming for a political event and showed up for a homicide analysis. I looked past the bandstand, the campaign signs, and even the bagels and marble cake.

Behind Martin Barlow was his prized rose bush, in full bloom, affording an office seeker the finest background for the finest photo-op in American political history. If you looked carefully, you could see the tiny specks of blue in the pink petals, almost in the shape of diamonds.

Martin Barlow had gotten his rose bush from Arthur P. MacKenzie.

# Chapter 18

"Did you really say, 'give me a by-line or give me death'?" Abigail asked. She and Mahoney were staring blankly at me across the kitchen table as I finished our chicken and couscous. I kept eating, having devoted most of the day to not eating.

"You had to be there," I told her. "It was more a spur-of-the-moment kind of thing."

"What were you thinking?" Mahoney wanted to know. "You don't have anything on these people. Not yet, anyway."

"I wanted to make them think I did. I wanted to force them into a stupid move that I can exploit."

"And you wanted to piss them off," Abby added.

"Well, yes, that too."

Abby stood up to clear her plate, and picked Mahoney's up while she passed, since he had finished as well. He nodded thanks.

"I don't know that I'm crazy about this, Aaron," she said, scraping couscous into the garbage so she could put the plates in the dishwasher. "If the Barlows were involved in killing Madlyn Beckwirth, and you make them think you can prove it, they might come after you."

"That's why *he's* here," I said, pointing at Mahoney. "While I'm taking my little drive tonight, the galoot here will be watching you and the kids."

"Galoot?" Mahoney said, raising his eyebrows.

"I meant it in the most affectionate way possible," I said.

"You stay on that side of the table, Pal," he said. "I still have my knife."

Abby put the dishes in the dishwasher and sat back down at the table. "So you were just trying to irritate the Barlows today?"

"Well, there were plenty of news organizations there, too. If somebody wants the complete story, they now know there's a reporter who has the inside track."

"Oh yeah," said my wife. "Screaming 'Don't vote for Mayor Murder' while you're being thrown out of a suburban backyard cookout is going to look really good on your resumé. Not to mention I don't know how I'm going to get through the supermarket now. Everyone will be staring at me."

I stood up. "They all stare at you now, Honey," I said. "At least the men do."

At the door, she kissed me a little more passionately than she normally would. "Drive safe," Abby said. I gave Mahoney the eye over her shoulder. He understood the message, and I left.

The ride to Emmaus seemed a lot longer this time, even though I could listen to A.J. Croce, Elliott Smith, Janis Ian, and Ella Fitzgerald on the way. But Mahoney's absence meant two things: no friendly banter, and possible danger at home. It was difficult to resist the urge to call home on the cell phone every three minutes. But I managed to call only twice en route, and things were fine both times, although Leah couldn't make up her mind whether to take a bath or a shower. Some decisions are just too big to be made quickly.

I had wanted to talk to MacKenzie on the phone, but his number was unlisted. And I didn't have time for Barry Dutton to come home (where he wouldn't be overheard consorting with the enemy), get the number from Verizon, and call me back with it. But this way, MacKenzie wouldn't know I was coming beforehand, and with his hearing, it could be a while before he knew someone was at the door, especially if he was in the greenhouse.

He took a couple of minutes to answer my ring, and did seem surprised when he saw me at his door. The trip had taken twenty minutes less than the first time, mostly because this time I knew where I was going. MacKenzie invited me into the living room for coffee, but I asked if we could talk in the greenhouse. He seemed puzzled, but agreed. He didn't walk as quickly as he probably had at fifty. Or sixty. The walk to the greenhouse was probably more than he was prepared for, but he didn't complain.

Once there, he asked if I was here to buy some flowers or a shrub, assuming that I'd asked to come into the greenhouse to choose the one item I wanted to take home. I assured him that wasn't the reason for my trip.

"Then I can't say I completely understand," he said slowly. "I've already told you I can't help with the matter of the phone call."

I walked to the drawer where he had gotten the cell phone on the last visit, and asked if I could take it out. MacKenzie nodded, but still seemed puzzled. I turned the phone on and pushed a couple of buttons.

"You see, Mr. MacKenzie, you and I were both thrown off the track the last time. Could you do us a favor, and get for me the card with your cell number on it?"

He thumbed through the index cards again, and retrieved the card while I talked. "We forgot to think that someone might have wanted to deceive both of us, that they'd know we'd check the phone number on the threatening phone call."

MacKenzie found the cell phone number on his card, and I walked to him to get it. "I don't see why that would make a difference, Mr. Tucker," he said. "I still know I didn't make that call."

"And I don't think you did, sir, but I do think that someone you know made it."

His eyebrows jumped up. "Really? But the only ones who come

back here are me, my daughters . . ."

" . . . and the people who come to buy your plants," I said.

There's a button on every cell phone that will tell you what phone number it's using. That is, if you forget your own phone number, it will be glad to show it to you. And when I pressed that button on MacKenzie's phone, and compared it to the number on the index card . . .

"They don't match," MacKenzie said, his voice confused. "What does that mean?"

"That means this isn't your cell phone," I told him. "It means someone who has the same model phone came here, switched phones with you when you weren't looking, and took yours home with him. Since you never use the cell phone, you'd probably not even notice the one or two calls he made using your phone—it would hardly stand out on your bill. If you were scrupulous enough to check the bill when it arrived, it would be so long ago that you wouldn't remember this guy being here."

"I did notice an increase of a dollar or so on the bill the last time," MacKenzie said. "But I didn't bother to call. I figured the rates had gone up again. Goddam phone company, you know."

"Exactly."

"Why would someone do that?" he asked as I checked the number on the phone in MacKenzie's drawer again, wrote it down on the back of an ATM receipt in my pocket, and handed the phone back to MacKenzie.

"Because they didn't want the calls to be traced to them," I said. "They knew there'd be an investigation, and they knew that you were far enough away and unlikely enough a suspect to confuse everybody."

MacKenzie nodded. "Very clever. But you said you think I know who might have done this. Who was it?"

"I was at a party yesterday in Midland Heights, New Jersey, and I saw a pink rose bush whose petals had little blue specks in the shapes of diamonds, Mr. MacKenzie." "Do you know Martin Barlow?"

MacKenzie sat on a stool near a workbench, and slowly nodded. "I met him through my attorney, Milton Ladowski," he said.

"That figures."

"Mr. Barlow?" MacKenzie marveled. "Who'd have thought it? He speaks so well."

"Has he been up here in the last month or two to buy a plant?"

Again MacKenzie nodded. "Yes, yes he was. He bought one of the rose bushes, and a rhododendron. Didn't know how he was going to get them home, but he had a minivan, and they just fit in the back."

"Yes," I said to MacKenzie, who was still a little glassy-eyed over all the revelations. "Everybody in Midland Heights has a minivan. Even me."

# Chapter 19

I didn't attend Madlyn Beckwirth's funeral. I know it's something that Miss Marple would have done. Just as Sam Spade would have been there, or Dashiell Hammett's nameless Continental operative from all the short stories. Any of them would have gone, to observe the suspects and various untoward glances back and forth, but it wasn't for me. I hadn't been a friend of Madlyn, and I don't think she would have appreciated my presence.

Besides, I was going to visit her mother only a little while after the service. That was enough of a nervy move, I thought, and if the annals of investigative reporting judged me harshly for not watching Madlyn's "closed casket" (I later confirmed that) lowered into the earth, so be it. Instead, I woke up early, checked my email, and starting about nine o'clock made some phone calls.

Naturally, when Barry Dutton checked the number I had written down from MacKenzie's cell phone against Verizon's records, it matched Martin Barlow's. And according to the Verizon Wireless records, Barlow's was the same model as MacKenzie's cell phone.

It was Saturday, so I didn't have to worry about Colette Jackson or Westbrook being with Barry when he called from his office with the news. But when I suggested that this link should put a crimp in their case against Gary Beckwirth, Dutton chuckled.

"You want me to let Beckwirth off the murder charges because a nasty phone call to your house was made on Barlow's cell phone?" He laughed. "How do you know Beckwirth didn't just borrow Martin's phone? Or that anybody else on the planet did? Besides, there's no proof that whoever made that call was the person who shot Madlyn Beckwirth. And guess what? I have a credit card found in Beckwirth's wallet that bears the name Milton Ladowski. I still have a gun with Beckwirth's fingerprints on it. I have rumors that Madlyn was sleeping around on Beckwirth. And I have Beckwirth acting very much like somebody who shot his wife."

"I can tell you for certain that Beckwirth didn't shoot his wife," I told Barry. "He might have killed Madlyn, but she wasn't his wife." I then told him about the annulment records I'd found. Barry stammered for a moment, but held his ground.

"Doesn't mean he didn't shoot her," he said.

"No, but it sure is interesting," I told him. "First I'm hearing about this credit card, too. Do you think Milt Ladowski knows?"

Barry's voice dropped about one and a half octaves. "Mr. Ladowski does not take me into his confidence very often," he said.

Since I wasn't the chief of police, I figured there was no reason Mr. Ladowski couldn't take *me* into his confidence, but it was Saturday, and I couldn't go to his office and be annoying now. I'd have to put off that pleasure for two days. I hung up the phone and sought out my wife, who was sitting on our back steps looking out over the tiny expanse of concrete and cheap flagstone we call a backyard.

"What we need," she said, "is grass."

I sat down next to Abby and kissed her on the shoulder. "As an officer of the court, you should know that pot smoking is illegal," I said. She did not smile.

"This backyard is depressing," she said.

"So is our bank statement," I said. "And the phone hasn't exactly been ringing off the hook with editors offering me plum assignments—

only cranks who want me to come and explain the Madlyn Beckwirth murder to their tiny groups for free."

"You couldn't explain it for money, either," she reminded me sourly.

"Wrong side of the bed this morning?"

"I'm not crazy about having to have Mahoney play bodyguard here while you're away," she said. "I don't like worrying that you've gotten us into a situation that could endanger the kids, and you didn't even talk to me about it first. You worry me sometimes. You think you know how to control or fix everything, and you really don't. How do you know that whoever killed Madlyn Beckwirth isn't going to show up here tonight with a gun?"

"I don't," I admitted, "and I should have talked to you first. I'm sorry. But the Barlows seem like such a couple of pompous asses, I felt I had to annoy them just to keep myself sane. I don't like being manipulated, especially by people who consider me insignificant. I reacted emotionally instead of thinking it through, and I was wrong to do that. I'm a very emotional guy, you know."

She finally smiled at me. "I know. So what's on the agenda for today?"

"Going up to visit Madlyn's mom in Westfield," I said. "That's about it."

"How do you know the gunman won't shoot me and the kids while you're away?"

"Because you're all coming with me."

And three hours later, in Charlotte Rossi's living room, a very brown place with lace curtains and framed high school graduation pictures of two girls, my son slumped in an armchair, engrossed in Gameboy as only an Asperger's child can be, oblivious to all else going on around him. Leah sat very quietly on Abigail's lap, on a couch opposite Mrs. Rossi's television. Leah's attention was on the tape of *The Little Mermaid* that we had brought, and that Mrs. Rossi had graciously agreed to play on her VCR. Abby's attention was on Charlotte Rossi, and on me, since I was sitting next to Abby and asking the questions of Mrs. Rossi.

That is, I had offered condolences, declined an offer of coffee (which Abigail had considered accepting, but had a girl on her lap), and asked one question: "tell me about Madlyn," and Mrs. Rossi was off and running. After much talk and any number of old photographs, I managed to get a word in edgewise.

"How did you feel when she got married?"

Mrs. Rossi, a slim, vibrant woman with hair that might not have been its natural color (jet black) and large, very aware eyes, sat back in her armchair just a bit. This was not the memory she wanted to dredge up today.

"Well, I thought they were too young, you know. Madlyn was, what, twenty, twenty-one? But she was" — her voice dropped to a whisper for Leah's benefit — "*pregnant, and she wanted the pretty boy.*" Charlotte turned to Abigail, with whom she clearly felt more comfortable. "At that age, you can't tell them anything."

"At *any* age," Abby agreed, and Charlotte chuckled, the black dress she had worn to the funeral in sharp contrast to the laughter.

"You got that right," Mrs. Rossi agreed. "Later on, when they got it annulled, I thought she had come to her senses, but . . ."

"You knew about the annulment?" I asked.

Charlotte looked offended. "I'm the mother," she said. "Of course I *knew*. But by then, well, Maddie and I weren't really talking all that much."

Leah looked up from "Under The Sea" long enough to look amazed. "You didn't talk to your own *daughter*?" She looked at Abby, who hugged her and said, "watch the movie."

Mrs. Rossi put a hand to her mouth, and lowered her voice again. "I'm so sorry," she said. "I hope I didn't upset her."

"Not at all," I told her. "Leah likes to be dramatic. But I am

214

curious. What came between you and Madlyn, if I may ask:?"

Charlotte didn't want to answer, but she knew I was trying to do right by her daughter, and she knew her response would help. She bit her lower lip for a moment, and kept her voice to a barely audible whisper.

"It wasn't easy," she said. "But I'm a good Catholic."

Yeah, and I was a Jewish agnostic, but what did that have to do with anything? "So ... did Madlyn want to convert?" I asked.

"No," Charlotte said. "She still considered herself a Catholic. But, you know, the Church frowns on how she ... ended her pregnancy."

Huh? "Madlyn had an *abortion?*" I said stupidly.

Leah looked up at Abby again. "Mommy, what's an abortion?"

Abby smiled at her and said, "watch the fish."

"He's a crab."

I leaned forward, and probably blushed at my own indiscretion. "But I thought Madlyn miscarried the first baby."

"First? *Only* baby. And that was just what they told people—she miscarried. She ... actually terminated the pregnancy. And after that, we didn't talk very much. I would hear things from her sister, and then after the annulment, we really didn't hear from Maddie very often at all. A card at Christmas, my birthday, that sort of thing. She never called, and when she moved out, she didn't let us know where she was living. I found out about ... *this* from the newspapers." Her eyes misted.

"Was there anyone who did hear from her regularly?" I asked, and Charlotte nodded, although she seemed to find it hard to speak.

"She kept in touch with Marie Aiello," she managed, and opened the 1974 high school yearbook on the coffee table to a picture of Marie, a very attractive girl with dark hair and eyes. "I think Ree-Ree heard from her quite often." Her voice was getting shaky, and she was staring bravely at Leah. Charlotte was trying very hard not to break down in front of my daughter. I thought that was too much to ask of her.

"Well, thank you for letting us come on such a hard day for you,"

I said, and stood up. Abby looked a little surprised, but patted Ethan on the leg to let him know it was time to go. He stood and walked to the door without taking his eyes off the Gameboy, a skill at which I have often marveled.

"It's all right," said Mrs. Rossi. "I appreciate being around the young people. And I appreciate what you're trying to do. If I can help in any way, please let me know."

I stood and walked to the door, and Abby picked Leah up off her lap and informed her we were leaving. Leah stared at the TV, and moaned, "but we were just getting to the good part."

# Chapter 20

Mrs. Rossi gave me Marie Aiello's address in Westfield, but when we stopped by the house, nobody was home. I left a business card wedged in the door, the one with "Aaron Tucker, Freelance Writer/ Screenwriter" and my phone numbers, fax machine number, email address, home address and, if I remember correctly, hat size. On the only open space, the back, I wrote, "Please call re: Madlyn Rossi."

Then we took the kids to see some god-awful movie. If some non-Asperger's 11-year-olds saw a poster for this dog, they'd have stayed three blocks away—it was that uncool. But Ethan and Leah, the whole way home, re-enacted the film's supposedly hilarious highlights.

I had just been paid for a *Parenting Magazine* piece the day before, and was feeling flush, so, on the spur of the moment, headed to dinner at the Italian restaurant where we knew Ethan would be able to find pasta prepared to his exacting standards. By the time we got home, it was late, and Leah had fallen asleep in the car. Ethan attached the light to his Gameboy and remained relatively quiet, occasionally humming what he considered to be mood music appropriate to the game he was playing.

We hadn't planned on being out this late, and hadn't turned on the front porch light before leaving, so the house was unusually dark when I carried Leah up the brick steps to the front door. I had my keys in my right hand, and was about to lean over the lock, when something stopped me.

"What's the matter?" said Abby, but I put a finger to my lips the best I could and shushed her. I motioned to her to take Leah from me and back to the car, which isn't so easy to do when you're trying not to wake a sleeping seven-year-old.

I put a finger to my ear, and then pointed toward the door. "I hear something inside."

Abby immediately turned and walked back down the steps, carrying Leah. She made it to the car, huffing and puffing, and put down Leah, who was finished pretending to be asleep because this was just too darned interesting. I followed her to the car. Ethan was still in the back seat, playing Gameboy. We'd left him there until we were inside because, well, it's just easier that way.

"What did you hear?" Abigail asked.

"I don't know. It sounded like somebody knocking around in the living room. But the lights were out. I'll go in and take a look around."

Abby gave me a look which froze me in my tracks, and opened the passenger side door of the car. The dome light came on, which made Ethan smile, and Abby reached in for the cell phone. She handed it to me.

"Nine-one-one," she said.

I called police headquarters at the regular number, and got a dispatcher I didn't know. I asked for Barry, but he was not in the station, and the dispatcher asked what my problem was. I didn't have time to provide a long explanation, so I told him I thought there was some intruder inside my house.

"Are you inside the house now?" he asked.

"No, I'm outside in my driveway. We just got home, and I heard something inside the house."

He asked for my address, and when I gave it to him, there was a long pause. "Aaron Tucker?" he asked. I acknowledged that I was, indeed, myself. "It may be a while before we can send someone, Mr.

Tucker," he said with a sneer in his voice. "You know, Saturday nights are awful busy, and ..."

Abby, who had been listening at my shoulder, grabbed the phone out of my hand. "This is Abigail Stein, attorney at law," she snarled into the phone. "If you don't get a patrol car to my house in five minutes, I'll see to it that the department is investigated by the state Attorney General's office and you personally will be under indictment by the end of the week." More than just a pretty pair of legs, my wife.

The cops showed up in three minutes—two cars, each with a uniformed officer. The lights were flashing and one had the siren on as he pulled up.

"Good," I said to Crawford as he got out of the car. "I think you snuck up on him."

"Just keep the children out of the way," he said without looking at me, and got out his flashlight. He motioned to the other cop, whose name, according to his badge, was Morgan. Morgan went around the back of the house to make sure nobody got out that way.

"Any sign of forced entry?" Crawford said to Abigail, who shook her head. He turned in my direction. "Any enemies you might want to mention?"

"None you don't know about."

"Is the door locked?" I nodded, and held out the key. Crawford took it, and motioned us back toward the car.

Crawford approached the front door very slowly, tried to see into the living room through the front window, but couldn't get a good look. It was too dark inside, and the streetlight, instead of illuminating the interior, was reflecting off the window glass and made it more, not less, difficult to see.

"Daddy," Leah said, "is there a robber inside our house?"

"We'll see, Honey," I said. "If there is, the police officers will get him."

Abby told Leah to get in the car with Ethan, but she didn't want to. The only way Abigail could get our daughter to sit inside the car was to get in the front seat herself and close the door. The dome light went off, which made Ethan scowl.

Crawford picked up his walkie-talkie and said something into it, then listened. He nodded, although Morgan certainly couldn't see him from the back of the house. Crawford took the key I had given him and slowly turned it in the lock. When the door was unlocked, he took his gun out of the holster on his hip, and Leah's eyes grew wide. Crawford checked the gun, put his hand on the doorknob, and his lips started to count: one, two . . .

Abby, her car window open, reached out and grabbed my hand.

Crawford abruptly slammed open the front door, holding the flashlight in one hand and the gun in the other. "Police!" he shouted, and started moving the light around the room. His head turned abruptly, and Morgan came in from the back, also with his flashlight on. They both scanned the living room with their lights, and suddenly, Crawford shouted, and held open the screen door as wide as it could go.

Just then a little brown bat flew out through my open front door. He headed directly for the trees across the street, then toward the park, and was out of sight in a matter of seconds.

The cops turned on the living room light and looked around. Morgan even went upstairs and turned on the lights in all the bedrooms.

"Did we make the bed this morning?" Abby asked me quietly. I shrugged.

Crawford walked out the front door, smiling. Morgan, behind him, merely waved, got into his car, and drove off. Crawford couldn't resist the temptation. He walked over to me.

"Got rid of your intruder, Mr. Tucker," he said.

"Thanks," I said sincerely. "Glad nobody was hurt."

"Better get a cap for your chimney. And next time, before you call the cops, try the old tennis racket bit," he said. "I hear that works real well with flying rodents."

He got into his car and drove off.

"Bats aren't rodents," Ethan said in the back seat. "They're chiroptera mammals." Abby just stared at him, then turned her head to me.

"I guess we were worried for nothing," she said.

"No, we weren't," I told her. "We just weren't right this time. And I'm tired of it."

"Next time we'll know better," she said as she opened the car door for Leah.

"There's not going to be a next time," I said. "I'm putting an end to this show right now."

# Chapter 21

This time, I wasn't going to devise a plan, much less put it in motion, without first discussing it with Abby. And I did. She said she wasn't crazy about the particulars, but overall didn't see any other way to end this whole mess. So she finally consented. Secretly, I'd been hoping she'd suggest some improvements.

I couldn't start anything on Sunday, but I could prepare. Abby took the kids to a children's museum we like in Staten Island so I could do some research.

The freelance writer's best friend used to be the public library. Now it's the Internet. You point your browser toward any keyword you happen to like, and the next thing you know, all sorts of information about your friends and neighbors pours into your living room.

In this particular case, I used a search program called Copernic, which consolidates a number of search engines, to get me some background on "Respa, Worthington and Mattingly," the Wall Street firm that Gary Beckwirth worked for before hitting it big in the Internet stock lottery. A number of the search engines that Copernic uses found sites that mentioned the firm, and eventually I was able to come up with the information I wanted, which was a personnel list for the years Beckwirth worked there.

I printed out that screen, then went to Beckwirth's current company's web site, and compared the personnel roster against the paper. There were three matches. One was Beckwirth. The other two were Miriam Lybond, a bond trader, and William Ryan, who worked in the accounting department.

I was willing to bet that Miriam knew Beckwirth better personally, and that Ryan knew more about his finances. As it turned out, Beckwirth's finances were not the most interesting part of this story, so I looked up Miriam Lybond on the Internet White Pages, and found her in North Brunswick, New Jersey. I called the number, and found Miriam at home.

When I told her I was a reporter working on the Madlyn Beckwirth story, she almost hung up. "I don't believe for one minute that Gary had anything to do with her death," Miriam said boldly.

"Neither do I," I told her. "I'm working on the story to see if I can prove he *didn't* do it."

There was silence on the other end of the line. Miriam clearly hadn't expected to hear that. She began to reconsider. I could practically hear the wheels turning in her mind.

"What do you want to know?" Bingo.

"I'm working on background," I said. "Nothing really pertaining to the crime itself. You knew Gary when he was working at Respa, Worthington, right?"

"Yeah. He was setting up the web trading, and I was selling municipal bonds."

"Was he married to Madlyn then?" I asked.

"That's right. It was when they were married the first time."

"Sure. The ... first time. Do you know what happened after they broke up?"

"Well, Gary was devastated. I mean, you never saw a man pine for his wife like that. He couldn't believe she'd leave him for another guy."

The surprises were coming too fast for me.

"Did he manage to get over it?"

"Well, you know that he got married again, don't you?"

The way she said it, Miriam made it clear she *didn't* mean that Gary had married Madlyn again, or at least, that wasn't what she was referring to. When in doubt, tell the truth. It's too hard to remember the bullshit.

"No, I didn't know," I said. "This is exactly the kind of background I need. Who was the new wife?"

"Well, she was this blonde who started as a secretary, like me, and eventually ended up running the whole futures division. One of those. A real cheerleader type. All the guys were after her. Except Gary. Maybe that's what made her set her sights on him. And once she decided she wanted him, there wasn't any doubt. God, I wish I could remember her name . . ."

"Rachel," I said. "I think her name was Rachel."

An awed pause. "That's right!" shouted Miriam. "How did you know that?"

"I'm not really sure," I said.

"Rachel Aston," she said. "Now I remember. I guess they didn't stay married that long, because he went back with Madlyn again. Whatever happened to Rachel? Do you know?"

"I'm not really sure." It was the only thing I knew how to say now.

"I'll bet she's the CEO of some big corporation," said Miriam. "That woman was the most ambitious person I ever met."

I hung up feeling absolutely dizzy, and felt the immediate need to recap our game of "Marital Musical Chairs." Gary Beckwirth marries Madlyn Rossi because he gets her pregnant. For some reason, they decide to abort the pregnancy, and in a matter of weeks, Madlyn leaves Gary for an as-yet-unnamed guy.

Rachel Aston, who, the smart money would wager, now goes by the name of Rachel Barlow, nabs Gary, after an extended bout of the bummers. But Gary and Rachel don't stay married, because by the time everybody decides to move to Midland Heights, Gary's back with

Madlyn and Rachel has married a proper-sounding English professor whose connection to this wacky story was, so far, somewhat hazy.

After downing a salad, I really didn't want lunch, so I went to Richardson Park, just a few blocks from my house, for a rally in honor of our beloved Mayor, Sam Olszowy. Actually, I went to the preparations for the rally, which was going to start at four. It was one o'clock, and Olszowy was already there, watching his minions build a tent for the speeches and inevitable coffee. Nobody ever furnished hot chocolate at these events.

I don't know why I wanted to talk to Sam. I guess I figured it was only fair. Part of the "Equal Time" law maybe. If you cover a murder affecting one side of the political fence, you have to get the reaction from the other side, or something like that.

Olszowy didn't have a reaction to Madlyn Beckwirth's murder. In fact, he didn't know who Madlyn Beckwirth was. He had been mayor of Midland Heights for so long, and a non-rising non-star in the local Democratic party for so many years, he was just running on auto-pilot. There's a murder. There's not a murder. It's all the same to him.

Sam Olszowy, maybe sixty-two years old, was dressed in a suit and tie, and had very little of his original hair left. What hair there was he had clearly bought from some mail order outfit. The color didn't match his sideburns, and it looked like he was walking around with a bird's nest on his head. It was a wonder he could get from one room to another without dislodging the silly thing, but he seemed oblivious to appearances.

"I don't have much time, young man," he said, although he had three hours before anyone would ask him to smile and shake hands, and they were the most strenuous things he'd do that day. "What's on your mind?"

There are times you go into an interview with prepared questions and an agenda, and other times you simply ask the first thing that's on your mind. These free-association type interviews are generally more interesting, because you're flying without a net, and you can crash and burn much more easily. And that's what I was in danger of doing with Sam Olszowy. I didn't expect anything from this interview, so I winged it, throwing out the first name I thought he'd recognize.

"Milt Ladowski," I said.

"That son of a bitch," were Olszowy's first words. "I don't know how many times he's tried to get me thrown out of office. Technicality this, Sunshine Law that. Lawyers. Can't trust a one of 'em."

"I'm married to a lawyer."

"Lock up your wallet at night," he said. "You're not safe in your own bed."

"So why have you kept Ladowski on for all these years?" I asked, ignoring the slight to my wife.

"The mayor in this town has less power than the deputy in the animal control department," he said. "I've tried to get rid of Ladowski five times. And if I'm re-elected, I'll try again. But he's assured of a position if that bitch is elected. She's already promised him he can stay on, and she'll even raise his salary so he can buy another goddam kraut car."

I left before he had time to offer me coffee. I wasn't sure what I'd found out, but I did know one thing: neither candidate was getting my vote for mayor in less than two weeks.

# Chapter 22

Milton J. Ladowski, Esquire, has a very nice private office on the thirty-second floor of an office building in Edison, New Jersey, right near the Metropark train station. Ladowski's office features real maple doors, thick pile carpeting, a wet bar, seven telephone lines, computers networking together Ladowski's sixteen associates, a stereo system (which usually plays Mozart and Brahms while Ladowski is working), and a view of the surrounding area, which includes parks, highways, shopping malls, and condominium complexes.

I've never actually been inside Ladowski's private office, only his borough office. That description comes from a piece that *New Jersey Monthly* magazine ran on Ladowski in 1998. The feature was written by a freelancer I know casually, who would believe you if you told her that King Kong used to date your cousin. So take the information for what it's worth.

I have, however, been outside Ladowski's building, and I was there at about 10:30 the following Monday morning, in the blue 1991 Plymouth minivan that Abigail forced me to buy. Her reasoning was that when Leah or Ethan wanted to go somewhere with their friends, I could drive more of the kids together at once. My reasoning was that this was, at best, a dubious advantage. Her reasoning prevailed, I signed the purchase agreement against my will, and we have a minivan. What the hell? If we didn't have one, we'd probably be voted out of Midland Heights, though we're in serious danger of that, anyway, these days.

Detective novels go to great lengths to explain to their readers exactly how tedious and awful stakeouts are. They seem to think that the movies have made stakeouts seem glamorous and exciting, when in reality, movies and TV generally show two grungy men sitting in a nondescript car while, inevitably, it rains, and lots of time passes, as seen through lap dissolves.

This was my first stakeout, and so far, it had been brief and quite pleasant. I had gotten there about fifteen minutes before I knew Ladowski would be leaving the building. I had called his office that morning and asked if he'd been in all day. No, his secretary said, he'd be leaving around 10:30. Thanks, I said, and that pretty much did it for sitting around for long periods of time fogging the window with my breath and hot chocolate steam. In the movies, it's coffee steam.

Also, it was sunny and about sixty-five degrees, this early but pleasant April day. I had my tape player on, and Ella Fitzgerald was singing "Someone To Watch Over Me" when Ladowski walked out of the building, into the parking lot, and to the door of a silver Infiniti. Don't ask me the model. All obscenely expensive cars look alike to me.

I started up my pain-in-the-butt-minivan, checking my disguise in the vanity mirror, which is on one side of my sun visor. I had pulled down, over my eyes, a New York Yankees baseball cap—a real one, not the kind with the adjustable band in the back. I was also wearing dark sunglasses with a little image of Mickey Mouse in the lower part of the left lens—a pair I bought for an emergency during a trip to Orlando two years ago. A denim work-shirt filled out the image. That's all that mattered because, if Ladowski saw me at all in the minivan, he'd see me only from the steering wheel up.

You follow most people so you can observe them without their observing you. But I had just the opposite in mind. I very much wanted him to see someone following him, though not clearly enough that he'd recognize me, because let's face it, I don't cut what they'd call a threatening figure. So a little finesse, but not too much, was called for here.

Milt drove out of the parking lot and toward Route 27, which takes you either north toward the Garden State Parkway and Newark or New York, or south toward New Brunswick. I muscled the minivan, which has steering like a Sherman tank, out of the lot behind Ladowski, and stayed two cars back of his fancy-shmancy Infiniti heading toward 27.

Once at the two-lane highway, he made a left, which would indicate he was headed south. Good. A trip into the city today might have taken me too far out of the way to be back home when the kids trooped in after school. Different gumshoes have different concerns.

Milt was driving calmly. He didn't notice me yet. Probably wanted folks to believe he was listening to Mozart and Brahms on the onboard CD changer. More likely he had a Metallica album on. (I never believe it when people say they only listen to classical music or watch only public television.)

I decided to push it a little and get his attention. So I pulled the van out from behind an original Volkswagen Beetle I was tailgating and passed it and a Chevy to get directly behind Ladowski. The Chevy driver wasn't pleased when I nosed my way in between him and Milt, but I wasn't getting paid to make friends with the Chevy guy. Come to think of it, I wasn't getting paid at all.

Milt still didn't seem to notice, so I got closer, and started to tailgate him. This got his attention, and he speeded up a little bit. So did I. He went a little faster. Me, too. Soon, we were doing 65 in a 45-mile-an-hour zone. He must have begun wondering what the hell was going on.

He changed lanes. Whaddaya know? So did the minivan behind him. Then he headed for the fork in the road where Route 27 runs into Midland Heights, and coincidence of coincidences, so did the minivan.

Ladowski, I hoped, was now sweating behind those very expensive sunglasses of his. He was, in fact, driving like a man who was sweating, all right. He wove back and forth in the right lane, wondering if he should call the cops on his cell phone or if he was just being paranoid. Why would this old, beat-up hunk-of-junk minivan behind him be tailing a classy piece of machinery like his?

I'm assuming he let out a sigh of relief when I passed him on Edison Avenue. But because I knew where he was going by this point, I had made a quick change in my plans.

I wrestled the minivan into the Borough Hall parking lot, and backed into a space. Now I wanted him to know exactly what he'd seen in his rear view mirror. I pushed the button to open my back hatch, and got out through the back just as Ladowski was pulling into the lot. He didn't notice the minivan right away, but did a double-take when he saw it. But it was too late. He was already out of his car.

Ladowski stared at the minivan, frozen. He couldn't know if the evil tormentor who had tailed him here was still in the vehicle, or if he was walking into an ambush. The thought processes were practically spelled out on his face like that ribbon news line that used to run on Times Square.

I settled it for him by circling around behind his car, crouching until I was right behind him, and grabbing him from the back. He let out a sound similar to that of a gosling pushed in front of a tractor. (I'm only guessing here.)

Since I'm considerably smaller and lighter than Ladowski, I knew I couldn't hold him long. So I snarled into the back of his neck, "this is what it feels like to be followed around by a blue minivan, Milt. How do you like it?"

When I let him go a little, he spun around. When he recognized me, he began to sputter.

"Aaron, are you out of your mind? What's the idea of . . ."

"Of having someone followed by a minivan, Milt? I could ask *you* that same question, couldn't I?" My facial expression was the one I use on Ethan when he's decided he's not joining a Saturday night dinner with the family because they're showing "a very special episode of *All That.*"

"I don't know what you're talking about," Ladowski said, in the least convincing voice since Regis told Kathie Lee he'd miss her.

"Yes, you do. The only one who would have wanted me followed was Gary Beckwirth. He was the only one obsessive enough about what I was doing to care. And Beckwirth wouldn't have known how to go about finding people to trail someone. If he had, he'd have cracked open the Yellow Pages to find himself a private detective. No, he'd go to his friend and legal advisor, and you'd go through your files of clients whom you'd kept out of jail. And since they weren't technically break-ing any laws except the speed limit, they'd be happy to do it. For a small fee. How'm I doing so far, Milt?"

He said what everybody says when you catch them red-handed. "You have no proof."

"I don't need any proof. I'm not having you arrested. I'm not even going to get you disbarred. But I'm going to get to the bottom of Madlyn Beckwirth's murder, Milt. I'm this close as it is"—and here I held up my fingers, millimeters apart. "I know about Gary and Madlyn's annulment, and I know Gary was married to Rachel Barlow. I know that Gary took out a credit card in your name—it's easy, if you know the other person's Social Security number—and paid for Madlyn's trip to Bally's. That's only a taste of what I already know. This whole sick story is going to come out, and when I put a couple more pieces togeth-er, your name is going to figure prominently, I'm sure. Look for it to show up in some very prominent publications. I doubt the coverage will be as flattering as the profile in *NJ Monthly.*"

I dropped my hands off his biceps, turned, and walked back to the minivan. Ladowski's expression was a mixture of amazement and some-thing else.

Fear. That's what it was.

Now, I'd better turn something up, or I was going to look extremely foolish.

# Chapter 23

When I got home from harassing Milt Ladowski, which I have to admit had been, for me, the most satisfying chapter in this whole sorry story so far, there was a message on the machine. I pushed the button next to the flashing light.

"Hi, uh, my name is Marie Aiello. You left a card in my door a couple of days ago . . . Anyway, I'm looking for Aaron Tucker, and here's my number . . ."

It took me as long to dial Marie's number as it does for Bernie Williams to turn on a fastball and drive it into the right field bleachers. But it seemed like an eternity, and my inner voice was chanting the entire time, "be home, be home, be home, be . . ."

"Hello?"

"Hi, this is Aaron Tucker. Is this . . ."

"Oh, hi. Yeah, this is Marie. I called you maybe an hour ago. You're the one who's investigating about Maddie Rossi, right?"

"That's right."

"You know, I wasn't going to call you. I've been getting calls from the papers. But every one of them wanted to talk about Madlyn *Beckwirth*. Not you. You asked about the Maddie I know."

I had written the name that way—Madlyn Rossi—because I figured Marie would recognize it more fondly. But I hadn't really given it all that much thought. You never know which details are going to make the difference.

"I spoke with her mother the other day," I said.

"And don't think I didn't call Mrs. Rossi to check you out," Marie answered. You had to like a friend who was still loyal after death. "She said you were a nice man, and you had a very cute daughter."

"Well, she's right about my daughter."

Marie didn't have time for me to come over and talk to her right then. She was going to her job as a dance instructor and had to be there in an hour. I heaved an inward sigh of thanks, since I'd been going to enough people's houses and refusing coffee lately. We agreed to a phone interview, and Marie asked that I "cut to the chase," and only ask the things I hadn't be able to find out elsewhere. Mrs. Rossi must have told her that she'd provided enough detail on Madlyn for a three-volume biography.

"I knew Maddie since grade school. She was my best friend until I went to college," Marie said. "We kept in touch, you know. I think I was the only one in Westfield she ever spoke to after she had the falling out with her mom."

"That was over the abortion."

"Yeah. Maddie didn't want to even tell her mom she was pregnant, but Gary insisted. And the two of them talked her into having the baby. But when push came to shove a couple of weeks later, she decided she was too young, and you know what? She was right. If she'd gone to delivery, Maddie would have resented that baby forever."

"Did she resent her mom for making her feel guilty?"

Marie's voice was changing into the dreamlike sing-song people use when they're remembering fond friends. "No, that was the funny thing," she said. "Maddie always felt bad about her mom, but she wasn't mad at her, you know? The one she never forgave was Gary. If he hadn't badgered her, she'd have had the abortion, and her mom never would have known. I don't think things were ever good between

Maddie and Gary again."

"Well, they annulled the marriage not long after that."

"That was Maddie," Marie Aiello said. "She called me up right before, straight shooter, ya know? 'I'm dumping him,' she tells me. 'Can't take it anymore. He's cute, but he's a pain. I can do better.' And she did."

"She did? She got married again?"

Marie took a deep breath. "Okay, here's where the story gets a little weird," she said.

*Here? Here's* where it starts getting weird? "I'm bracing myself," I said in all seriousness, and she chuckled.

"Okay. Maddie annuls the marriage, but Gary Beckwirth keeps calling her, trying to get her to go out with him. Maybe they can patch it up, that kind of thing. Not exactly a stalker, but he doesn't go away. Finally, after this goes on for, like, years, they're still friends. And Gary marries this Rachel *person*." The tone on that word spoke volumes. Had she lived in Midland Heights, Marie Aiello most definitely would not have cast her mayoral vote for Rachel Barlow.

"So that's good, right? Now Maddie doesn't have to worry about Gary anymore." I'm now calling her "Maddie," more from repetition than calculation.

"Well, you'd think so," said Marie. "But they start double dating. Gary and his new wife, *Rachel,* and Maddie with this guy she's really getting to like, this guy Martin."

My throat was dry, and what I tried to say was "Martin Barlow?" But it came out "aaaaaaarffffilik?" Marie chuckled.

"That's right. Martin Barlow. Maddie was nuts for him, like you never saw. Worshipped the ground he walked on—couldn't get enough of him. I don't think they left their bedroom even once in the next year. I barely heard from her that year. And eventually, she wore Martin down, and they got married."

I've always enjoyed the expression, "his head was spinning." For me, it conjures up images of Linda Blair in *The Exorcist*. I mean, your head isn't really *spinning*.

My head *was* spinning.

"Martin Barlow and Madlyn Rossi were *married?*"

"Yeah, they were married about five years. Actually, depending on how you look at it, they were married close to thirteen years."

"Okay," I said. "Let's pretend I'm a complete and total idiot who's just learned the English language, and you're going to explain this situation to me. In nice, small words that the average goat would understand."

Marie laughed. "Mrs. Rossi was right, you are a nice man. Okay, let's see if I can explain this."

"I'll bet you ten bucks you can't."

"Try me. Maybe twelve, thirteen years ago, Maddie and Martin Barlow are married. They're trying to have a kid. Maddie says, at least, *she* wants one. Rachel and Gary are married, and they *have* a kid, but Rachel really hates being a mom, right? Because the boy gets more attention than she does."

"Okay, so now you're telling me that Rachel Barlow is actually Joel Beckwirth's mother."

"See, you *can* understand. So one night, the four of them, pals that they are, are over Gary's house—this is when he and Rachel are living in West Windsor—and they smoke, let's say, a few 'special cigarettes,' and down a couple of bottles of wine, okay?"

"So they're high and tight."

She chuckled. "Very good. And somebody—probably Martin— says, 'Hey, it's back to the Seventies night, with the pot and all. Why don't we go all the way, and have a wife-swapping party?'"

People's first reactions to unexpected news is always interesting. It's the most honest we ever really are in our day-to-day lives because we don't have the time to edit our responses. And so, with great decorum and class, I just burst out laughing. When I finally got myself back into serious reporter mode, I said, quite clearly, "oh, *no!*"

"Oh, yes. And everybody's for the wife-swapping but Maddie, who very much likes being Mrs. Martin Barlow and doesn't want to have all that much to do with Gary Beckwirth again. But they wear her down, and give her a few more drinks, and the next thing you know, she's over at Beckwirth's place re-living the bad old days, and taking care of a kid who isn't hers. Meanwhile, the not so pretty man she really loves—Professor Martin Barlow—is having his mind blown by Rachel, a woman Maddie really can't stand."

"Okay, so that's one night," I said. "That doesn't explain how ..."

"Well, that's what Maddie thought," Marie said. Her voice started getting more serious. This was the bad part she hadn't wanted to tell, and the fun of shocking me was not enough to overcome that. "She figures the next day, she'll get up, take a really long shower, and go back to her husband Martin. The problem is, she sleeps late, and everybody else decides this is a great arrangement, and they should just stick to it."

"Why?" It seemed a logical question.

"It solves everybody's problems," Marie said, a tinge of disgust and anger in her voice. "Everybody but Maddie's, but then she's the only one who'd truly been happy up to that point, and they couldn't allow that. Gary gets back the woman he really wants, though she doesn't much want him or his kid. Martin gets the hot blonde he's always wanted. And Rachel gets to ditch Gary, who's a loser in bed, for a guy who talks like Lord Byron and is an up-and-comer at this big university. So everybody's happy, right?"

"Except Madlyn. So why doesn't she just refuse?"

"I've never really been clear on that," Marie Aiello admitted. "She just couldn't take on the three of them. One or the other she could deal with, but not all three at once. Maybe she just couldn't bear to tell Martin 'no.' And I think she figured Martin would get tired of old *Rachel* in a day or two, and that would be that."

Imagine living all that time with someone, hating every minute of it, and waiting for years for the person you really love to come to his senses and return to you. Having to endure the thought of him in bed with someone other than you *every night* for twelve years? It should have driven Madlyn Rossi Beckwirth Barlow mad. Maybe it had.

"But it kept on going," I said. "Why didn't they just get divorces and make it legal?"

"They didn't just trade *wives*," Marie said. "They traded *families*. Maddie raised Rachel's son for her, because that bitch never wanted to have a kid—he was an accident. And then, Gary suddenly hit the jackpot. At that point, there's no way Rachel's divorcing him and giving up her right to all his money. So she makes Gary pay big for getting Maddie back."

"And," Marie continued, "there's no way Gary's giving Rachel half the money he just made. Not to mention, if Rachel divorces Gary and marries someone else, like, let's say Martin, she loses alimony, too. Better for Martin and Rachel to blackmail Gary, because he doesn't mind trading them money in return for the chance to keep Madlyn in his household. He starts paying for Rachel and Martin's house, their cars—all that stuff. And no matter how much Maddie complains, Gary stays in the driver's seat, and he knows it.

"That is the weirdest story I ever heard," I admitted. "And I lived through Watergate."

"You want the rest?"

"There's a *rest?* ... Sure."

"Maddie's trapped, but she has information they don't want her to share—mainly that she's not Mrs. Gary Beckwirth, and that Rachel Barlow isn't really Mrs. Martin Barlow. Once everybody moves to Midland Heights, reputations start to become a really big deal, since Gary wants everything nice and tidy, and Rachel, well, she wants to take over the world."

"So what does Maddie get for her silence?"

"She gets vacations. Every once in a while, she just takes off, rents herself a hotel room, and calls Martin Barlow. He shows up, they go at each other like a couple of bulldogs in heat for a few days, and she goes back to Gary, flaunting it over him that she likes Martin better in bed, and making sure that Rachel knows she's using Martin up over and over again."

Martin Barlow, sex machine. Go figure. "Is that the end?" I asked.

"No, but I don't know the end. Maddie always calls me every week, except when she's on what she calls her 'Martin breaks.' Well, she doesn't call two weeks ago, and she doesn't call last week, so I figure she must be on some kinda break. Then I read in the paper that she's dead."

"That must have hit you right in the gut."

"Tell you the truth, all I could think was, at least it doesn't hurt her anymore. She had what she wanted, and they took it away from her. And the guy she really loved was one of those who did it to her. That must've really hurt."

"I would guess."

"So who killed her?" Marie Aiello asked.

"I don't know," I said, "but if you call me tomorrow, I might have another answer."

"Well then, I'll call you tomorrow."

"I hope I'm here to answer the phone," I said. "Oh, and Marie, I owe you ten bucks. You *could* explain it after all."

# Chapter 24

When he opened his front door to my knock, I blew past Gary Beckwirth and shouted over his protestations that Milt Ladowski had told him not to talk to me. He looked drugged. He might very well have been on a number of different tranquilizers.

"I know it all, Gary, every bit of it," I rattled on. "I know that Madlyn wasn't really your wife . . ."

"She *was* . . ."

"You're not talking now. *I'm* talking. She wasn't your wife. Rachel Barlow, or whatever her real name is now, is your wife. You guys decided to play Swinging Seventies one night and swapped families. It's not unheard of. A couple of Yankee pitchers did it in the *real* Seventies."

Beckwirth was now looking nervously toward the staircase. He motioned, palms down, for me to lower my voice. But I was in full annoyance mode, and would have none of it.

"What's the matter, Gary? You afraid Joel will hear? Doesn't he know Madlyn wasn't his real mother?"

Beckwirth sagged into a chair in the hallway, his face impassive. "He knows," he said. "He knows."

"So what's to hide?" I asked. "I know, you know, he knows. There's no reason for secrets anymore. The thing that I don't get is why you're not defending yourself. You know you didn't kill Madlyn. You never could. You loved her too much, didn't you?"

Gary started to cry. He buried his face in his hands and sobbed, but he nodded "yes" just the same. I sat down next to him.

"But it ate at you, didn't it? That you loved her so much, but she didn't love you. She loved *him.* She loved Martin Barlow. Her real husband. And when she'd go off on her little holidays, it probably tore you up inside. It bothered you so much you hired a private detective with a blue minivan to watch her day and night, but he drove her off the road the night she left. Right? Because you loved her so much?" I thought of him going through the photographs in his bedroom and weeping.

"So if you knew where she was, why in the name of Anthony Quinn did you send me after her? Why, Gary? It doesn't make sense."

He looked up, his cheeks wet. His eyes were disbelieving. "You don't know? You don't understand?"

"No. I'm asking you," I said, voice gentler now.

Beckwirth didn't even try to compose himself. The combination of prescription drugs and strain was too much to battle. "She used to go away for two days, maybe three. But this time ... she just disappeared in the middle of the night. I really did think she was kidnapped the first day, until Martin called." The way he said "Martin" was similar to the way Marie Aiello had said Rachel Barlow's name. "By then, I'd already talked to the police. And then it dragged on and on, and I thought she might never come back. The thought of her ... you know, *with* him like that ... I needed someone to make her come back. I knew you could do it."

That was it? I was supposed to deliver Madlyn Beckwirth, um, Barlow, from the seductive grip of Martin Barlow, and then back to Gary? I was supposed to convince her that she really loved Gary, even though she knew she didn't? Who the hell did he think I was, a combination of J. Edgar Hoover and Dr. Ruth?

"But somebody killed her. Was it you?"

Beckwirth looked as if I'd suggested he'd jumped up one morning and landed on Mercury. "Me? Kill the woman I loved? You alread said I didn't do it."

I shrugged. "It's happened before. Jealousy, crime of passion. It's not a new thing."

Gary shook his head violently. And started to cry again. "Not me," he said. "Not me."

"Then who?"

He shook his head again.

"Are you telling me you're still covering up for them? After they permanently took away the one person on this earth you loved, you're going to let them get away with it? What do you owe these people, Gary?"

He vibrated in the chair, but said nothing. I decided that playing good cop wasn't working, and I'd have to switch into bad cop mode. So I raised my voice again. A lot.

"Fine!" I screamed. "This whole thing is coming down tonight, Gary! And if you don't do what's right, it's going to come down right on your head! I know all I need to know, and tomorrow morning, you can kiss this pretty house of yours goodbye! Enjoy your last day as a wealthy man!" I all but ran for the door and let myself out, fully aware that I had no idea what I was yelling about.

First, I scared Milt, then I threatened Gary, so next were the Barlows. Pissing them off again proved to be considerably more fun than dealing with Gary. Just the sight of me at their front door was enough. Martin tried to slam it in my face. But I had seen enough traveling salesman cartoons. I wedged my foot inside the door. It hurt a little, but New Balance makes a damned sturdy little shoe, and Dr. Scholl will be getting a new customer as soon as I can get to the drug store.

"If you want to win this election, you're letting me in. Otherwise, you can hear what I have to say nice and *loud* on your doorstep, where everybody else on the block can be in on it, too," I told him, and I saw Rachel, behind him, nod her head. Martin relieved the pressure on my foot, and I walked into the house. Martin made a point of closing the door as quickly as possible. I did my best not to limp.

"Say what you have to say," Rachel said, biting her upper lip. It gave her the rather dubious appearance of a chimpanzee in a polyester doubleknit.

"I know all about the goofy wife-swapping deal with you and the Beckwirths," I started. Martin's eyes widened, but Rachel simply watched me with practiced calm. "It probably wouldn't play well with Martin's tenure petition, would it? Or with the voters. But then, neither would a murder conviction."

"Murder?" Rachel spat. "We didn't kill Madlyn. Gary did. Don't you read the papers?"

"Gary Beckwirth enjoyed his suffering way too much to end Madlyn's life that way," I countered. "He loved her. If he was going to kill anybody, he'd have killed Martin for having better sex with Madlyn than he could."

Martin flushed and made some stammering noises. Rachel, again, was icy cool, but the lines around her mouth were showing just a little bit.

"We didn't kill anyone," she repeated, "and I don't hear you proving otherwise."

"I have all the proof I need," I said, knowing I had none. "I know that Martin called me and threatened me on a cell phone he stole. By the way, Marty, Mr. MacKenzie wants his cell phone back, and he expects you to pay the long distance charges on his bill. But I doubt there were any threatening, anonymous calls to Madlyn. You just made those up, didn't you, Rache? I know all that. And I'll hand it all over to the cops tomorrow unless you two decide to cooperate."

Rachel turned to the man everyone thought was her husband. "It all comes down to money," she said. "I told you." Then she turned to me. "How much do you want?"

"Four hundred thousand dollars."

Rachel laughed. Martin looked like he was going to swallow his tie. "Four hundred thousand?" she asked. "Why not ask for an even half million?"

"Okay."

"We don't have that kind of money," Martin managed to say.

"You have a decent amount stored away," I said. "You don't pay for your house. You don't pay for your cars. Your son is being raised by a man who's considerably wealthier than you. I don't care where you get it. Just get it. By tonight. Or I'll be calling Barry Dutton and a few of my newspaper editors in the morning. And Martin?"

"Yes?" he asked bravely.

"That whole wife-swapping thing? The 'you-take-mine-I'll-take-yours-and-don't-tell-anybody' plan? That is, without question, the dumbest arrangement I've ever heard of in my life. What in the name of Charles Dickens made you think you could keep it a secret forever?"

Saying that felt especially good. It's one thing to stumble across an intricate, brilliantly conceived, maddeningly logical, ruthlessly executed plan. It's another to dig for weeks on a story and find out it's about a plot that Isaac Asimov would have rejected as too far-fetched, and executed by a group of egos that put Chuck Barris to shame. It was insulting to have uncovered it.

I turned on my heel, careful to make sure that Rachel Barlow didn't have a dagger in her hand, and walked through the door.

Once outside, I felt a tight pull inside my stomach. My plan had gone just the way I'd thought it would.

Damn it.

# Chapter 25

It surprised me how little time it takes to annoy a bunch of murder suspects. Back in my office, I was trying to get my screenplay characters into that inevitable argument that would threaten their budding romance. I had been staring at the screen for an hour, and written for fifteen minutes, when Ethan got home from school.

He was in "oblivious boy" mode, seeing nothing but the place to leave his backpack and the jar in which we keep the sharpened pencils. Ethan barely said hello before he was at the table, doing his homework at the speed of light so he could get upstairs and log Nintendo time before *Pinky and the Brain* came on. Ethan leads a very full life.

I struggled further with the two obstinate bastards I'd been writing when Leah came in from school, gave me a kiss on the cheek, and headed straight to her homework, too. It was just about that time that Barry Dutton called.

"Tucker, are you out of your mind?"

Cool! Somebody had called to complain! Maybe we could eliminate a suspect. "Who called you?" I asked.

"Called? Nobody called. I'm just wondering why you're dialing nine-one-one when there's a little brown bat in your house." Oh, that.

"I didn't *know* it was a little brown bat. I thought it was a large menacing person of undetermined color."

Ethan walked over and dropped his homework on my desk, then turned and ran up the stairs. He knew if I found anything wrong, I'd be up to discuss it with him when I got off the phone.

"It's nice," said Barry, "that you don't discriminate against large intruders of one skin tone or another. Now, why did you think someone called me about you?"

I picked up the top sheet of Ethan's homework. Right up at the top, he'd written his usual "Math—Ethan," in near-perfect block letters, but his numbers below were barely legible. He spent more time practicing his name than he did his numbers. It's part of his Asperger's— the kids tend to have in fine motor skills deficits, and writing is a problem best dealt with by occupational therapy, or compensated for with a computer keyboard.

"Lately, you haven't been calling during business hours," I told Barry. "I thought maybe you were calling now because there'd been complaints. I haven't been leaving everyone alone like I'm supposed to."

I did the calculations on Ethan's math, and as usual, he had gotten the problems right. At least, the ones I could figure out myself. See, I was an English major . . .

"*Who* haven't you been leaving alone?" Barry's voice took on a long-suffering tone.

Ethan's next page was for social studies, and of course on top it read, "The Civil War—Ethan." A number of questions about the Civil War were below, and this time, I could figure out the answers all by myself. He had gotten only one answer wrong.

"Don't worry, Barry," I said. "Your job isn't in jeopardy."

"No," he said. "But if you get killed, I'll have two murders on my hands, and how will that look when it comes to salary review time?"

"I'll do my best to avoid that," I said, and hung up. I picked up Ethan's last page, an English assignment called "Ethan's Favorite Time." It was an essay about the child's favorite time of the day, and of course at the top, he had written, "Ethan's Favorite Time—Ethan," like Mrs.

Fisher didn't know that Ethan had written something called "Ethan's Favorite Time." I started to read, and then looked at the top of the page again. And I stared at it for a few moments.

Oh, for crying out loud!

I got up and walked up the stairs to Ethan's room. The door was open, so I didn't knock. He was sitting at his computer, not at the Nintendo.

Ethan writes poetry. Two years ago, he wrote a poem for a school assignment, and got enough positive feedback from adults that he just continued to write poems. And he's actually pretty good. I've never had much use for poetry myself, but my son communicates through his poetry in ways he can't always manage in ordinary conversation.

On his computer screen was the beginning of a new poem, called "Wavelength." Of course, it said "Wavelength—Ethan" at the top. And it read: "Nobody else is on my wavelength, I know/It bothers me sometimes, but I try not to show." That was as far as he'd gotten.

He saw me reading over his shoulder. "No one, I think, is in my tree," I said. "I mean, it must be high or low." Ethan stared up at me, confused. Was the old man going off the deep end?

"Did I get something wrong?" he asked. He assumed if I had come upstairs, it was about homework. I sat down on his bed and looked at him. Ethan was puzzled, and swiveled back and forth in his chair absent-mindedly.

"It was you, wasn't it?"

"What was me?" Now he figured he was in trouble over something, and got ready to explain how it was really Leah's fault.

"It was you with the barbecue sauce. You wrote 'Fuck Ethan' out on our sidewalk, didn't you?"

He looked down at the floor and shrugged.

"It wasn't until just now that I figured it out," I told him. "First you wrote the word 'fuck' on the sidewalk, and then you signed it with your name. Just like you do on all your homework."

He shrugged again, wondering what punishment he would now face. Ethan stole a quick involuntary glance at his Nintendo machine, knowing that inappropriate behavior usually resulted in a loss of video game time.

"Did you just learn the word?" I asked. "Was that what it was, and you just felt like using it?"

He tried shrugging again, but saw from the look on my face that shrugging wasn't going to be enough. "I guess," he said. "But I didn't just learn the word. I just felt like writing it."

"Where'd you get the barbecue sauce?"

Ethan's eyes were still avoiding me, but he doesn't make eye contact much under the best of circumstances. "Matthew stole it from Big Bob's, this place by school. And he kind of . . . dared me."

Good old Matthew. The kid who had taught Ethan how to make the fart noise under his arm. You could always count on Matthew.

"You did it to show Matthew?"

He started to shrug, and decided to nod instead. "And some of the other guys. Warren Meckeroff, Avil, and Thomas. They said I was a baby and I wouldn't do it. When they saw me write my name, they ran, and I didn't know what to do with the barbecue sauce, so I threw it by the garbage cans, because Mom was coming."

"Why didn't you just tell us this?" I asked, and immediately realized how stupid that sounded. "Because you figured you'd get punished?"

He nodded, and slowly started to cry. I kneeled next to his chair and put my arm around him. "It's never easy being Ethan, is it?" I said. He stopped crying and looked at me.

"What do you mean?" he asked.

I smiled. "Forget it." I got up and started to leave the room.

"Dad?"

At the door, I stopped and turned. "What is it, Pal?"

"Am I . . . do I . . . um, what punishment . . ."

I smiled a crooked smile. "Don't worry about it, Chief. Just don't do it again. And Ethan ..."

"Yeah, Dad?"

"Don't tell your mother, okay? Oh, and one more thing." He looked up. "Your printing is getting much better."

I walked out as he was shaking his head at his unexpected good fortune.

# Chapter 26

"Are you really sure this is the best way?" Abigail asked. "I don't like it."

"I'm not nuts about it myself," I admitted. "But as far as I can see, it's the *only* way. Besides, I've already spent the day irritating people."

"As only you can."

I ignored her. "And the die is cast."

She doesn't often look at me the way I look at her: a little dewy-eyed, smiling wistfully. So when I caught that expression across the kitchen table, I knew what she was thinking.

"Relax. This isn't the last time you'll ever see me."

"Are you sure?"

"Sure I'm sure. Unless you get hit by a bus on the way to Mahoney's house," I said, although I wasn't the least bit sure of anything these days. Since yesterday, I'd followed an attorney and threatened him physically, been given a magical mystery tour through marriages, annulments, wife-swapping, child-swapping, and for all I knew, dog-swapping (although I hadn't seen a dog at either house), I'd yelled at a murder suspect, I tried to blackmail a couple of political wannabes out of a half a million dollars, and I figured out that my son had cursed himself on our own sidewalk. This kind of stuff tends to shake one's belief system just a tad.

Abigail stood. "It's necessary for us to go to Jeff and Susan's? We could all just stay upstairs ... If somebody comes, it'd be easier for us to call ..."

I walked over to her and put my hands on her shoulders. "Abby," I said, "I'll be fine. But I *won't* be fine if I have to worry about you and the kids while I'm doing this. Go to Mahoney's. I know you'll be safe there, and I won't have to think about that part of it."

She gave me a long kiss, which is also somewhat unusual in the middle of the kitchen. Behind us, I suddenly heard Ethan going "woo-woo." That's my boy. Abby broke off the kiss and looked around at him. Since our talk upstairs, Ethan had been a model citizen, and Abby, though a little suspicious, had decided, I think, not to question his good behavior. Leah sidled up next to Ethan, her shoes already on.

"You ready to go?" Abigail said.

"Yeah!" Leah cried. "Dinner at Uncle Mahoney's house!" Ethan smiled and shook his head at his sister's enthusiasm. He hadn't gotten that jazzed up about anything since Keenan and Kel had starred in their very own movie.

"All right, then," said my wife. "Let's get going." She gave me what I'm sure she'd refer to as "one last look," and shepherded the kids toward the front door. I followed.

Leah looked up, a puzzled look on her face. "You're not coming, Daddy?"

"Not this time, Puss. I have to work. But I'll see you later." Leah made her "disappointed" face, sticking her lower lip out, and I laughed in spite of myself. I made her give me an extra-long hug. It's better to be safe than sorry. Then she turned and walked out to beat Ethan to the "good" seat in the car.

Ethan stopped at the door, too, perhaps sensing something unusual in how Abby and I were looking at each other. You never know what Ethan's taking in, and what he's not. "See you later, Dad," he said, with a conspiratorial smile on his face. Then he came over and gave me a hug, which isn't unheard of, but is also not terribly common. Either he was grateful I hadn't grounded him or he knew something was up. I stroked his hair for a moment, and then he was out the door, too.

Abby was doing her best to look normal. She looked around for her keys, found them on the kitchen counter, and picked up her purse from the foot of the living room stairs. "Okay, then," she said. I stopped her before she reached for the door and gave her a long, serious kiss. When I finally let go, she had that look in her eye again.

"That was for luck," I said.

"I hope you don't need luck."

"Who knows? Maybe nobody will show up at all," I said, knowing she wasn't buying that for a second.

"I dunno," Abby said. "You are awfully good at pissing people off when you want to. The right one, whichever it is, will probably come by. Do you know which one is coming?"

"I think I do, but I hope I'm wrong," I said.

She nodded. "I hope nobody comes." I didn't answer. I couldn't tell her what I was really thinking—that I couldn't stand it if no one came. I needed this to be over, tonight. "Call me as soon as we can come home," Abby said.

"I will." She gave me another kiss, a normal one this time, and left. I stood in the doorway and watched her drive the kids away in the Saturn. Mahoney's house was only ten minutes away—not even a long enough trip for a tape to keep the kids from killing each other in the car.

I spent the early part of the evening quite pleasantly, really. It was a warm-ish April night, and the Yankees' game against Baltimore was on the tube. I made some pasta and watched the game's first few innings, making sure I was somewhat visible through the front window, but not so visible that I'd be a good target, though that wasn't a tremendous concern. I'd seen the wounds on Madlyn Beckwirth, and whoever the killer was, s/he certainly wasn't much of a marksperson.

In true Madlyn fashion, I left my front door unlocked, although I stopped short of opening it just a crack. When somebody decided to come in, the creak of the door would be enough warning for me.

About nine, I closed the drapes in the front room and turned on the outside light. Wouldn't want the killer to fall down the stairs and break a leg. In America, it's better to get killed than get sued. I did open the front closet door at one point, and during the course of my visit there checked to see that my thirty-six-ounce Bobby Mercer bat (which dates me pretty seriously) was where I could get to it quickly. I slid the closet door closed only half-way.

It was a little after ten, and the Yankees were ahead of the Orioles by two runs in the ninth inning, when the front doorknob started to turn. And the first thing I felt was annoyance. This murderer was not only coming to do me harm, he was going to make me miss the end of the game, too. After a microsecond, though, my heart started pumping double-time, and I stood and prepared to greet Madlyn Beckwirth's murderer. The front door creaked ominously. I made a mental note to plane that door down one of these days.

Joel Beckwirth walked into the living room. He was carrying a handgun.

"Oh, Joel," I sighed. "I was really hoping I was wrong."

He closed the door behind him and leveled the gun at me, but his face was scrunched up. "What the hell do you mean?"

Best to keep him talking. The more he talks, the less he shoots. "I knew somebody would come to try and kill me, but I was hoping it was Madlyn."

"Madlyn? Madlyn's dead." He was forgetting why he was here. That was good.

"I thought maybe the woman in the hotel wasn't Madlyn," I babbled. "I thought maybe she and Martin had trumped it up, you know, found themselves a prostitute in Atlantic City, convinced her to come up to the room, and shot her so Madlyn could pretend to be dead. Go on the ultimate vacation, you know? That would have been good, huh?"

Joel was in about two feet over his head. "What do you think this is?" he asked. *"Murder, She Wrote?"*

"I didn't know kids your age watch that," I said, talking much faster than usual. "Does it run on some cable channel, or ..."

"Shut up," Joel said. "I'm not here to talk." Uh-oh. He remembered again.

"No," I said, facing him. "You're here because you shot your own mother."

"She *wasn't*..."

"That's true," I said. "But she raised you. Your own mother didn't *want* you, did she? Madlyn pretty much adopted you. And you shot her."

He took a couple of steps closer, and let his eyes scan the room, making sure the drapes were closed enough to block the view of him from the street. "You weren't there," he said. "You don't know what it was like."

"Oh, I'll bet it was bad," I told him sincerely. "I'm sure she took every opportunity to tell you she didn't want you, didn't love you, hadn't asked for you. But still, she had been there when you had a cold, and your own mother hadn't. Madlyn might not have loved you, but she took care of you. Did that mean Madlyn deserved to die?"

Joel shook his head. If he'd known I'd engage him in an emotional debate, he might have prepared more diligently. "Just shut up!" he shouted. "Shut up and leave me alone!"

"Madlyn wasn't going to come home this time, was she, Joel? She was going to stay away, and blackmail the others into letting her do it. Am I right?" He stayed silent, but didn't actually raise the gun to kill me, so I figured I was ahead. Delay is all. "And when she tried to pressure Martin and Rachel, they got scared. Something like this hits the fan, it's gonna be hard to get elected mayor." I circled the whole time, trying to get closer to the closet door, but Joel was keeping his back to the closet, and blocking my way.

Joel actually seemed interested in our discussion, like he hadn't heard it put exactly this way before, and was seeing things from a fresh perspective. "So they decided Madlyn had to go, and when Rachel couldn't talk Martin into getting rid of her, they tried Gary," I said. "But Gary, unlike everybody else in this bizarre little story, actually loved Madlyn, and refused to discuss it. How am I doing so far?"

"I wasn't there for all of it," he responded, quite reasonably, but he didn't seem to consider this whole thing to be all that serious. It was like we were just talking about a little dust-up at school. The worst he was looking at was a couple of days suspension, and he could watch TV and eat pizza at home. How bad was that?

I finally managed to get near the closet door, but when I reached, Joel raised his gun. "What are you doing?" he asked.

I dropped my hand and ignored the question. "I'm betting that when they came to talk to Gary, you were upstairs, and you heard them, just like you heard me talk to Gary today. And you volunteered, didn't you? You hated Madlyn enough to actually volunteer."

At this, Joel became quite animated, and shook his head vigorously. "No, no," he said. "I didn't ask to do it. They came to me. After my father left the house, Rachel came back."

"Your birth mother."

"Yeah, and she said she knew Madlyn had been bad to me. She said Madlyn was being bad to them, too, and somebody had to do some-thing about it. I finally said I would."

I circled away from the closet, and he followed me, lowering the gun but still watching my every move. "Did Rachel get you the gun?"

"Nah. My dad had it around the house. He didn't tell Madlyn about it because he knew she was scared of guns." Joel was proud of himself now. He'd been smart enough to find a gun without help. "But Rachel and Martin gave me a ride down to Atlantic City in a rental car, so if anybody saw the car, they wouldn't think it was us."

"And you went up to the room and shot her."

"Jesus, man, you should have seen her. Waiting for her precious Martin to show up, all dressed in dirty underwear. I couldn't look. I just pointed the gun and pulled the trigger without looking. Then I went home."

It was perfect. Rachel and Martin got what they wanted, Gary would protect Joel out of parental guilt, and Joel, little budding sociopath that he was, didn't even see the wrong in what he'd done.

"You killed her, Joel. You ended her life. She can never have her life back again. Is that fair?" Maybe I could get him to feel something.

"She got in the way, and she deserved it. Just like you deserve it." Then again, maybe I couldn't.

"I don't think you want to kill me, Joel." Joel shrugged and raised his left eyebrow. I could almost read his thoughts: "What the hell? Kill one person, kill another. What's the difference?"

"You're a problem. You need to be solved."

"Where'd you get *this* gun?" Keep him talking.

"From Rachel and . . . oh, no," Joel said. "Not this time." And he raised the gun to fire.

I moved quickly to my left as Joel shot. The sound of a gun going off in a small room is truly jarring, not like it sounds in the movies. Stunned, I stopped and stared at Joel. The bullet missed its intended target—me—by several yards and blew out the woofer on my left stereo speaker, four feet over my head and way to my left. If all this took two seconds, it was a lot, but it was enough to throw off my rhythm, and my composure, and I became rooted to the spot where I was standing. This time, Joel held the gun with both hands and aimed it straight at my chest, and he squinted.

Jeff Mahoney came barreling out of the front closet on slightly shaky legs. The barstool he'd been sitting on inside the closet fell over and Joel half-turned, reacting to the sound. But it was too late. Mahoney, a good six inches taller than Joel and fifty pounds heavier, had a bear hug around Joel's arms, causing him to drop the gun even before Joel knew what was happening.

I, of course, bravely dove behind the couch until the whole thing blew over. Joel shouted, but was quickly subdued. Mahoney held him tight while I picked up the gun with a pencil.

"So," I said to Mahoney, "finally out of the closet, eh?"

"Just tell me one thing, Joel," Mahoney said. "That rental car—what company was it from?"

# Epilogue

The Yankees gave back the lead in the ninth inning, but managed to eke out a win in the thirteenth. Ken Singleton, the former Oriole who now announces Yankee games, called it "a typical game between these two teams."

Barry Dutton showed up with Westbrook, and promised to let me have all the information on the arrests of Martin and Rachel Barlow/Beckwirth, who would be charged with conspiracy to commit murder, among other juicy crimes. Barry scolded me for not warning him beforehand, and Westbrook said some things so stupid I chose not to remember them.

I called Abby as soon as the cops left. She and the kids were home in maybe twenty minutes. Abby gave Mahoney a longer hug than she gave me, which was probably his reward for saving my life, and my punishment for putting her through this. Mahoney, for his part, gave his statement to the police, hugged Abigail and Leah, shook Ethan's hand, and left, after shaking his head at me and laughing. Sitting in a closet all night—some plan.

Joel Beckwirth would probably not be tried as a juvenile, Colette Jackson told me the next morning, but as an adult. This came as no surprise to me, since Abby had predicted and explained it the night before. But there was significant evidence Joel had no earthly idea what he did was wrong. He'd been screwed up on so many levels for so many years that it was hard to know exactly what had penetrated his defenses, and what had merely bounced off. He'd either be declared incompetent to stand trial, or be declared not guilty by reason of insanity. When he'd shot Madlyn, he'd been glad he could rid himself of someone he saw as a tormentor, but he couldn't look at her while he did it. In all likelihood, he'd be hospitalized for a good few years.

Marie Aiello called, as promised, the next morning, and I told her the whole story. She was shocked, but sounded relieved that she could put the whole thing to rest. She said we should meet someday, so I could pay her the ten dollars I owed her, but neither of us tried to make a firm date of it.

I didn't call Charlotte Rossi. There are some things even I don't have the nerve to do.

Milt Ladowski called, too, but he wasn't sure why. We talked for a few minutes, and he blustered and tried to get mad at me, but his heart wasn't in it. He didn't face any criminal charges, and wasn't going to be disbarred. He did, however, resign as Borough Attorney. Luckily, he had something to fall back on.

I had something to fall back on, too, so I started going to the Y again the next day in an attempt to get rid of it. But that morning, the first day after Joel's visit, I had work to do.

Once I had all the facts, I called the night city editor at the *Newark Star-Ledger*, the biggest newspaper in New Jersey, and offered her the story, although we'd never met. She asked me to fax a couple of clips, I did, and she bought the Beckwirth story. For a lot less than a thousand dollars, but hey, it was an "in" at the *Star-Ledger*. You could do worse. I used the money to replace the stereo speaker Joel shot out. My first murder investigation, and I had managed to break even.

The next morning I deleted from my computer files the romantic comedy screenplay I'd been struggling with, and started work on a murder mystery. They say "write what you know."

Gary Beckwirth actually called me later that day, his voice almost robotic. He said he wanted to apologize, and for the life of me, I couldn't imagine why.

"For sending those men to follow you in the minivan," he said. "They had Madlyn under surveillance, but they panicked when they saw her outside that night, and look what . . ." He couldn't finish the sentence.

"Forget it, Gary," I said. "Until you just mentioned it, I had."

"Well, Milton said you were upset," Gary said. "It wasn't my intention to upset you."

I didn't know how to answer that, so I asked, "How are you holding up?"

"Oh, I'm fine," Beckwirth said. "Really." I wasn't sure if he'd be facing any criminal charges, but I never thought for a moment he'd spend a night in jail. Sad to say, it wouldn't surprise me if he killed himself within the year.

Barry Dutton asked me to come to his office and give a full statement in the presence of Colette Jackson and a videographer, and I did, explaining what I knew and how I knew it. It took quite some time, but when it was over, I managed to pull Barry to one side.

"Okay, what's the latest?" I asked him.

"It's okay," Barry said. "I can talk in front of this crowd. The killer's been found."

"Yeah, and he was a fourteen-year-old kid. Jesus!"

"The interesting ones are the Barlows. Or, at least, Martin and Rachel. Renting a car to drive the kid to the casino. Suggesting he kill his own, um, stepmother?"

"I'll bet they say it wasn't them," I said.

"Are you kidding? According to them, they never *heard* of Joel Beckwirth, much less gave him a gun. They don't drive cars, they've never been to Atlantic City, and, I'm guessing, they probably never met Madlyn Beckwirth in their lives. And all this because they were afraid Rachel would lose the election."

"At least you don't have to worry she'll fire you."

"You never know," he said seriously.

They held the primary election the following Tuesday, and sure enough, Sam Olszowy managed to beat the accused conspirator to homicide by a neat thirty-five votes. Maybe if Sam had been convicted of a sex crime, the margin of victory would have been wider. Rachel, from her jail cell, vowed to call for a recount.

I was going to ignore the election entirely, but decided instead that I'd use my vote as a protest against a system that makes us choose between an old, bigoted moron and a homicidal, scheming moron. I punched the little key that allows for a write-in vote and very carefully recorded my choice for the job of Midland Heights mayor—Abigail Stein. I was crushed when she lost.

Margot the Agent continued to call every Wednesday, presumably out of boredom, and I continued to tell her I was writing a mystery. She maintained that there is no market for them. I asked how that would be different from anything else I'd ever written, and Margot suddenly remembered a veterinarian appointment for her Pekinese.

I hadn't actually indulged in a full-blown midlife crisis yet, but I was getting concerned about my way of making a living. I've seen fifty-year-old freelancers, and they're a sorry lot—begging editors half their age for jobs, and showing up at press junkets strictly for the free food. It's not the kind of thing one sees as an attractive Golden Years option.

Even so, it took me by surprise when at dinner one night, after the kids had retreated to the living room to watch *Kablam!*—it's an animated TV comedy —my wife said, "you know, you turned out to be a pretty good detective after all."

"Oh, I dunno," I said. "If the murder victim and the murderer hadn't actually come looking for me, I probably would have slept through the whole thing."

Abby started clearing dishes from the table, and I got up to help. I opened the dishwasher, which was full, but hadn't yet run. Typical.

"Yeah, but you maneuvered the killer into coming after you. And the victim called because you were doing too good a job. Not to mention, you solved the mystery of the barbecue sauce obscenity all by yourself," she said.

Bending to get the dishwasher detergent from under the sink, I stopped. "Now, how did you find out about that last little item?" I asked.

"Ethan told me."

Shaking my head, I poured the liquid into the little holes in the dishwasher door, then closed it and started the dishwasher. "I specifically told that kid not to mention it to you," I said.

"This is Ethan we're talking about. You know Ethan," said Abby as I put the dishwasher liquid away and moved the dirty dishes from the countertop to the sink.

"Yeah, I know Ethan."

She turned from the table, which she had just wiped down with a sponge. "I still think that showed some investigative skill," Abby said.

I put my hand on my hip and looked at her. "What are you trying to tell me?" I asked. "That you think this is a promising career opportunity for me?"

"Not if people with guns are going to keep coming after you," she said. "The next time, you might not think to keep Jeff Mahoney in the closet."

My lips pursed involuntarily, and I let some air out through them. "Very nice," I said.

Abby came over and put her arms around me, throwing the sponge into the sink behind my back. "It was just a thought," she said.

"A thought," I said. "You really want to be married to a private dick?"

She gave me a tight hug, and looked into my eyes. "Better than a public one," she said.

# Praise for *Minivan*

"Jeff Cohen's *Minivan* rolls merrily along—accent on the merrily. Mr. Cohen's ideas on marriage and murder (often cut from two ends of the same bolt) are wise, wicked, and witty. Surprisingly tender, too, regarding the responsibilities and trials of being a parent—fathering a delightful book in the process."
—**Larry Gelbart,** *Writer (M\*A\*S\*H, Tootsie, Oh, God!, Bedazzled, A Funny Thing Happened on the Way to the Forum, Barbarians at the Gate, etc.)*

"Jeffrey Cohen's *For Whom The Minivan Rolls* is hot. An authentically fun switch on the oft-used amateur sleuth theme, it debuts Aaron Tucker, a suburban stay-at-home dad who never asked to become a detective. Witty, with great characters and nifty twists, it should delight mystery fans, and, above all, anyone who enjoys a good puzzle and big laughs. His wife and kids may not realize it, but Aaron Tucker (and his creator) have glistening new careers ahead of them."
—**Tom Sawyer,** *Novelist & Former Head Writer, "Murder, She Wrote"*

"In my long and semi-illustrious career, I have been beaten to various literary punches by lots of dead white guys and by lots of others who, pending test results, are still alive. Among them is Jeffrey Cohen, who has written a comic mystery novel that is (a) comic, (b) mysterious, and (c) a novel. *For Whom the Minivan Rolls* had me rolling, which is no mean feat considering I don't drive a minivan. At least now I won't have to bother writing a comic mystery novel because I couldn't do it nearly as well as Mr. Cohen. His book is great. I could put it down, and sometimes did, but I didn't want to."
— **Jerry Zezima,** *Humorist, Journalist, & Public Nuisance*

"Author Jeffrey Cohen has written a sly, entertaining mystery whose twist-laden plot will truly puzzle and entertain. The voice of his protagonist, Aaron Tucker, is unique and delightful. And above all, his Minivan is immensely funny."
—**Michael Levine,** *Hollywood Publicist and best-selling author of 12 books.*

"*For Whom the Minivan Rolls* is not just a humorous look into American suburbia and what happens when a freelance reporter is asked to solve a local murder. It is a fresh, modern-day murder mystery with real-life, quirky characters that range from eccentric, obscure, and spirited to witty, guilty, and just plain nosy. Liberally infused with humor, it all beautifully blends together into great entertainment. You'll enjoy it so much you may even want to try visiting the story's fictional setting—Midland Heights, New Jersey."
—**Chrissy Blumenthal,** *Vice President of Production, Escape Artists (Sony Pictures)*

"How rare! *Minivan* was as enjoyable as they said it would be, and then some: good, tight story, humorously told by a fictional character I actually cared about. If author Jeffrey Cohen isn't soon spinning a published Aaron Tucker tale once a year for the next bunch of years, I've been wasting my time reading five mysteries a week for the past two decades."
—**Rita Bortz,** *Hollywood, FL*

"Aaron Tucker—aspiring screenwriter, loving house-hubby, and doting father— protests that he could never become a detective. Yet, he's wrong. He's nothing less than the consummate snoop, and makes up for his lack of investigative experience with canine-like persistence and a bloodhound's instinct for following a crime trail. Jeffrey Cohen has managed to write a mystery that is not only full of engaging characters, but features the likeable and witty voice of Aaron Tucker, who is (doggone it) naturally humorous. His *For Whom The Minivan Rolls* is thus an engrossing, entertaining read. That it's a first novel makes me think and hope that we'll soon be hearing a lot more from Jeffrey Cohen, and Aaron Tucker as well!"
—**Elliott Light,** *author of* Lonesome Song *and* Chain Thinking, *the first two book-length installments in his critically acclaimed "Shep Harrington Smalltown Mystery" Series*

"I thought I'd sit down one night and read Jeffrey Cohen's Minivan for just an hour or so, but then I couldn't stop myself, and went on reading until the finish. It's a remarkably funny, twisted tale of murder and mayhem. Aaron Tucker is you, me, and every-man. And I can't wait to read his next adventure!"
—**Lou Grantt,** *Editor,* Hollywood Scriptwriter, *the trade paper for screenwriters*

"What fun! *Minivan* is a crackerjack mystery with a prize inside: it's laugh-out-loud funny to boot! How can you not like a detective who has to carpool? Or worry with equal effort about dinner, murder, and checking his kids' homework? It's a great setting and a great crew of characters, and I hope Aaron Tucker's lack of success with screen-plays translates into a long and full career solving crime with wit and whine."
—**Dan Fiorella,** *roving editor,* Cracked *magazine, and contributing writer, "Prairie Home Companion"*

"Pick up Jeffrey Cohen's *For Whom the Minivan Rolls* and you get a funny, quirky, insightful look into human nature wrapped around that rarest of all things: a good story, well told."
—**Cary Solomon and Chuck Konzelman,** *principals, Numenorean Films*

"As the mother of a teenage son with Asperger Syndrome and President of ASPEN,® I am especially sensitive to any portrayal of the disorder. In *For Whom the Minivan Rolls*, Jeff Cohen has done a wonderful job of conveying the lovable quirkiness that's so often a part of these children and the day-to-day living that goes with it. It's the laughter that gets you through the day, and Jeff has certainly shown us how interesting life can be for the family of a child with Asperger Syndrome! Aside from all that, though, *Minivan* was the first book I had read in a very long time that I absolutely could not put down and that I thoroughly enjoyed. I was hooked into the story line right from the beginning and looked forward to turning each page to find out what next plot twist was in store. The only thing better would be a movie based on the book, or the next installment in the series, which I'm anxiously awaiting."

—**Lori Shery,** *Co-Founder and President, Asperger Syndrome Education Network, Inc. (ASPEN®)*

"I thoroughly enjoyed *Minivan,* which is replete with LOLLs (Laugh Out Loud Lines). Some of my favorites: a) When receiving a threatening phone call, Aaron Tucker answers, 'Who is this?', as if the caller would actually identify himself. b) 'It would never occur to a New Jersey driver to park his car, even when trailing a pedestrian.' c) 'It's hard to be macho when avoiding unnecessary carbohydrates'; d) 'It's better to get killed than sued.' So as not to overindulge myself as a blurber, and to avoid author complaints, I'll stop there. Suffice it to say, Jeffrey Cohen has written a very funny story and infused it with an awful lot of laugh-out-loud material!"

—**John Homans,** *aka Wilber Winkle, author of* Wilber Winkle Has a Complaint

"I loved *For Whom The Minivan Rolls.* The characters were quirky and endearing, the plot kept me guessing, and the jokes were funny. I hope Aaron Tucker has a good, long career of not being a private investigator, so he can come back in more books like this one."

—**Marcy Gross,** *Gross-Weston Productions, Inc.*

"Bringing a new and upbeat voice to the much-populated mystery scene, author Jeff Cohen has succeeded in doing what many another writer knows not even to attempt—tell an engaging mystery in a humorous way. *Minivan* is thus not only an easy read, but a breath of fresh air for all of us desperate to briefly escape the real world. It thoroughly entertained me for the few hours it took to read it."

—**Shauna Kelley,** *student, Goucher College*

"This book is a hoot. I laughed. I didn't know who dunnit. It made me want to tell other people to read it. Here's a hero who shows his mettle by moving away from the buffet table, and by making those little extra efforts to be a good dad and husband that most men don't bother with any more. When he puts himself on the line, it isn't just another day at the office. And you talk about sexy—give me a man who fills up the dishwasher and I'm there. I not only like that, I want to know more! I hardly ever read fiction any more because it's just no fun ... I prefer true crime personally. But this Jeff Cohen is a different sort of egg who might turn me into a 'mystery junkie' even though I swore no one ever would. Please consider this my highest endorsement for a fine read and good story, with plenty of mirth on the side."
—**Phyllis Murphy,** *story editor, NBC's "Profiler," and personal friend of Ted L. Nancy (Author, "Letters from a Nut")*

"With *Minivan,* Jeff Cohen takes the mystery genre and stirs in a generous helping of laughs. He's created a character whose voice is as much fun as the story he's telling. After only a couple hundred pages, Aaron Tucker already feels like an old friend. I'm looking forward to spending a lot more time with him."
—**Ian Abrams,** *creator of the TV series "Early Edition," and head of the Drexel University dramatic writing program*

"*Minivan* is a delightful and diverting read. Its chief character, Aaron Tucker, amusingly reminds me of John Corey, Nelson Demille's smart-alecky NYPD homicide cop. I find Demille's stuff to be great and irresistible fun. Likewise *Minivan!*"
—**Dr. Ellen Taylor,** *Pikesville, MD*

"Against his better judgment, a short, middle-aged, Jewish family man and freelance writer gets tossed into his first detective work, whereupon he must tap into every resource he knows to keep his head above water. It's so hard to write funny. For me, a true mysteryholic, finding a really funny mystery writer is something to tell the world about. Jeff Cohen, where have you been all these years?"
—**Ginny Levin,** *President, Oheb Shalom Sisterhood, Baltimore, MD*

# Author's Note

First of all, I'd like to thank the Academy and all the little people who made me what I am today. It's not easy being a first-time author, but luckily, you only have to do it once.

There are a few people I would like to acknowledge by name, however: first of all, to Jessica, Josh, and Evie, thanks for letting me borrow their personalities and exaggerate them so Aaron would have a story to tell. And to Jeff Pollitzer, for being much too good a best friend not to write about.

Thanks to my mother, for instilling in me a love of a good story and the thrill of reading, and to my father, who loved mysteries. I wish he could have read this one. To my brother, thanks for taking my writing seriously way back when.

Of course, thank you to Bruce Bortz, for taking a first-time author and making him a published author, and for raising his own concerns and listening to mine.

To voters for the Edgar Awards: the checks are in the mail, but don't let that sway you. They'll probably bounce anyway.

There are people in the town where I live (and don't think for a second I'm going to tell you where that is) who will recognize themselves in this book. With the exceptions I've mentioned above, they are all dead wrong; I made everybody up. But hopefully, they'll still buy the book to find that out.

I'd like to express my gratitude to everyone who encouraged me to write this book, but since nobody knew I was working on it, that would be a very short list. Aaron's story was originally going to be a screenplay, so I'd like to thank all the producers who wouldn't have bought it for convincing me I should write a novel instead.

For general encouragement, thanks to Lou Grantt, Ken Walz, my agent Amy Winokur, Judy Storch, Leonard Nimoy (although I'm sure he wouldn't remember), Marcy Gross, Ann Weston, Chrissy Blumenthal, and all my writer friends at PAGE.

And because I can't say it enough, thanks to my wonderful wife for believing in me, even when she shouldn't.

## About the Author

Author Jeffrey Cohen has been a full-time freelance writer/reporter for 16 years, and has written more than 20 feature-length screenplays. His work has been published in *The New York Times, TV Guide,* and *Entertainment Weekly,* among many others, and his screenplays have been optioned by Jim Henson Productions, CBS, and Gross-Weston Productions, among others.

He lives in New Jersey, with his wife and two children.

He is a graduate of Rutgers, the State University of New Jersey.

*For Whom The Minivan Rolls,* Cohen's first novel, is the first in a planned series of Aaron Tucker Mysteries.